Hidden Company

Company

A Dark Psychological Thriller

By
S. E. England

About the author

Sarah England is a UK author. Originally she trained as a nurse before a career in the pharmaceutical industry, specialising in mental health – a theme which creeps into much of her work. She then spent many years writing short stories and serials for magazines before her first novel was published in 2013.

At the fore of Sarah's body of work is the bestselling trilogy of occult horror novels – *Father of Lies, Tanners Dell* and *Magda*; followed by *The Owlmen*.

You might also enjoy, *The Soprano*, a haunting thriller set on the North Staffordshire Moors, or *Hidden Company* – a gothic horror set in a Victorian asylum in the heart of Wales. *Monkspike* is her latest novel.

If you would like to be informed about future releases, there is a newsletter sign-up on Sarah's website. Please feel free to keep in touch via any of the social media channels, too. It's good to hear from you!

www.sarahenglandauthor.co.uk

www.twitter.com/sarahengland16

www.Facebook.com/sarahenglandauthor

Acknowledgments

Raven Wood, a traditional witch of Germanic and Celtic roots. Thank you for your invaluable contribution on pagan witchcraft – from the incantations and herbs to the rituals and first-hand experience with the fae – it's a fascinating subject and I am most grateful for your help. etsy.me/2L6rVih

Scott Radke, US artist and sculptor. Thank you immensely for permission to use your incredible artwork on the cover of this book. www.scottradke.com

'And those who were seen dancing were thought to be insane by those who could not hear the music.'

Widely attributed to Friedrich Nietzsche

Prologue

Flora George
Winter, 1893

My name is Flora George, I am nineteen and have a child. Somewhere, I am sure...yes quite sure... that there is a child.

Yet here I am. In a squeaking, juddering carriage racing over God-forsaken moors through driving rain at the dead of night. At some point there was a change of horses – a rush across cobbles towards a dark inn, gaslights held high in the wind - but now once again the pace is furious, and seems to quicken with every mile. Why the urgency? Why? I am sickly...and so confused...where are we going? And where is Amelia? And Samuel?

The blanket placed around my shoulders affords little protection from the chill, the view through the window grimly awash – a barren plateau rippling with ebony lakes in the sodden dawn. Something is badly wrong. And with every pounding hoof on this barren heath another cog of terror rams into my bones. This carriage is heading far, far away from home – across mountains into an alien country.

Several hundred feet below, a ravine almost totally obscured by cloud, wends its way through a narrow, wooded valley. This is the route drovers and such people use to take their sheep to market - gypsies and wild folk riding bareback from outposts. It is not a road for carriages such as these. Full of ruts and hidden bogs the track is treacherous, the horses made wild with nerves and icy sleet. Yet the driver whips them on, faster, faster, faster…

But the panic is short-lived, and soon the oily blackness of opium claims my conscious mind once more. I cannot think…Occasionally my eyelids lift just enough to observe a scurry of raindrops rolling across the glass like beads of mercury, before closing again. I cannot keep awake…and I am so sick, my head so heavy…

Then through the fog of dreams it comes to me. I am alone. Being taken somewhere…at night…An explosion of renewed alarm kicks me hard in the heart. *I have to get out.*

"Madam, no! Don't! You'll fall."

"Stop! Driver! Stop the carriage and turn back at once! Do you hear me? Stop the carriage. We must turn back."

"Madam, please. Sit down or you'll do yourself an injury."

The maid's hands are all about me, prising my own from the window.

Maid? This woman is not my maid. Her voice is not at all familiar.

Her face looms in and out of focus. No, she is no maid of mine. There's a vague memory now, of Amelia holding both my hands, imploring me to take a short

2

holiday. And Samuel, yes Samuel, talking about the best place in the country, one that would save me from a far worse fate. Yes, yes, they painted such a picture - of a leafy private retreat for gentlewomen, a place to rest and recuperate, in which to take stock of matters and receive appropriate help. It seemed to make sense. I have been ill, have I not? And for such a long time. So that is where we are heading. To the retreat...

For a while the rocking motion lulls all further thoughts. Until another flare of panic flashes into the dark recess of my mind. This carriage came clattering into our stable yard at midnight! And why do I travel alone save for this broad-beamed woman I do not know? Nor were there any good-byes...And this is a long way from Derbyshire – how would my family visit? Something is badly amiss.

"Oh no, Madam, no you mustn't!"

The woman all but shoves me back onto the seat.

Such impertinence as I have never known, to be handled in such a way.

"You must stay seated now, Madam. And hold on tight or you will fall."

Any attempt at further conversation is quite impossible. The carriage is tipping steeply downhill, hurtling at breakneck speed. It is a wonder the horses do not stumble to their knees, and the carriage topple over. The maid and I are at pains to grip the seats for fear of being thrown off. This is alarming. Such speed when the driver surely cannot see ahead, and the horses may slip on the scree?

This new day has brought with it bouncing, needle-sharp rain; and silvery slithers of moonlight flash through an electric sky. It is said the lakes are gateways to the Other World, that men have been lured by strange orbs of light from lonely mountain paths to the sucking, hissing black bogs beyond. Then down they go, horses and all, without leaving a trace. I've read about the Black Mountains - in fairy tales, in folklore. Perhaps then, this is another dream and none of it is real? I have them all the time, wake up screaming, with laudanum held to my lips.

The maid's disembodied voice rattles into my thoughts. "We'll soon be down this steep hill, Madam, then into the forest where it's less windy. Not far then - we'll be there by eight I expect, just in time for breakfast. I'm dreadful hungry and no mistake."

Her lips are moving but not in tandem with her words, as if the chirpy voice comes from elsewhere and is not attached to her at all. Her flour-white face bobs up and down like a balloon on a string. What a vacuous expression. Self-satisfied. Superior. As if she knows something I do not. Come to think of it, was she not packed and ready to go at the dead of night, my belongings already stowed in trunks and a travelling outfit laid out? For a good long minute I stare at her, my eyes burning into hers…until eventually she turns away. It has all passed in a daze and I have a feeling now that a terrible mistake has been made.

The thing is, I never quite know what is going on anymore, drifting as I do across the boundary towards insanity with pained self-awareness. What has happened? How did I let myself be led away from my comfortable home onto this perilous journey?

"Oh, Madam, don't do that to your hands." She

passes over a pair of gloves. "Here we are – pop them back on, you're making an awful mess and no mistake."

Scratches. Oh dear Lord, look at them - the skin is quite raw, gouged and bloody…blackened nail beds as congealed and sticky as burnt jam, the nails themselves pulled clean out.

Suddenly the wheels slam violently into a rut. The horses stumble badly and the whole carriage whips around sideways. Luggage flies off the roof and we grind to a halt. Amid clanging metal and a blast of freezing night air, rain whips inside and the horseman is shouting. One of the horses is lame and we have to get out.

Standing there in the half-light with raw wind stinging our faces, we are still wrestling with hats and shawls when the resounding shot of death cracks over the moors. And when hours later I wake once more, it is to a stiff neck and to find the light has changed. Three horses not four now, their breath steaming on the early morning air, the pace a brisk trot on crunching gravel.

Skeins of ethereal mist hover over acres of fields and forests to either side. But the eye is drawn to what lies ahead. To the imposing stone mansion flanked by turrets. Bay windows dominate the ground floor, with two rows of sash windows above. This must be the retreat. Certainly there is no other building or village or sign of life within miles.

The fatigue of travelling all night without sleeping has taken its toll. I hope I will be shown to my room straight away – to bathe and take breakfast before resting. Oh yes, to sleep and sleep. I can hardly wait – to feel the soft comfort of bedding, the shutters drawn.

The carriage clatters into the forecourt, coming to a

stop outside the front door, and standing on the steps is a woman dressed in a uniform of grey serge, her hands folded neatly in front. I trust she is the housekeeper and do not pay her much attention. There is something else…something that sits uneasily within me…

"Here we are, Madam. Lavinia House."

Even as the woman on the steps begins to walk towards us, smartly and with purpose, I do not glance up. It is only when her hands are wrenching open the carriage door that the cause of my disquiet hits me like a bullet.

Those upstairs windows…they have bars across them.

***

Chapter One

Isobel Lee
1st February, 2018
Blackmarsh, Mid-Wales

It had gone five o'clock when Isobel drove past the sign for Blackmarsh, and fog had rolled off the mountains settling into the valley. Squinting into the murky evening the density of it caught her unawares and she only just noticed the white-painted fingerpost in time. It stood at a crossroads, the pub on the corner looming into view along with a small, cobbled square opposite. It sure was an easy place to miss.

The Drovers Inn had clearly seen better days, with stone walls covered in moss and grubby nets strewn across darkened windows. Still, a pub was a pub and her needs were pressing in more ways than one. It was also where the keys had been left for The Gatehouse.

Parking on the square between two rows of low-roofed cottages, she turned off the engine, the cessation of motion oddly abrupt in the muffled silence, and sat for a moment. Her head throbbed and her eyes were scratchy and hot. Behind the cottage curtains, lamps and fires had been lit against the dusk, and at the far end of the square a church spire tapered into the gloom. After a day of travelling the last few hours had, without doubt, been the most arduous - the concentration required on hazardous mountain passes with visibility down to nearly zero, taking its toll. But she was here now, well almost – just the key to collect.

Her high heels echoed loudly on the cobbles, a fine sheen of rain quickly coating her hair and face. Instinctively she glanced back, surprised to see the car had already been swallowed by the fog, and shivering, hurried towards the inn. The plan was to collect the keys, order a coffee and have a warm by the fire before continuing to the house and unpacking. With luck they would serve food too.

There were however, no lights on.

This was definitely the right day, wasn't it? She'd said after four, so…She rapped several times on the front door, then stood back and waited before rapping again, this time a little harder.

Still no answer. How annoying. The place gave every appearance of being closed. Not a sound - not even a dog bark. Perhaps if she went around the back someone might be in the kitchen? The agreement had definitely been for today at this time.

Night was drawing in rapidly now, drops of rainwater tinkling off gutters, the air pungent with wet earth and lichen. Fatigue and hunger weighed heavily and the pressure in her bladder had become urgent. Still she hesitated. It seemed intrusive to walk around to the back door. Maybe there was another entrance – on the main road? She walked around the corner to look, but the pub wall ended with empty fields and a solid bank of fog. Okay, it would have to be the back door, then! She tramped back, following the curve around to the narrow lane leading out to Lavinia House. Here the wall eventually gave way to an overgrown driveway littered with upside-down crates, dumped beer barrels and a dilapidated caravan.

She bit down the frustration. Sighed. Pulled out her mobile for the landlady's phone number. No signal. Of course, no signal. No streetlights either. No sign of life and not a sound, except the drip-drip-drip of damp coursing off roofs and the gurgling of marshy fields in every direction. Glancing down at her court shoes she resigned herself to picking through the long grass and debris to what would hopefully be a back door. Oh well, here goes…

"Esgusodwch fi!"

A man's voice caused her to wing around sharply.

"Oh, I'm sorry." She'd got as far as the corner of the garage and was holding onto a rickety drainpipe, already sinking into a squelch of mud. "I…I, um…don't speak Welsh. Sorry. Um…I was looking for Delyth Edwards? Is she–?"

"Ah, you want Delyth, do you? I think she had to go to the 'ospital – I'll give her a ring, see if she's back." A stocky man with his hands in his pockets stood in the lane, his back hunched against the rain while he gave her the up and down treatment.

"Thank you."

"And who shall I say wants her?"

"Oh, sorry, it's Isobel. Mrs Lee."

"Mrs Lee, is it? All right, give me a minute."

"Thank you."

As soon as he'd gone, she skidded and slipped back the way she came, hands stretched out in front for the wall. But at least by the time she was back on the pavement again, stamping her feet in an effort to scrape the mud off, there was a light in the pub window and the sound of bolts being drawn back.

Thank goodness! The thought of being stuck out here in the cold and dark all night...

A woman peeked around the side of the door. She had a large, bloated face the colour of uncooked dough, and wispy light hair that barely covered her scalp.

Pulling a chunky brown cardigan over her chest she said, "Oh, 'ello! Isobel Lee, is it? Sorry, I forgot it was today only I've been to see my mother in the 'ospital, see?"

Isobel followed her into a swirl of orange and brown from a bygone era – a lounge crowded with brass knick-knacks and hundreds of tankards hanging from the beams. God, it was horrible and it stank too. What was it? Boiled cabbage or old drains?

Slipping behind the bar, Delyth picked up a mug and drank with a succession of tiny slurps. "Oh, that's better, that is. I'm so cold. Been out all day. With my mother–"

"Yes." Isobel suppressed her irritation at the woman's lack of hospitality and then checked herself, offering a smile. *Low thyroid function, I wonder if she's having treatment?* "Of course–"

"Oh, sorry, it's the key you want, is it?"

"Thanks, yes. Look, I hate to ask but do you have a toilet I could use? Only I've had a long journey and there wasn't anywhere to stop." She looked around. It really was stuck in a time warp. The fire surround was made of ornate cast-iron with a bread oven to one side, the grate unlit and full of soot. Above it hung pictures of dead-eyed folk in Victorian dress.

"Ty bach's down the corridor." Delyth took another series of noisy slurps and hugged herself tighter into the cardigan.

Wondering why she didn't put the heating on or light the fire, Isobel thanked her and headed down a tiled corridor towards the ty bach, trying not to inhale the all-pervasive smell of body odour, boiled vegetables and general staleness. At the end there were no clues as to which of the three doors would lead to the Ladies and which to the Gents. One of the doors was locked and bolted like a prison cell and another, she quickly realised, opened into a broom cupboard. So, there was just the one ty bach then? With dismay she baulked at the state of it - no lock on the door and no soap, towel or loo roll. The bare bulb dangling on a wire only added to the sense of neglect, and by now it was hitting her just how travel-weary she was, the need to get to her destination suddenly overwhelming.

Delyth's sister, Gwen, was the cleaner, hence the key being left here. She could only hope her new home was considerably more spruce than the public house. *Ugh!* Cleanliness was her thing and this was just…ugh.

Back in the bar, Delyth had acquired company. An old man sat pint in hand, the two chatting away in Welsh as she reappeared. Her name, she was sure, had been in that last sentence of indecipherable consonants.

"I'll just get you that key then," said Delyth. "I know

Gwen left it somewhere…"

"Thank you."

With the old man eyeing her, she smiled politely and nodded hello, not sure if he spoke English. He wasn't particularly easy on the eye - with a coarse reddened face, bulbous nose exploding with purple veins, and peg teeth that stuck out in all directions; and Delyth was taking her time. A little awkward with him smiling and nodding but not speaking, she decided to casually examine the pictures on the walls. Most were line-ups of people from the Victorian age, too old for school photographs, too formal for factory or even church outings. Villagers, then? Perhaps they were taken for clubs or ceremonies?

Men with severe haircuts and ill-fitting three-piece suits stared out of sepia worlds. In others, a hotchpotch of women in long, drear dresses stared equally vacantly…There seemed to be something so poor about these people, so…

Without warning, a blast of crowd noise rushed into her head along with the unmistakeable stench of blood, human filth, illness and disease. So powerful was the assault on her senses that she had to reach out and clutch the mantelpiece for fear of falling. *Deep breaths…deep breaths…*

God, she should have known better than to stare at old photos.

Stupid…stupid…Swallowing down the surge of hot nausea, she turned away from them and hurried to the other side of the room as if something new had caught her eye, acutely aware of the old man's eyes boring into her back. *He'd noticed…damn…why couldn't he mind his own business?* For years she'd perfected the art of disguising the effect these attacks had on her. No one must know. If there was one thing to set people talking behind your back it was this.

At this end of the lounge a high-backed wooden bench lined the wall, instantly conjuring a row of miners and farmers sitting cheek by jowl drinking pints and smoking after a long day's work. Above the bench several oil paintings had been hung, and assuming they were by a local artist, Isobel peered in, genuinely interested. Paintings were safe.

Initially, she thought the effect might have been because of shadows cast by the single light bulb, but later – much later, when she would lie awake in the early hours – she knew that was not the case at all. Right there though, with the old man staring and her heart pumping hard, she was just grateful no one could see her face.

"Here we are," said a voice from far, far away. "I knew she'd put them somewhere."

Isobel swung around, disorientated. "What?"

"Good, aren't they - Branwen's paintings? Your keys, lovely."

"Oh…yes…thank you. Thank you so much."

Delyth clasped the mug of tea. "Well, I hope everything will be to your satisfaction, anyway. She's very good is Gwen."

"I'm sure it will be. Thank you."

By now she was hurrying away, unable to think clearly, blindly grabbing for the door handle. It was only when she was standing outside again on the damp, dark street that she realised she'd clean forgotten to ask for directions to Lavinia House let alone for a coffee.

There was something slightly wrong here, which didn't seem in keeping with the small church community described by the lettings agency. A darkness…something hidden and unsettling…amid layers as changeable and moody as the mountain mists.

***

Chapter Two

The Gatehouse, Blackmarsh

A few hours later Isobel woke violently, as if someone had shouted directly into her ear. Had they? Who was it? Where? She jumped to sitting position. There'd been a noise…banging or knocking…Surely not at the door? God, what time was it?

The digital alarm clock glowed in neon green: 02:23.

No, it must have been a dream, albeit a bad one.

Flopping back against the pillows she stared into the darkness for several long, heart-thumping seconds, struggling to remember where she was and why the hell it was so black in here. There wasn't a breath of air, the room icily still, and so completely devoid of noise or light that the creeping panic suddenly became over-whelming and she hit the light switch. This had been a mistake. A terrible mistake. To be so alone like this. Miles and miles from anywhere.

The last time she'd lived in rented accommodation was back in her early twenties, never dreaming she would be living out of a suitcase again at forty-one. How impersonal it was! The paper balloon in the centre of the ceiling now starkly illuminated white-washed walls, a serviceable brown, nylon carpet, and mismatching furniture that smelled of mould and mothballs. Floral curtains festooned a large bay window in shades of orange, reminiscent of hospital accommodation – those spacious Victorian residences converted into nurses' flats as cheaply as possible. Probably this had once been a beautiful house, with its generously proportioned rooms and long, sash windows; no doubt gutted and replaced with functionality for rental income.

Still, it could be made homely enough - a few rugs, plants and pictures would make all the difference.

And those had been her thoughts when drifting off to sleep a few hours ago - of sourcing rugs and throws, paintings and candles - but something was very different now, the atmosphere no longer one of simple emptiness. With a puzzled frown she registered the new reality. While she had been asleep every drawer in the pine chest had been pulled open. And the wardrobe door was ajar.

A sickly lump lodged in her throat. Had she left them like that?

No, no I didn't….

For a good few minutes the rapid thudding of her heartbeat banged in her ears. Before the rational side of her brain cut in. Okay, this is what must have happened – on arrival, tired and tetchy, she would have had a quick scout round checking everything before crashing into bed. Yes. And left the drawers open. Must have.

Certainly she'd been exhausted.

Obviously hadn't been thinking clearly.

In fact she'd been more tired than ever before, even on a ward at five am on a night shift. The fog had thickened during the short time spent in the pub waiting for the key, and the car headlights were rendered useless, reflecting only a dizzying white glare.

16

It had been a struggle to follow the directions issued by the letting agency, with one wrong turning after another. Nor had it been easy to turn round on those winding, mountainous lanes.

She had just come to the point of despair when the driveway to Lavinia House loomed quite suddenly, its distinctive stone lions towering over the gateposts. She'd almost cried with relief. A grand stone archway stamped with the family coat of arms announced what was an imposing estate, although the wrought iron gates now hung from their hinges, rusting into the ground. Reputedly one of the largest private houses in Wales, it had belonged to an English family through successive generations and was said to have been used as an asylum at one point, the gentleman of the house being what was termed an alienist or mad doctor. These days, however, it served once more as a private residence.

The Gatehouse was located immediately by the archway, and since she had neither the time nor energy to do anything other than quickly unload the car and grab the box with the kettle and coffee in it, there was gratitude to be had in that. She really had done precious little – the absolute necessities only - before falling into bed exhausted.

Attempting now to stay calm, Isobel forced herself to mentally comb through her actions from the night before. It was as difficult as having to recall a dream or period of drunkenness, her conscious mind continually blocking the train of thought. After locking the front door behind her she'd flung her suitcase in the cupboard under the stairs, put the box of kitchen items on the table and then run upstairs while the kettle boiled.

What then?

All right, well she knew herself pretty well – definitely she'd have whipped back the bed sheets and more than likely checked the wardrobe and drawers for cleanliness before hanging up her coat. Yes, and then neglected to close them again because she'd been so darned tired. Okay, right, that made sense. But...

No, *something had* woken her up...a knocking noise, a persistent banging...

A shiver suddenly goosed up her back. The ceiling light barely reached the four walls, which seemed blacker than ever. Was that her own breath or was there another...?

Christ, something else is breathing in here...

Oh good God no, this was no bloody good. She had to do something – make tea, anything. Wide awake and fully creeped out, she pushed back the covers and sat on the edge of the bed. The night air was as cold as a morgue.

There was definitely something knocking in here...it woke you deliberately....those drawers were being pulled out...one by one...and you know it!

Hurriedly now, she shoved on slippers and grabbed her dressing gown. It was those damn paintings in the pub. They'd given her nightmares. Those tiny, wizened figures with wrinkly faces and twisted mouths. It wasn't just that they were macabre, that the artist clearly enjoyed creating malevolent looking creatures, it was more the shot of recognition they'd evoked - the sudden overpowering aura of moss-ridden woods and sickly disorientation. Even more than that though, was the conviction of having been here before. And being punched in the gut with the fear of it.

Padding downstairs in the full glare of the landing light, she wished now she'd closed the curtains. Outside, the fog lay thick and damp with not a thread of light to permeate the moonless night. And with the house lit up like a stage it lent a curious feeling of being watched. The dining room was empty of furniture, with bare floorboards and a blackened grate. Swishing shut drapes of chintz she hurried across the hall and into what had been the front parlour, marching straight in to find a figure standing under the bare lightbulb.

It caught her completely off guard.

Less than a second. A flash of blue light. A vague impression. And then it was gone.

Christ!

She stood with her hand to her heart. Panting. Still holding onto the door handle where she'd burst in a moment ago.

Had that happened?

Or was it a trick of the light?

It had to be a trick. No one had been registered as living here. And definitely not a woman. For it was a woman. Elderly, black dress….long skirts….

No, no – it had been her own reflection - in the glass!

She breathed a long sigh of relief, laughing at herself. *For goodness sake Issy, get a grip. It's a new place, you've had a bad dream and you're spooked. Everything will be perfectly all right when the sun comes up.*

Shaking with relief she closed the curtains, left the room and clicked shut the door.

At the end of the hall the kitchen lay in darkness, the

outlines of fitted units and furniture shadowy. She should make some tea and go back to bed, get some sleep and put everything in perspective. These were only her nerves talking, bad dreams and fears coming to the surface.

On nearing the doorway, however, a cold draught blew against her cheek. As if a door had opened somewhere.

No...there was definitely something sinister here...and the sense of that was chilling her back like a dark shadow. As if whatever it was had followed her from the parlour.

Light! Get the light on!

This was getting silly.

Get. The. Light on!

Damn, where was the switch?

She fumbled blindly around the door frame, the feeling of rapidly escalating dread now overpowering. Something or someone was behind her. That woman in the parlour. Oh God...

Got it!

The kitchen lit up in a surgical glare.

At that exact moment, the dull, repetitive thudding she instantly knew had woken her, began again...a steady bump...bump...bump...against an upstairs wall. As if someone was banging their forehead against it. And even in the bright, white light, fear clutched at her heart.

There was no way she could stay here. No way.

***

Chapter Three

1893
Flora George
Lavinia House

"No, I will not stay here. Take me home at once. Driver, turn the horses around!"

This is no retreat. This is an asylum. A madhouse. The woman standing at the carriage door stares with such insolence. No curtsey from her - merely a nod to the maid as if the two of them are in league. And what is this? She has the impertinence to reach inside the carriage and...

"Now Madam, Mr George said you were to be brought here for a few days, just until you were well—"

Rage explodes inside of me. "How dare you! No, I absolutely refuse. I will not get out of this carriage, no—"

I can scarcely believe it, but the awful woman is grabbing at my arms, and the maid who last night brushed my hair is helping her. It is beyond all manner of belief.

"Let's get you inside now, shall we, Mrs George?"

She has the nipped face of a harridan indeed, and her grip is one of iron. Another of her ilk now hurries down the steps and takes hold of my other arm so that I am quite pinned between them, hauled away like some common prisoner. Vaguely I am aware of the spectacle I must present - bucking and kicking – whilst helplessly looking over my shoulder at the sound of the horses being led away, the maid scurrying alongside them with her head down. No doubt she is heading for that breakfast she's been so looking forward to. Shameful! Damn her to high hell for keeping me drugged and fed with lies.

"Get off me. Get your damn hands off me."

"Come on now, Flora. The doctor's waiting for you and you really don't want him to see you like this, do you?"

"What doctor? I wish to go home immediately. I have been tricked. And how dare you address me in such a way."

But this time when I turn around the horses have gone, the sound of their hooves a muffled clip-clop in a stable yard I cannot see.

The fear is a knife blade to my stomach.

"No, no! I will not go in. Let go of me!"

It is impossible to break free, the vice grip tightening as a noose with every struggle. One of them calls out and now a man…oh God, the humiliation of it…is approaching with a stretch of cloth.

"Bit wild, isn't she? Don't let her kick now. Just bloody hold her." And in less than a breath he's got it fastened round my waist, adeptly pinning my arms to the sides. He's laughing, chuckling away through rotten peg teeth, wafts of his sour breath nauseating.

And thus it is with great indignity that the four of us shuffle and skirmish our way into the cavernous, wood-panelled hallway of Lavinia House.

Behind , the heavy oak door clicks firmly shut. A bolt is shot. A key turned in the lock.

It has a sobering effect.

With the finality of that resounding clunk, standing silent and shocked, the fight suddenly drains out of me and tears erupt in torrents of despair. The great gasps and stuttering intakes of breath are as a child's even to my own ears. Alas, I am so wretched with tiredness. What have I done to deserve this? And what fate awaits me beyond those double doors to the doctor's consulting room?

There is no chair, no glass of water, no arm of comfort around my shoulders. Instead they simply wait until the worst subsides.

"Is she calm now?" someone asks. "Shall we take her in?"

In the oak door there is a large knot and it is this which now arrests my attention as the sobbing quietens and tears dry. It resembles the face of a man - with tiny, close-set eyes and wild hair...So they are here, too - the wood sprites?

The old man's face twinkles. I think he winks.

My God, they are everywhere...they have followed me all this way.

"Come on, Gwilym, she's calm enough. The doctor hasn't got all day - undo her, is it?"

Trembling from head to foot, it takes all the strength I have to stand up straight while the ties are yanked un-done and the harridan taps on the door.

It is a strange house. The corridor behind is dark, air-less and gloomy, the staircase leading to the upper floors narrow and oppressive. From somewhere high above us a woman's screams, rising and impassioned, rent the air. To what have my husband and dear sister abandoned me? Nothing bodes well. Dried tears sting my cheeks. This doctor – he is going to ask me what happened, isn't he? Why Samuel and Amelia consulted with a local medic and had me sent here.

And I do not recall. That's the thing - I really cannot remember. A lurch of panic rises in my throat. I do not know how to save myself.

***

Doctor Edgar Fox-Whately, the Alienist and owner of Lavinia House, is a man with a pale, glassy stare and a twist of razor wire for a mouth. I draw, I paint, I pick out what others do not always notice – and were I to depict this man it would be to the exclusion of everything that is ordinary about him, such as the religious severity of his black waistcoat and starched white collar, in order to highlight the sheer force of contempt in that stony-eyed scrutiny. His thin lips, moistly aglow in a forest of facial hair, he licks repeatedly, and revulsion twitches inside my empty stomach.

"You have made quite a fuss," he says by way of introduction.

"Thank you for asking, I had an unpleasant journey and I am most dreadfully tired. I would like to be taken to my room immediately, please."

"You will be going to your room soon enough, Mrs George. First we must document your arrival here, after which you will be bathed and provided with clean clothing–"

He appears to have forgotten his manners. "May I sit?"

He indicates a hard-backed wooden chair in the middle of the room. The harridan seems to be standing in attendance and I wish she would leave. I do not wish for the embarrassment of having the staff know my personal details.

"I would like that woman to leave, please."

"Mrs Payne is here for your protection and you should be grateful to her. She will be your personal attendant during your stay. Thus, she needs to know everything about you in order to offer you the best of care. Do you understand?"

"Of course. I am not without wit, sir."

On his desk is a large copy of the bible, and a ledger. The latter he pulls towards him. This, it transpires, is what is known as a Letter Book, in which our diagnoses, histories and prognoses will be recorded for the Commissioner of Lunacy. He takes his time writing, dipping the nib into ink, deliberating on each word. Occasionally his gaze flicks to my face, while presumably he judges and describes my appearance. At long last he puts down the pen. "Would you take off your gloves now, Mrs George?"

"I beg your pardon?"

"I asked if you would take off your gloves, Madam."

"I would rather not."

"Please do as I ask. I am a doctor and I need to examine you."

I could flee the room right now, run down the drive to the road and flag a passing carriage. But in that flicker of a glance to the double doors, the harridan steps a little closer. Perhaps for the moment it would serve better to feign serenity and do as the doctor says. He is my best chance of an early discharge.

Alas, on taking off my gloves his eyebrows shoot up at the sight of the shredded skin and congealed blood where my nails should be. "What caused you do that to yourself, Flora?"

"I really do not know. And my name is Mrs George."

He pauses from scribbling, looks up. "You do not remember doing it or you do not know why you did it?"

"I had something irritating my skin. I expect I must have done it during the night.

His gaze locks on mine. "You pulled your nails out in your sleep?"

"I must have."

"Did you see a physician?"

"Yes."

"And what was his diagnosis?"

"An irritation of the skin. I had to wear gloves and apply cream."

"I see."

He stares directly into my eyes. Several minutes pass in this manner. Voices from the far reaches of the house carry like ghosts on a breeze. And only after the longest time does he apparently allow the matter to drop.

"I would like you to remove your bonnet now, please." He motions to the woman behind me. "Mrs Payne, would you–?"

"No, do not touch me. I am quite capable of removing my own hat."

My hair is coiffured to perfection day and night and

with good reason, but Mrs Payne is already marching forth and unpinning the bonnet, tugging at my coil of hair… Letting it fall in long, burnished tresses to my waist…exposing the all too visible patches of shiny, bare scalp the size of guinea coins.

There is a tiny gasp from someone.

Shame roars into my ears.

Like my hands, I do not know how or when this happened. Sometime during those weeks…days or weeks…in the dark chamber…Oh dear God, I cannot remember…

"What happened to your scalp, Flora?"

Amid the thumping in my head, my ears, my chest, a small voice is saying, "My name is Mrs George. I would thank you to address me in the proper manner."

"What happened to your scalp? To your hair?"

"Yes, yes, I believe it was after the child was born. It started to come out… in my hairbrush. Nurse said it would grow back and it happens to everyone, well to many people, lots of times, and…and…" Grief seizes hold of me with an almighty squeeze to the chest. My voice falters as desperately I'm trying so hard to think of something else and failing. Anything…but not that…

"Child? Hmmm, I am particularly pleased you brought up the subject of the child, Mrs George. Good, yes, very good indeed " He puts down the pen and leans back in his leather armchair, eyeing the top of my poor scalp in the harsh, grey light of morning.

"And what do you recall about this child, Mrs George?"

A sudden flashback. Of the sash window slicing down like a guillotine…of the howling pain in my black, empty soul….

"Mrs George?"

There were faces…everywhere…whispers...

"Flora? Can you hear me?"

I can see them now, just as they appeared to me then - faces, spirits from the woods – in the fabric of the wallpaper, carved into the bedposts, hidden in the patterns of the curtains, the knots in the floorboards….chattering, whispering. It grew louder and louder, ever more incessant.

But then one morning the maid came chattering in and stopped dead in the doorway, dropping the tray, hands cupped to her face. "Oh, Madam."

I turned then, and saw clearly a reflection of myself in the dressing table mirror. An emaciated, hollow-eyed woman with plugs of hair pulled clean out of her scalp, her hands and arms all covered in blood.

After that a different doctor came – one wearing a top hat - and instructed the maids to tie my hands to the bed posts with sheets, to nail shut the window

His voice is harder now. Louder. More insistent. "Flora! Mrs George! I am asking you a question. What do you recall about the child? Most particularly the birth?"

They would not tell me. No one would tell me anything. I was lying in the dark…

"Your husband informs me you tried to take your own life. Do you remember–?"

"He lies."

"What does he lie about?"

"He lies, all the time, about everything–"

"Flora, do you recall if your child lives?"

Does he? Oh pray to God he does. But where? That is the thing. Where is my child? What happened to him? I simply cannot remember. I travel so far along a tunnel of recollection and then it just stops. There is no more. It is akin to picturing infinity - what happens outside the expansion of the expansion of the expansion? Every single time the mind blanks out.

Dr Fox-Whately's red worm lips are moving but his voice is projecting from another part of the room entirely - a distortion of sound from a faraway place just like it was with the pudding-faced maid back in the carriage. An age ago. A lifetime. I should have jumped. But I have a child, I know I do. I gave birth. My breasts leak and my womb aches.

"Well, perhaps after six months here at Lavinia House you will start to remember, hmm?"

Why can I not remember? Why? Every time I try to recall the birth or the baby's face, there is nothing there. It is quite as if all memory has been excised, and because of that, part of myself is lost forever - my history, my life. How can that be? How?

He is scribbling again in the ledger, dipping the nib in and out of the ink pot with painstaking pedantry. "I'm prescribing laudanum and a moral treatment regime. You must work hard and have a healthy diet. I am confident that with the help of the good Lord and our capable staff you will make a good recovery. You are very ill, Flora. You do see that?"

"I must see Amelia. May I write to my sister? I cannot be simply left here."

"Your sister and your husband may correspond with you, of course." He turns away, done with me now.

"Mrs Payne, please take this lady to the admissions room—"

I hear no more. His words have caught up with me. And registered most fully.

Six months, he said six months!

***

Chapter Four

I hear no more... I hear no more...

I must have screamed myself hoarse, and thus it is with a sore throat and a pounding head that I jump awake. There is a weight on the bed like that of a small animal...and the sound of malicious chuckling.

I had been dreaming, careering in a horse-driven carriage over mountain tops, telling the baby I was clasping not to fear the Otherworld. That we were travelling far too quickly to be caught...that no one could catch us...faster, faster, faster...

Alas, it was merely a dream. In reality the night is black as pitch, and staring at me - a matter of inches away - is a most unearthly face.

"Oh, dear God!"

At my sharp lurch backwards, the creature skulks closer, stealthy as a cat, its weight straddling my chest. Its skin is parchment white and crinkled as tissue, its darting eyes of madness peering into mine with a fiery glee. The overwhelming stink of urine and sulphur catches in my throat. This creature, this repulsive, filthy creature, is squatting on my bed, and fingering my scalp.

Scalp!

Oh God yes, I remember now. They held me down,

cut off my hair….I cannot bear it. Oh God! I have no hair! I have no hair!

The creature starts in delight at my sudden consciousness. Its eyes search mine, enthralled with the expression of what must be profound horror. Fascinated to the point of excitement, its bony fingers begin to trace down my cheek, down and down…to the neck, before, in a sudden jerk of movement, it pins my arms with a grip belying its fragile form and snatches back the covers. Sniggering now, it shuffles down the bed to further examine, prod and poke, yanking up my nightdress.

"No! Get off me. Christ!"

It stops instantly, glancing up in surprise, eyes of black flint. Then suddenly my head is rammed so hard against the metal bedhead it knocks the breath clean out of my chest with shock. Swiftly followed by one bony hand winging back. Too late I see it is clutching a shoe. As with sickening pain it wallops into the side of my face.

Something cracks. Sears. Skin splits open.

And through the blinding tears of my scream the creature recoils, hops from the bed and scampers across the floor on all fours. The image is only on the periphery of a vision blurred with pain, already dissipating into the gloom, but I am not mistaken. It skitters like a dog, scuttling sideways on spidery limbs, cackling hysterically.

I cannot stay here.

I cannot…will not….

That thing, that unworldly creature, no – it could not be human – it had to be a hallucination, yes an opiate-induced dream. That would explain it. None of this is real. I have had terrible dreams before - during those long days and nights in the chamber...batting away giant spiders on the bedspread that swelled in size and ran into my hair...being unable to stop them because my hands were tied. It was punishment, you see? That is what the whispers were about. And the more I screamed the more they ran across my face and into my mouth...

Alas, my cries have brought her forth.

Myra Strickland, the housekeeper, holds a lantern over my bed, her long, coffin shaped face swinging in and out of shadows. "What on earth is all this screaming for? Lie down in your bed properly or you will have to be restrained."

"I was woken...I think one of the—"

"Silence! Do not answer back. Go to sleep. Nor do I expect to be wakened from my bed again this night, do you hear?"

Her voice is a bark laced with barely contained loathing, one which triggers the padlocked memory of that belonging to a nurse I once had as a child. It claws now into the vessels of my heart and squeezes. Certainly it is one I will never forget to my dying day. And why it is so easy for her to thrust a spoonful of laudanum to my lips.

Slowly after that, the unnatural cries, moans and banging noises from within this dreadful place, begin to mute and fade.

It is a respite. A hazy, grey place of limbo.

Before the full horror is revealed.

***

Morning is a chill, grey dawn of rain smattering across barred windows, coupled with a stench like no other. Wild screams and deranged moans resound in what is a cold, hollow dormitory lined with sash windows jammed shut. There is no fire to warm the freezing, fetid air, the small grate at the far end a gaping black hole.

Someone is shouting the same words over and over again, 'Get out of my head, get out of my head, get out of my head…' One or two of the women have soiled themselves and are being cleaned up in full view of the rest of us; a mobile basin unit wheeled from one bed to another without the water being changed. Surely they will not bring that filthy water to me? Surely?

A few yards from the foot of my bed a used commode has been parked, left uncovered for all to see its contents. The whole floor stinks of human waste, disease and filth. It is a smell I am sure I will never forget, mixed as it is with that of unwashed bodies and entrenched sickness – an all pervading, sour stench of sepsis. This will stay with me. Haunt me. As will the bursts of maniacal laughter, screeches of rage and howls of torment.

How long must I stay?

I pray like I have never prayed before, that it will not be the six months cited. Please God, please God I beg you – set me free from this appalling plight.

In the opposite bed a woman lies staring at the ceiling. Bald and cadaverous, half her face has decayed, bones and toothless gums exposed, facial tissue wasted away. What is left of her skin is covered in lumpy warts, the hands clutching at the sheets weeping with open sores. She resembles a corpse ready for the ground. How can she still be alive? Is she still alive? From time to time a wet, gurgling moan escapes from her throat, her sunken eyes rolling back in the sockets.

I have been sleeping opposite this poor, diseased creature? They put me here?

And what of the one who attacked me last night, the one who lopes on all fours like a wild dog? Does she walk normally this morning or cower in the shadows. One or two of the rake-thin, half-naked people being herded into a communal bathroom take off their night-dresses in full view, exposing hunched spines and jutting ribs; others wring their hands and mutter to themselves; some lie still manacled to cots, their screams renting the air.

And now it seems, it is my turn. The harridan, Mrs Payne, stands over me, sleeves rolled up.

"Out of bed, Flora. Bathroom and breakfast."

Flora!

Instantly the memory of last night flashes before me - the stripping of my clothes, the confiscation of purse and possessions, even the locket with pictures of Samuel and I on our wedding day. How I stood naked and shameful while she and the other one scrubbed my body with cold water and detergent, before chopping off my hair to the scalp. I fought back with everything I had but those two women are not only as strong as farmhands but brutal with it, and I will not make that mistake again. The doctor was called and the horrible red-faced man, Gwilym held me to the floor while morphine was administered. After that I do not recall much, except the familiar sinking, heavy limbed feeling as the opiate took hold. And sniggers from corners I could not see.

She whips back the sheets. "Take off your nightdress and go to the bathroom."

There is little choice but to join the herd of disgusting imbeciles who talk to themselves and pick at their sores. We share hairbrushes, towels, and bath water. Misery streams down my face. I shut my eyes. Sliding into a filthy tub while she pours buckets of icy water over my head and scrubs my back with a brush just used on another.

"And you can stop that blubbering."

The dress she hands over is of scratchy grey wool with a red asylum label blatantly sewn on the outside. And on top of that there is an apron, worn like that of a maid.

"Why an apron?"

"Because after breakfast you will be starting work, Flora. It's called moral therapy – you're all treated the same here, we'll have no airs and graces."

Despite the sickly growl of hunger, all thoughts of eating anything in this foul dwelling are repugnant. "I do not wish to partake of breakfast."

"Oh, you will."

"I will not."

"You will, Flora. And if you don't you will be made to. It is not your place to deny yourself food."

But I will not eat. Not here. I would rather die.

The dining room is a madhouse full of toothless, dribbling lunatics shovelling slop into their mouths. Long wooden benches ensure close proximity, the food is rancid and the grain alive with crawling things.

It is the most diabolical breakfast hour, quite unendurable, with my neighbour constantly fingering my clothes, peering into my face, touching and pawing. Have they no social mores? Another sits in a pool of her own urine, clearly having some kind of dreadful fit, her neck and face contorting with jerks and tics.

I can take no more and bolt from the room.

Alas, it is at the foot of the stairs where they wait. Mrs Payne. And Myra Strickland.

For a second confusion clouds my brain.

And then all becomes clear. Myra is holding a length of tubing. And Mrs Payne is armed with restraints. Frantically I look for a way of escape but all routes are blocked.

You will eat, Flora. And if you don't you will be made to...

***

Chapter Five

2018
Isobel, The Gatehouse

04:00 hours and perishing.

The pilot light on the boiler would not ignite, and her breath steamed on the air. Isobel sat at the kitchen table staring into the blue light of her laptop and drinking scorching coffee. At least there was electricity and, thank goodness, an internet connection. At the time of choosing somewhere to rent, Wi-Fi hadn't featured high on the list of 'must-haves,' but right here and now it was a godsend. Half way through the email to Nina, her closest friend, she paused to listen once more to the silent house. The banging noise had finally stopped, but if she relaxed even for a moment it would start up again for sure. For pity's sake, this was precisely what she'd come here to escape!

Nina - half Indian, half Yorkshire - brooked no nonsense whilst holding deeply spiritual beliefs. Nina listened with an emotional intelligence rarely found in today's selfie-obsessed society, seemingly without ego and brimming with compassion. They'd come together in an environment mutually detested but unavoidable at the time - that of corporate meetings, workshops and seminars. Catching each other's eye during a particularly life-draining session, they exchanged a complicit smile and soon became experts at trying to make each other laugh at the most inappropriate moments.

It was hard to say exactly what it was about the modern business world that so alienated her, but if she tried it would be a toss-up between the falsity of its employees and the meaninglessness of her existence while doing it. Everything from the fashionable speak adopted by her colleagues who, 'like, literally guys, ended every sentence with an upwards inflection,' to the general loud sense of entitlement and pouting readiness to be offended, cut her further adrift. And the longer it went on the more the screaming pressure inside her intensified. Week on week. Month on month. Until there was no longer any choice but to change her life immediately.

But by then it was way too late.

Nina now ran her own fledgling business, still single, still gutsy.

Isobel, on the other hand, had walked away with nothing. Divorced. Lost. Drowning in alcohol and wondering what the hell to do next. Then again, few had to endure the barrage of psychic attacks assailing her on a nightly basis …sometimes even during the day…and even fewer believed it actually happened at all. She was not meant for the same world as everyone else, that was the truth of it - the pull towards what some may call talking to the dead and others would term spiritual mediumship, setting her apart. Little wonder her husband had become angry and one by one every single person she came into contact with backed off. They were all scared. Really scared. More than that

– terrified.

The painful realisation that she was different began as a child, when one night she opened her eyes to find a ghostly figure standing in the middle of the bedroom – a lady with an ashen complexion and hollow eyes wearing a long, ruffled dress. At her throat she wore a locket on a choker, and her hair had been fashioned into a fringe of curls beneath a fussy black bonnet. The woman told her she used to live in the house, and that a bottle lay hidden in one of the foundation walls, which contained both a newspaper of the day and some photographs. The apparition then faded softly into the upholstery, leaving five year old Isobel staring in amazement.

Next day at breakfast she excitedly related the event to her parents, urging them to seek the bottle and see if it was true.

What happened next, however, caused a rift in the family that never healed. Her father fixed her with a glare of dismay, his words shards of ice. Ghosts never had and never would exist, Isobel. He had expected better from a child of his, and she was never, ever again to mention such nonsense in this house, did she understand? Did she?

The shocked silence at that breakfast table with everyone staring at her, still occasionally replayed in nightmares, the way her reality had been exposed as an unspeakable thing. Worse, her mother said that people who saw and heard things that no one else did, ended up in lunatic asylums. In tears she'd sat and howled, learning from that day on never to mention the shadow people standing in the corner of a room, or to pass on information that flashed into her mind.

Many years later though, when the kitchen floor-boards became springy with wood rot and her father hired a joiner to rip them out, a bottle was discovered nestling in the brickwork. She watched her dad's reaction, how the colour drained from his face as the man fished out the contents. He could hardly tell him not to do it – it was an exciting find, after all. And then exactly as she'd described ten years before, the time capsule revealed a rolled-up broadsheet from 1891 together with several sepia photographs. Wordlessly, these were passed around to each member of the family, at which point Isobel's heart had almost stopped right there and then. Staring out of the picture in the newspaper article about a missing girl, was a woman in Victorian dress with a locket around her neck and a fringe of curls – without question the one who had previously shown herself.

After that, she knew she had the sight. And that it was real. She also knew to be very discreet about who she told - that most people either did not believe in the afterlife or were too frightened to want to think about it; and some, as her mother cautioned, would actually think her mentally unwell. Although that, as it turned out, was far less concerning than communicating with the spirit world itself. Many were not wholesome, and some could be downright dangerous, setting out to purposefully terrify or even possess. The truly evil ones, those from the lowest astral planes, often pretended to be a loved one, preying on the bereaved, heartbroken or recklessly curious in order to enter the material world. And it was these tricksters she had inadvertently meddled with. And let in.

Alas, as with so many things, the lesson had come

with far too high a price and was far too late.

Intrigued by her gift, a schoolmate had spread the word and before she knew it she'd become something of a curio, suddenly popular and in demand. One or two girls asked her to read their cards, which she quickly learned how to do, surprising everyone including herself with their accuracy. And then came the game of Ouija. It had been a dare, a laugh, with lights out and candles lit – the girls giggling, the boys swigging high percentage cider. She didn't let on that it wasn't a joke, that it was real and it seriously frightened her. Instead she played along with the horror movies, pizza night and cheap booze. Then laughing and flirting, pushed the planchette around the board with the others.

Hoping nothing would happen.

Praying inside that it would not.

Knowing in her heart that it would.

With her there, it definitely would.

All at once the teenage giggling and shrieking became muted as if from a great distance, replaced with what sounded like a tuning fork singing in her ears. Quickly followed by the queer sensation of falling backwards down a dark well. The fall was felt as a thump in the solar plexus, the same feeling as the lurch sometimes felt on falling asleep, except it continued and the fall went on and on. She must have gasped and gripped the table, trying desperately to stop the descent.

Are you all right?

Has she fainted?

I told you not to bring that home brew...

One or two candlelit faces swam overhead, voices echoing as if shouting down a drain.

Perhaps she was drunk or had been drugged and they were laughing at her?

But the place she was in had a hard, cold floor like a cellar or vault, and a chill wind whistled from a tunnel, along with the funereal toll of a bell.

The others did not hear. But she heard. Knew what was coming even as she began to surface with what felt like the worst hangover ever. Knew that when a bird banged into the window making the girls scream, and then a door slammed upstairs, exactly what had been invited in.

After that night she couldn't sleep, frequently starting awake with the conviction someone was in the corner of the room. Sometimes it felt as though a cat was on the bed, a purring weight, yet she had no cat. Other times there would be a sudden cold blast of air against her cheek in what was a warm, heated room. To escape the sensation of being followed and watched, she speeded up – kept busy, tried to never be alone, kept the lights on even at night, and made a concerted effort not to think about it, to zonk spark out with pills at the end of each increasingly busy day.

But in the end the darkness caught up with her. Just as she knew it would.

It happened one night walking home through the park from a club, initially in the form of solitary footsteps on the path behind. Time and again she winged around…only to find the park empty. Continuing at a more hurried pace, positive someone was right behind her, the fast walk became a jog then finally a sprint. It was not real. There was no one there…Over and over she told herself this was her imagination…even as the footsteps quickened along with her own…and the night darkened rapidly to the point where not even the outline of the trees could be seen. Was it still her imagination that the moon had vanished behind a sky now blacker than black, the lamplights in the park dimming? She broke into a flat-out run, the feeling of dread now overwhelming, until there he was – suddenly and impossibly. Directly in front of her stood a man in a coal black suit and hat, waiting by the church railings, the tip of his cigarette a singular red spark.

Drink, drugs, all-night parties and a punishing work-load helped, but not forever. The spirits pursued her. Relentlessly. It ruined her marriage. It ruined her career. It ruined nights out and it ruined friendships.

All except Nina's, that was. Nina got it. "Seems to me you haven't much choice, love. You've got to learn to control it or you're going to be a sodding victim all your life, and into the next."

"Oh, great." She eyed her friend. "Seriously, have you any idea, I mean any idea, how real this is? What it's like to be drifting off to sleep and feel someone sit down on the side of your bed, only you're the only one in the house? Or be talking to someone and see their face change into someone else's? And how do I know what's genuine and what's a trick?"

Nina, who believed in karma and reincarnation, shook her head and confessed she knew nothing of the dark side.

She told her then about the sudden drops in temper-ature before an apparition; the babble of voices - like a choir rising and fading on the breeze; and some but by no means all, of the disturbing events experienced during the times she'd dabbled, prodded and taunted the Unseen. It was hard to describe the confusing welter of howls and unearthly screams that had almost sent her mad; even harder to explain the echoing footsteps of someone not there that night in the park - how she'd run to the point of collapse until she reached the church, only to find him there first. She had pulled and pulled at the lychgate to get onto holy ground but it was padlocked, then practically vaulted over the railings and huddled in the porch until first light like a whimpering dog. That it had left her with a fear so great she'd spent the rest of her life running from it. She could never be on her own too long, couldn't sleep, and if she did it was to wear headphones playing audio books into her head for fear of hearing voices.

"Did you get help?" Nina asked.

"Kind of. I learned how to pray, to believe in God, to picture white light–"

"I mean with being psychic?"

"Well, no because I don't want to be–"

"But you are - a gift like that, you know - you can't *not* have it."

"But don't you see? It's what comes with it…it's like you acknowledge the Unseen and a door opens and…"

No. Stop. Isobel, stop! Don't go over this kind of stuff at this time of night, especially not here in this bloody house…

She must not re-conjure what happened that night. Mustn't think of all she had told Nina, and of that terrible time spent in the hospital…

Think of something else for Christ's sake!

She stood up and stretched. Then despite the hour,

rummaged through a box of groceries brought from the sold-up marital home, unscrewed the cooking brandy and began flicking through pictures on Rightmove and Zoopla – looking at houses on the coast, imagining the fresh breath of salty air and billowing white curtains. Calming down, thinking nice things.

Before resuming the email.

'You know I'm thinking, Nina, that maybe you were right after all, and I am going to have to confront this. I suppose I thought if I got away from people there would be less of a barrage of spirits, but they're here too, even in the middle of nowhere, in fields and mountains…It's as if I've run into the dead-end of a darkened alley and finally have to stop running–'

She stopped typing. What the fuck was that? Every single light downstairs was switched on for a good reason - spirits travelled in the dark much more easily. She emptied the last of the brandy into her coffee mug and took a good long swig. Spirits and spirits…*Yeah, well why not? Who wouldn't in my situation?*

Resuming typing, she scrubbed the last paragraph and decided to adopt the jolly, 'I'm fine' tone she used when at her absolute worst. 'Anyway, I have to say this valley is breath-taking. It's the right place for anyone who wants to stop the world and get off for a while, that's for sure. I imagine it's been the same for hundreds if not thousands of years – virtually unspoilt – I'll upload some pictures tomorrow. As for the asylum it's now in ruins and only a small part of it's lived in – by the local doctor and his wife, would you believe? Apparently she's very involved in church fund-raising activities. Oh, I must tell you, though – talking about things not changing for hundreds of years – the village is a bit weird actually. The pub was empty last night when I arrived, apart from this woman who couldn't be arsed to open up until someone phoned her. Anyway, there were some really spooky paintings on the wall – sort of tiny wizened creatures that were neither human nor animal – like trolls from a fairy tale. They had crinkly, tissue paper faces set on black canvas and they looked startled, as if caught out, not used to being seen...'

Again she paused. The silence fizzed almost like a living thing.

"Who's there? Is someone there?"

She stared through the atoms - at the fully lit, glossy white units, the steadily humming fridge, then down the corridor towards the front door. A light rain spattered against the kitchen window.

Did she dare begin to use her gift again? Attempt to control it? Here? On her own? Really...? What if there was an answer...?

Her heart squeezed in her chest. She reached for the mug and downed the dregs.

No, no, no....go away!

It was the fear. The one thing she couldn't describe - not to Nina, not to anyone. That sickly bang in the chest, a piercing awareness that this was either communication with dead people. Or entities that may never have even been human. Or insanity.

Again there came a creeping feeling of being observed like an actor on a brightly lit stage.

With shaking fingers she hastily finished the email. 'Anyway, Nina, don't worry, so far so good. I just wanted to tell you that I got here in one piece and it's an amazing place. Look, I promise to sort myself out, honest. I'll be fine. Keep safe. Hope all is good with you and chat soon… lots love, Issy xxx'

She closed the laptop. Well, she had to be all right, didn't she? Six months' rent upfront had used up the last of a pitiable divorce settlement. Question was, had she made a terrible mistake coming here or was this to be the making of her?

"Guess I've run out of options either way," she said aloud. "Right, come on then, Isobel Lee, you've got to do this. No one can do it but you because you're absolutely on your bloody own."

Methodically she began clearing the table, rinsed the mug, and made another coffee to take back up to bed. Soon it would be dawn and with it the light would come. Logic. It was important not to let fear overrun her mind. First it would be useful to know who the ghosts were in this house and communicate with them - find out what they wanted. Then have the whole place blessed.

Right, good, in that case what was needed was the history of Lavinia House. A few names would help. And a visit to the local vicar. Oh, and she must be in good physical health too - lots of walking in this stunning countryside – the forest, the lakes, the mountains…because God only knew this sleeplessness wore you down. Yes, here was where she would finally stand ground and face up to her demons.

"Come on then you lousy bastards," she muttered as she stomped upstairs. "Do your worst - I'm ready."

***

Chapter Six

Lavinia House

At nine o'clock, Isobel let herself out into the grey drizzle of a February morning. As she locked the door she noticed a pathway around the back, and decided to take a quick look at the garden before setting off for Lavinia House.

It looked as if it had once been properly landscaped and well stocked, but now lay sadly neglected. The orchard and hedges had been pruned to sticks, the boxed beds and borders covered with ivy and rubble from the recent laying of a patio.

It seemed a shame, she thought, picking through the long wet grass. This garden had once been full of scented roses...

Where did that thought come from?

Too late, she'd missed the aura of warning, the air all too quickly sweet and cloying, the drone of bees, omnipotent.

No, no... I don't want to see anything...

She hurried around the side of the house towards the gate. A vision was coming and she wasn't ready, didn't feel at all well - suddenly sick and dizzy, the atmosphere static, colours too bright. Lurching along the path like a drunk, she staggered and almost tripped over the body of a small bird. It lay on its side, neck broken, on the ground beneath her bedroom window. Prey to an early predator, the eye had already been pecked out of its socket, entrails prostrate across the gravel.

"Ah! You poor thing."

Wait! The knocking noise last night? Had it been a bird flying repeatedly into the window, then? Her mood picked up. Yes, that might explain it…

What, at that time of night?

No. Enough. It was just a bird that had flown into the pane and died.

She walked briskly now towards the gate and through to the driveway, making a concerted effort to think positive thoughts and do positive things. Hopefully Lorna Fox-Whately would be at home. It would be reassuring to have a friend close by – someone to call on if necessary, not to mention enlighten her about the history here. One thing she did know about being a spiritual medium was that information helped enormously, especially - and here she gulped at what might lie ahead - if you had to persuade an earth-bound spirit to move on. Wasn't that the job? What Spirit wanted her to do? Oh God!

In reality the driveway was longer than the half mile cited by the agents, but pleasant enough, lined by a post and rail fence, and gravelled, albeit with grass growing through the centre. Grass, grass everywhere…for miles either side. Dotted with sheep the landscape was so green it shone like polished emerald, despite the trees not yet being in bud and the brooding mountains towering over the valley. It was easy to see why this was the country of The Mabinogien, and home to tales of the fae and gateways to the Otherworld. Pure heaven for the storytellers of old.

As if to enhance the image further, Lavinia House loomed out of the mist in true fairy book splendour and she stopped for a moment to marvel. At exactly the same time several colonies of rooks burst screeching from the treetops. For a good few minutes the cacophony was deafening, raven wings blackening the air, as with beaks full of straw and nest debris, they evacuated the premises with screeching haste.

The birds gave her a creepy feeling, although she could not say why. Graveyard birds they were, she thought with a shiver, as once more the morning fell to that of a soft, muffled grey.

The house, as she grew nearer, gave every appearance of being uninhabited, and like The Gatehouse garden, appeared neglected. A thin mizzle coated the stones, and moss clung to the shaded walls. As she climbed the steps to the door she glanced over her shoulder. Fog had rolled off the mountains and settled into the valley behind, enveloping the house and surrounding fields in a thick cloud. That was something, she noted, to watch – the weather changed quickly in mountainous areas like these - one minute sparkling, the next impenetrable gloom.

She knocked on the door, the echo of iron on wood enough, as her late father would have said, to wake the dead.

With no answer after several minutes she tried again. Blimey, was no one ever at home round here?

Still no reply. And no possibility of a passing

neighbour to phone the lady of the house this time, either! Hmmm, perhaps the doctor had left for work and his wife was not in residence? Then again, only part of it was lived in so perhaps this was the part that was unoccupied? Oh dear, what to do? In two minds, she retreated down the steps and cautiously skirted around to the west wing. Was this intrusive or…?

This part definitely wasn't lived in. The paintwork was chipped and peeling, the gravel was stained green around the drains, and weeds pushed through cracks in a crazy paving path that wound around to the back. Hesitant at first, she walked towards a heavy, wrought iron gate barring entry to what could only be described as a magnificent expanse of gardens. Expecting it to be bolted, it was a surprise therefore, when it cranked open without so much as a scrape of protest.

"Hello?"

No, there really wasn't anyone home.

But my, what a place!

Dominating the sweeping lawns an ancient oak stood in the centre. Flower beds to the fore had been arranged and bordered in classic Elizabethan style with little walkways around each one, and a now dysfunctional fountain adorned the terrace. Whoever had owned this house had been seriously moneyed. It did not however, look as though the present occupants were. In fact, on closer inspection it was apparent the beds had run to seed, the grass was mossy and bald in patches, and the outdoor furniture weather-bleached and rickety. Nor were there any curtains at the windows of the house, and as she walked further towards the atrium, something else became clear. At some point the whole place had been badly fire-damaged. Ravaged, in fact.

She cupped her hands and peered into the darkened interior. Wiring looped down from the ceiling, a staircase hung loose from the wall like a dislocated arm, floors were strewn with piles of plaster and abandoned buckets, glass panes had smashed and the bare walls were blemished with graffiti. Perhaps local kids had broken in? Recalling her own forays into abandoned old houses to play Ouija, she screwed up her eyes to try and read what had been daubed in red and black across the bare walls. Probably something like, 'Gary loves Tanya,' she thought.

Only they didn't say that.

She reeled back.

Lunatics! Mad pigs!

Oh God, that was nasty. Vile. Was that because this had once been an asylum? It wasn't like anyone could help being mentally unwell, was it? Bloody hell that pissed her off. Some people were so ignorant and cruel. Frankly, it was a wonder the Fox-Whatelys had left it like this – it hadn't been an asylum for decades now, not since way back in the eighties.

And on a purely aesthetic level it was a shame too, because this had once been a stunning house, with French windows opening onto expansive lawns with a view of mountains and forests beyond. This house deserved to be loved and appreciated, did it not? At a guess this room had once served as a ballroom. It would have been magical. A truly beautiful home. She shook her head. What a travesty.

Okay, well maybe the Fox-Whatelys occupied the

east wing of the house? They definitely did live here. Perhaps if she left a note to say she'd called and would drop round another time? She'd phone ahead, though, because this did feel uncomfortably like snooping. Walking past deadened windows, her footsteps echoing dully on the path, her full intention was to find a door or letterbox and scribble a note, when the most intriguing sight caught her attention - a small arched gate partially hidden in a stone wall overgrown with ivy. There was just a chance that was an old fashioned walled garden and the pair had moved into temporary accommodation, a static caravan for example, while the house was being renovated? Well it was worth a quick check because frankly the east wing didn't look inhabited either. Downright scruffy, in fact!

Walking purposefully now and wanting to head back, she pushed open the gate and stepped through. Ah, it looked as though it had once been a kitchen garden. Segregated into sections it also housed a long greenhouse and several garden sheds. All overgrown, of course, but once it would have fed everyone here – even when it was a hospital. Beyond the far wall fields full of sheep bleated from out of the mist, and fringing the forest a lake rippled darkly.

Oh, a lake…how wonderful…

Shielding her eyes to better take in the scene, it was something of a shock however, to notice a figure on the opposite shore looking right back at her. Blinking she shook her head as if to clear it, scrutinising the horizon with renewed intensity. No, there wasn't anyone there – it had been a trick of light and shadow, a weak February sun pushing through the clouds. This was a painter's dream - absolutely breath-taking. She smiled - for the first time in weeks, probably months. My God how nature soothed the soul. This really was a little piece of heaven.

Still, she ought not to linger. It was time to go.

And was about to do so, when the jewels of a tiny chapel window flashed at the corner of her eye. Her hand flew to her mouth. Oh, my goodness, so they even had their own church! And look at it! The stones shone white in what struck her as a divine glow, a tiny graveyard to the side with ivy-strangled Celtic crosses toppling into weeds. This must be centuries old, built she could see now, over the original foundations of a much larger building. Unable to resist she gravitated towards it, dazzled by the leaded glass which glinted sapphire and ruby red...when a sharp voice cut through the morning air.

"I say! What the blazes do you think you're doing?"

She swung around, lost her balance and almost fell into the overgrowth.

"Oh no, I'm terribly sorry, I was looking for Lorna Fox-Whately but I didn't find anyone at home so—"

"How dare you! Get off my property this instant!"

The woman had her hands on her hips. An old English bulldog was the phrase that came to mind. Wearing a pleated swing skirt worn with a quilted jacket and wellies, the woman had a frizz of grey hair trapped in an alice band. Not more than forty, Isobel decided, but going on sixty. The accent was pure Home Counties, although there was an edge to it, something she couldn't quite put a finger on. She looked like a woman who employed others anyway, the sort who terrified Isobel and always had.

"I'm sorry. Honestly, I was looking for a door to knock on–"

"Well, you're a jolly long way from the house to find a door to knock on! Who are you? What's your name?"

She held out her hand, feeling for all the world as if she was bowing and scraping to royalty. "Isobel Lee. I'm at The Gatehouse. And you must be–?"

Lorna ignored the proffered hand, instead looking Isobel up and down with obvious distaste. "Mrs Fox-Whately. Good thing I was back from London this morning and caught you snooping. What was it you wanted?"

"I erm…well just the history really, of the area, and to erm…" Her words tailed off. *Make a friend?*

The woman stared back. "Surely you could have googled it? Or asked in the village? Frankly, we pay an agency to deal with the tenants."

"Right. Well I'm very sorry to have disturbed you."

"Follow me for the way out. Come this way."

Yes, Ma'am!

If she wasn't so mortified she'd laugh, tagging along behind Lorna Fox-Whately's fat arse. Pity the poor horse, her dad would have said. After a couple of minutes of uncomfortable silence, they emerged by a garage. And from here it was obvious this side of the house was lived in, although for rich folk she despaired at their standards - Venetian blinds haphazardly drawn half way up windows that needed a clean, sills cluttered with empty wine bottles, and paint peeling off the walls. In front of the garage, which had a half-closed door unable to tamp down an overspill of junk, an old Mercedes estate with tape stuck across fractured headlights had been parked at an angle. The passenger seat was littered with sweet and crisp papers and as she passed, two beefy black Labradors sprang at the window in the back, smearing it with saliva.

Lorna didn't pause, strutting briskly out towards the drive, before pointing to the distant road. "That way! Anything you need in future, I'm sure you'll find help at the shop or the public house. Do you know the way to the village?"

"Yes, I found–"

"Jolly good."

Lorna was already stalking back towards the frantic dogs, and since she didn't fancy being mauled, she hurried away. So much for finding a friend. More like a fiend....She grimaced at her own joke, muttering to herself about manners and the woman being right up her own arse. Her heart, however, was jabbing in her chest, thoughts in turmoil. Okay, it was true she shouldn't have been in the garden...

But for God's sake, did you have to be so bloody rude, you rotten cow?

It was only when she was almost level with The Gatehouse again that her indignation subsided enough to process something that didn't sit right, a scene that had been unfolding just before Lorna interrupted. And which now replayed in slow motion.

With every step nearer to the little church more details had come into focus - a kaleidoscope settling of coloured glass in the lead-crossed windows...of gargoyles sculpted into faces with lentoid eyes, protruding irises and sinister, upturned lips.... and the family coat of arms placed above the arched oak door.

Nothing was quite as it should have been. The images on those windows were not of roses or of Christ or of saints. But of those same wizened creatures hanging on the walls of the inn. And the lions were not lions on the coat of arms either....

She stopped walking. They had been altered. Smudged into different shapes.

To that of pigs.

***

Chapter Seven

1893
Flora George

So then, I am still here.

A single gaslight on the ceiling throws the walls into folds of darkness, and from that central point a long, jagged crack splinters outwards. It fascinates me as cracks in ceilings and walls are wont to do. That is where the weakness lies you see, where the spirits of a place can push through. And if you stare long enough the gap will widen sufficiently for them to reach in and…

I cannot move.

The realisation comes with a wallop to the chest. Christ, help me! It is true - I really cannot move an inch. They have tied my wrists to the railings of a crib. The restraints are rigid cuffs of leather. And my legs too… tied together at the ankles.

The panic that rises is blackening, deafening and all consuming.

Screams rip through the air. Mine. Oh God, they are mine!

Alas, it is a huge mistake. The hum of the dormitory

- of snoring, muttering, sniggering and restless pacing….all ceases in a heartbeat, the atmosphere throb-
bing now with the glee of watchers in the dark. They
know, of course, that the quickening footsteps outside
in the corridor are not coming for them this time. But
for me.

Myra Strickland. It is night. Of course. It will be her.

And now she stands over the bed once more,
candlelight flickering over the gaunt contours of her
face, hollowing the sockets of those deadened eyes.

Utterly at her mercy, my throat scraped raw from the
tube she rammed down it, I shake my head, tears coursing down to my hairline, drops rolling into my ears. I
cannot even swipe them away. "No-"

"Be quiet! This is the second time I've had to get up
in the middle of the night to attend to you. Be sure I
will make sure you pay for this, my lady."

Her withering glare is filled with such a loathing as
to send a shaft of coldness through to my very core.
This woman is merciless. Without soul. Her stare travels
the length of my body as if she finds what she sees disgusting.

"Doctor Fox-Whately was good enough to take you
into his home to help you recover from your folly and
your weakness. Good enough to try and teach you the
ways of the Lord and this is how you behave. You must
be fed. You have to be tied to a crib to stop you scratching off your own skin. You are a disgrace, Flora George,
and make no mistake you will stop waking me in the
night and disturbing my sleep. I shall most personally
see to that."

From out of her apron she takes a bottle. And before

there is time to protest, one of her great hands has the opiate down my throat. And thus she floats away like a dark queen, with a dance of princely shadows in her wake.

There is no way of knowing how long I have slept or whether this is still a laudanum-laced dream, but a ghostly creature in a white nightdress paces continually past the blue mist of the windows - up and down the length of the dormitory, back and forth, wringing her hands, muttering incessantly. Repeatedly she gets into her bed, only to hop out again moments later. Someone else moans and whimpers in the darkness, another quietly sobs as if her heart will break. Another is laughing, not a nice laugh, but one of cackling spite, the sound of drawers opening and closing and contents thrown about. I suspect this is the same creature who scampers around like a dog, the one who jumps on and off beds, pinching and pushing. It is a bizarre carnival indeed, and one which comes alive at night. There can be little rest in a place such as this.

Perhaps I have drifted away a little, slipped into dreams once more, but suddenly I sense a presence at my bedside and jump awake.

A child stands there as silent as a spectre, watching, waiting...and my heart almost stops with the shock. No ordinary child this one – her complexion is ghoulish white, eyes those of a quick and clever monkey. Beneath the feeble gaslight it looks as though half of her face has melted and been left to set in dribbles of candlewax. Searching my face with fervid intensity, her whole expression switches to something else entirely on gaining my attention. Our eyes lock. She smiles. A demonic hobgoblin full of mad mischief.

Let this nightmare end. Please dear God, let me never wake up again in this hellish place.

She sniggers, strokes my head as if I am a pet, examining every aspect of my face; now pushing fingers into my eye sockets such as an errant toddler might. Determinedly I keep my eyes closed and pray she will grow bored.

"One day I will poke out your eyeballs," she says in a sing-song voice. "And we will have them in a pie."

Do I scream again and risk the wrath of Myra? Or dare hope this demon child will stop at stroking and refrain from digging her thumbs into my sockets? Oh God, make this terrible hallucination stop...please make it go...

Suddenly there is a clatter from outside the dormitory. Instantly the nocturnal antics freeze, before dying back in a hissing cackling recoil, vanishing into the shadows as if they had never been. Someone is there - the disembodied giggles of a young woman, a maid perhaps, and the low murmur of a man, reeling drunkenly along the corridors. Lord, my eyes are so heavy, body sinking through the mattress into a crazy jigsaw of fractured memories and dreams.

Is there a baby crying somewhere? Is it mine? Yes it must be. I have found him then. He sleeps in the cradle beside me, does he not? In the chamber...in the dark where the drapes are drawn, and the flocked wallpaper shimmers with flickering faces in the candlelight. Whispers fill the room, those of the wood spirits residing in the bedposts... We had the oak most intricately carved from our woods...it is how they got in... This is what I told my husband. Yes, I told Samuel that the wood sprites still live in there, but now they've taken form, you see. Why will he not believe this? Can he not hear them too? *Listen...listen...*I tell him to press his ears close to the wallpaper, to the whorls in the wood...

Samuel's face looms in and out of focus. There is a change there, a darkening behind the countenance that once shone with pride and desire. He wanted me dead, I could see it the minute I told him what I knew. Even as I lay there bleeding. The sheets were soaked crimson. The blood ran like a tide to shore, dripping over the sides of the bed, rippling across the floor, oozing underneath it to surge down the hallway and plop-plop-plop down the stairs. So everyone knew I was bleeding to death. Everyone in that house knew.

There is a weight on my bed.

It is akin to looking through a muslin cloth. Where am I? This is not my bedchamber. My arms are held tight. I'm coated in cold sweat, heartbeat speeding up and up...something here in the dark, next to my head...breathing quick and sharp...

Through bars on the window a full moon bathes the walls in a grid of black and silver. And now, eyes adjusted, there is just enough light to see what it is. The delighted demon with bright black eyes I hoped had been a hallucination is not, after all, a figment of dreams. A sliver of moonlight catches the waxy distortion of molten skin on the side of her face as she begins to bounce on her haunches. A gleeful troll waiting to poke out my eyes with a stick.

"No!"

I cannot get free. My hands won't move.

Terror seems to feed the demon child. And others now join her, crowding around, peering like crones into a pram.

A vile stench permeates the air, the effect like smelling salts. Along with the cold – freezing, stone-cold damp.

I can't move.

So it is true, and real. I am in an asylum. For lunatics and imbeciles.

My whole body convulses into sobs.

"She's awake. She's awake. Look she's crying!"

***

This morning, however, there is no icy bath. Or breakfast. The others are stripped and washed, some raging at unseen tormentors, one flinging herself to the floor distraught to find the contents of her dresser emptied and strewn about.

But no harridan comes for me. Instead there is more morphine swiftly followed by the velvet blackness of opiate-induced oblivion. I do not know for how long I lie in its stupor. All I know is that when the world switches back to grey, and light criss-crosses the walls once more, the melancholy is like no other. My heart sits as a rock.

Through the bars a weak gauzy sun struggles to permeate heavy cloud, the green haze of fields merging with mist. Once I would have wished to capture such ethereal beauty but not today, it has nothing to do with me – I am no longer a part of it. At least all is quiet. The mad nocturnal circus acts have dissipated and for that I am profoundly grateful.

Gradually, the murmur of a foreign tongue seeps into my consciousness. Maids perhaps? Are they maids? Are they kind? Will they help me?

Half way along the row of beds opposite, two chattering women are whipping off sheets and flipping mattresses. One looks more severe than the other, with steel hair pulled tightly into a knot at the nape of her neck, and I recognise her as Mrs Payne. Ivy, the other calls her. This is the one who stripped and scrubbed me, who held me in a vice grip while Myra Strickland pushed a feeding tube down my throat. Pray she hasn't seen me wake, although I need the lavatory quite desperately. The whole place carries the stench of a sewer. The sheets being peeled away are wet and stained, these women wearing gloves just to change the bedding.

The one opposite Ivy is slightly younger - Nesta, I think. She's the one facing this way, and doing most of the gossiping - the throaty 'uch' and 'cluch' rapidity impossible to understand. But gossip it certainly is, the way her speech undulates, pausing here and there to emphasise a point, shaking her head in between dipping a scrubbing brush into a bucket and scraping at the floorboards. One or two of the names mentioned are familiar – Gwilym and Myra, for example. Other words catch and repeat several times – 'cwm, llyn, twp, gwynt, cwtch.' The language is beautiful and lilting but ultimately elusive. I must try to understand it if ever I am to fathom a way out of here. All the while, chatter, chatter, chatter. Something she is not happy about for sure. Softer to look at than Ivy, she has the same swarthy dark skin, bird sharp eyes and sinewy frame. Her forearms are like Ivy's too – knotted and muscled with raised veins on the backs of her hands. I imagine she slaps hard. I see those hands imprinted on my face and make sure to keep still and not call out. They will get to me soon enough. I can hold onto my aching bladder a little while longer. Let me take stock. There has to be a way out of here.

Iron grilles block every window along the entire wall, each sash tightly shut. And although icy in here, it is also cloying and stuffy, the grate at the end unlit. No fireguard. No trace of ash. Clearly never used. There is one light in the centre of the ceiling, and twelve beds opposite. Presumably the same number on this side? So I have twenty-three companions with barely enough space between us for a narrow cabinet each.

Thuds and thumps occasionally sound from upstairs along with isolated screams and drawn-out wailing. I wonder who is up there and why – perhaps those not fit to work? Is it the same as down here or worse? Are these for men or are there more women? Either way I have to assume it is a similar layout. Perhaps if I gained a position in an outhouse such as that of a laundry maid? From there it may be possible to run to the main road and implore a passing traveller? But money…they took my purse. And, oh, I remember now, they cut my hair. And what about clothing? How does anyone ever get out of here? I cannot stay six months. I will die. How could they have done this to me? What did I do to deserve this? Was it so wicked as to merit imprisonment without trial?

Where is Samuel? Where is Amelia?

Why do they not send word?

It takes effort, a great deal, to quell the rising panic and not call out.

Ivy and Nesta have been busy and are now scrubbing down the mattress on the opposite bed, the one which contained the diseased woman of yesterday. Was it yesterday or was it days ago? I wonder if she has passed away. Where was her body taken? Did they have a funeral for her?

They sweep off the bedding, exposing the metal frame. Along with the bolts. Iron bolts, in fact, hold every piece of furniture – from the beds to the little cabinets in between – firmly to the floor.

Perhaps Ivy senses the change in energy, or did I gasp?

Because all at once her back stiffens. She stops what she's doing, pauses, then slowly turns around. My bladder aches. I need so badly to visit the bathroom. I know my features are set to a grimace and I know she smiles inwardly at my discomfort.

"Nesta–" The rest of her sentence is lost on me, spoken in the foreign tongue. But the meaning is not.

The two of them are walking over now, slipping off their gloves.

"Morning, Madam!"

***

Chapter Eight

Dr Edgar Fox-Whately is seated behind a polished desk of oak, and a fire roars in his grate. Beside him stands a woman in a long dress of black taffeta, which rustles with the silky crepitation of birds wings. Behind a pair of spectacles she stares at me as if looking forward to the admonishment of a rambunctious child, her bloodless lips pressed together as if they have never, laughed.

What a pretty sight I must present – shorn and wretched in an asylum uniform, with bleeding wrists and a cut, blackened eye. The extreme distress causing tears to smear my cheeks however, is not due to this but the hacking of my long, flaxen hair. Now replaced with the close crop of a convict, it resembles that of unfortunates I used to visit in the course of my Christian duty - those facing the noose for murder. I avert my eyes for the shame of it. To stand here so debased…

Behind Dr Fox-Whately's shoulder, verdant fields glisten with dew. They stretch as far as a deeply wooded forest beneath a backdrop of snow-topped mountains. Its raw beauty stings my eyes anew. Far better not to have a glimpse at all.

On the periphery of both my mind and vision, the good doctor's voice drawls, "Mrs George, my housekeeper informs me you would not partake of breakfast. This will not do. It is part of your treatment and I rather thought I made that clear. Do you not understand? You must take three modest meals a day or you will be unable to tolerate a regime of hard work and treatment. Hardly a good start."

I wish to ask him why he does not partake of breakfast in there himself, among those screeching incontinent lunatics. But hold my tongue yet. His eyes are like wintry glass and I fear to look into them, instead fixating on a spot between his eyebrows. The hairs loop outwards in wiry disarray. "In that case I offer my apologies."

He nods. "Good—"

"But what I do not understand, Doctor Fox-Whately, is why I am incarcerated with those of the lower class. My family have paid. This is a private institution, is it not? The person who did this," I point to my eye, "is a filthy imbecile – a woman crawling around on her hands and knees—"

His countenance darkens with every word I utter, and has now reached such a degree that he can contain himself not a moment longer. "Mrs George, you are under my jurisdiction and I will decide where you reside and with whom. My wife, Cecily, and I are committed Christians and endeavour to provide for those in society who do not have the advantages people of your ilk are fortunate enough—"

"With respect, there are asylums for those people who would otherwise have been in poorhouses or prisons and—"

He holds up a hand. "Enough. We have far fewer facilities afforded to us here in Wales than in England. Therefore those of you who are able to pay help support those who cannot. I would have thought this would have pleased you as a Christian woman, Mrs George. May I also remind you, Madam, not to interrupt me while I am speaking?"

"I beg your forgiveness, sir."

Again he stares at me for far too long, before eventually deciding to continue. "As I was saying, my wife and I are devout Christians. We strive to provide church services and a moral regime for all those in need, not just," and here he spoke in the most scathing tone, "for the wealthy."

"So my fee covers theirs, is what you are saying?"

"Precisely."

"And I am not even afforded the comfort of a private room in return for the exorbitant fee my family has paid? Does my sister know of the circumstances I endure?"

"As a matter of fact your husband is in daily contact and would like to visit."

My husband? No, oh no, no...

"No! I will not see him. Tell him I refuse. I would rather see my child. And my sister...pray, why does she not write?"

The woman's eyes flicker.

They are keeping something from me.

Doctor Fox-Whately is scribbling now, scratching away in his damn ledger. Rage consumes me. Where is my sister? Where is my child? Why will he not answer my questions?

And then to my horror, quite as if I am watching someone else, my entire being lunges across the desk, swiping ledger, books and ornaments to the floor in one swoop. A river of ink streaks across the paper, the pen flying from his hand.

Both he and his wife jump back as if struck.

And for one tiny, dazzling, dancing speck in time they are thrown. Quite speechless. Until a bell is sounded and shouts go up.

Ivy, Nesta and Gwilym know what to do and they do it quickly – with spade hands and iron forearms, they slam me onto the floor face down, arms jacked up and legs pinned in less than a second.

Breathe...just breathe...

They have my limbs locked, cheek pressing into the floorboards. A light breeze soughs in the trees outside and the linen panelling creaks. Again distant howls echo down the flue and through the cracks in the walls, like those of distressed animals from somewhere high in the house – the attics, the turrets?

Breathe...just breathe...one day I will be out of here...my sister will come...

Doctor Fox-Whately is struggling to compose his features – the sinews of that flour-white face tightening into a grim mask of self-control. His razor-wire mouth twitches with distaste, the tongue flicking out to moisten his lips. "Well, it is quite clear to me, Mrs George, that you have made no progress whatsoever during your assessment period. Indeed you are a grave disappointment."

It is hard to retort when one's head is being yanked backwards.

"Where is my child? You must tell me. And my sister – why has she not written?"

He shakes his head. "You are most unwell, Flora.

Most unwell. And until you can learn to control your impulses and your violence, I am of the conviction that you remain a risk to both yourself and others. As such you will shortly commence a term of cooling treatments. These are commonly prescribed for a temperament such as yours and have shown excellent results." He nods to the three who have me thrust to the floor. "Mrs Payne, you will see this begins immediately. We will review the situation a month hence. Good day, Mrs George."

There is no point in screaming. This is indignity enough. "I wish to write my sister."

He nods. "You may write."

That, at least, is something. Amelia will secure my release once she is aware of these atrocious circumstances. Her soft, sweet face appears before me now, how kind she is, has always been. Oh, she will hear of this. I will have this before the courts. Taken to the newspapers. How a husband can have a wife who no longer grants him his pleasures…how he can have her removed in such a manner…

"And what of my child? You will tell me! You will!"

"Good day, Mrs George."

Back he goes to his scribbles. But all further thoughts of dialogue now fade rapidly following another dose of morphine. And with feet dragging along the floorboards, to my utter degradation, I am forcibly removed from the doctor's office.

***

Days pass. Weeks. Another phase of the moon.

Vigilant during the darkest hours, I lie awake night

after night listening to the pitiful moans and intermittent screams from the rooms above. Who or what is up there? I am quite unable to picture a human being making such a sound, night after night – the image more that of tethered wild animals with their pattering feet and pacing despair.

I am physically weaker now. But the morphine doses are much reduced and thus I have more wits about me. Enough to be aware of the danger here. I had thought the worst of this ordeal was to be imprisoned indefinitely without trial. But with every passing day the danger grows bolder, and the need to hear from my sister more pressing.

Still there is no correspondence from Amelia. I have written daily and sometimes more – carefully placing the letters in the postal box outside the dining room for collection. And when the mail is delivered I wait anxiously, only to be disappointed. I do not believe I can endure another day here. Oh, it is not the harsh treatments of which I speak, for they are bad enough, but that other. There are worse things here. Far worse.

It takes a while to see them. In a similar way to the eye adjusting to darkness and shapes to be revealed, so it is with the hidden layers within these walls. And they exist as surely as the umbra of a shadow. Everyone here knows it. Even the lunatics. Especially the lunatics.

Those dangerous layers swirl around the three of them like a noxious gas – Ivy Payne, Nesta Winters and Gwilym Ash. They whisper furtively in their native tongue, glancing my way far too frequently for comfort. These people are untrained and uneducated, yet quite unlike the maids at home, are utterly devoid of compassion and decency. Perhaps the vulnerability of insanity attracts a certain type? I have witnessed slaps, kicks and peevish pinches on simple, child-like creatures who mean no harm; and the beating of a young girl foaming at the mouth on the floor.

It does not bode well.

It most certainly does not bode well...

Each day my senses clear a little more and I have learned how important it is to appear meek, agree and obey, swallow down the castor oil and not grimace. To remain bodily free is paramount, restraints being one of the most distressing punishments. Yesterday morning a woman broke free of a leather face mask which had been fastened overnight at the back of the neck with straps. It had sent her quite hysterical. On being untied she bolted from the room, took the stairs at a rate and threw herself from the bathroom window. Her body smashed onto the terrace below, the neck quite broken.

I have seen others spun around in a chair whilst blindfolded, until dizzily disorientated they fall to the floor, vomit and lose control of their bowels. This is purging. And always seems to bring Ivy, Nesta and Gwilym an inordinate and inhuman amount of pleasure.

For myself the treatments prescribed are cooling, such as it is again this morning. The first time I was not sure what to expect as we were marched outside to stand in a row. Alas, with each successive treatment the dread builds. A cure is apparently effected by taking us to the brink of death in order we may be reborn without afflictions, thus each of us is dunked into a tub of freezing water while strapped to a board, and held under to the point of drowning.

I am not sure how much more I can tolerate. Each time the cold water treatment is carried out it leaves each and every one of us with wracking coughs, violent, uncontrollable shivering and lungs so painful it is nigh impossible to draw breath. Some cannot walk afterwards, but topple and fall to the ground. Others contract consumption. And one or two are not seen again.

Alongside me this particular morning are gibbering fools with no coherent thoughts in their brains, and I wonder what the good doctor hopes to gain by nearly drowning them. For example, there is Ada, with her neck jerking rapidly from side to side, grimaces and tics contorting her face, and wadding covering the oozing erysipelas on her skin. One moment she is laughing hysterically, the next sobbing and throwing herself to the ground for no apparent reason. At night she is heavily sedated to prevent her from dressing and undressing, getting in and out of bed and pacing around the dormitory or methodically ripping up sheets and clothing. Now, muttering to herself in an excitable, frantic language all her own, she nibbles her nails to the quick while Ivy and Gwylim muscle her onto the water board. Poor Ada, she has no recollection they did this to her yesterday and how badly it's going to hurt.

And Diane, dreadfully rotund, a pudding faced teen who shouts at imagined spectres and is forever either cowering like a terrified child or running around like a banshee threatening thin air. At night she repeatedly bangs her head against the wall to get the devil out. Now she too walks forward to be submerged once more. Shouting at the attendants with intelligible words she looks as if she's knitting something, always her arms are busy – as if she trying to communicate in a language which doesn't make sense.

My heart overflows for these poor wretches, long since abandoned by families who are shamed by their existence. Not so long ago I too called them imbeciles, idiots and inferiors, and shame washes through me for the person that I was. They are human. Not well humans. Traumatised or with some curious oddity. But mostly I am frightened. Because I think I am perhaps the only one who remembers each day what is going to happen and how close we are to dying, to contracting disease, to ceasing to exist, and for no one to even care that we once did.

The only one spared, it seems, is the demon child - Beatrice. She looks as if she is around nine or ten years old but those eyes, they shine and glint with a knowledge older than time itself. Sometimes I catch her watching me and when I look up, she grins. It is particularly disconcerting to be so afraid of a child.

She sits now, biting and scratching herself, bouncing up and down on her haunches as she watches the scene unfold. There is something particularly heightened about her demeanour this morning - a crafty, gleeful air about her - and I get a feeling she is set to do something.

And so she does.

Suddenly Beatrice rushes forwards and snatches Ivy Payne's hairpins from her head.

Ivy whirls around, grabbing at the air in futility.

But Beatrice has already lurched towards Ada, who is strapped to the board, and stabs her full in the eyeball.

***

Chapter Nine

Isobel Lee
The Gatehouse
2018

The episode with Lorna had left her shaken, far more than she cared to admit. She really was alone here, absolutely isolated and without a single friend. This had been a major mistake.

She stood in the drive staring at the front door, wondering what to do about it. Christ! Six months' rent was down...Get a grip, Isobel! You've had one rough night, that's all. You were over-tired, in a strange house in the middle of nowhere, and you're sensitive to atmosphere. It's far too early to throw in the towel. And as for that bloody awful woman, well she's just bad mannered – be thankful you're not her!

Having given herself a good talking-to, she decided to drive to the nearest town, fill up with petrol and stock up with supplies. It would be a couple of hours of relative normality and besides, her stomach was churning over with hunger and Delyth's hospitality wasn't up to much.

The nearest town was Lampeter - a busy centre bustling with shoppers and a choice of supermarkets -

and after a misty start the day began to brighten. After breakfast in a local café, a pleasant enough morning was spent looking around town before filling a supermarket trolley with everything needed for a week in the sticks. It was quite a long way to come, but then again probably a good idea to stay in touch with the bustle of everyday town life. Keep her feet on the ground.

In better spirits and with the situation once more in perspective, she finally headed back to Blackmarsh. By then it was mid-afternoon and beginning to spit rain, heavy clouds already rolling off the mountains. There were few other cars on the road, and by the time the village was signposted hers was the only one. It wasn't the way she'd come and looked like a shortcut – a back lane - and at the last moment she veered off. If it was quicker she thought, putting her foot down, so much the better because fatigue was setting and it looked as though it was going to pour.

The lane was narrow as it wended through the valley. Shrouded by heavily wooded slopes on both sides and lined with high hedges, passing places were few, and it became more and more difficult to keep track of where the last one had been. The further away from the main road the narrower it became. Grass sprouted in the middle, a skeletal canopy of trees arched overhead and occasional cobbled fords obscured by darkly rippling streams caught her by surprise, shattering the suspension of what was after all, not a car designed for off-roading. She pictured being stuck half way across one of these swilling pools. There wasn't a soul around.

Turn back…at the next passing place…turn around…

The road began to snake however, with blind bend

after blind bend and nowhere to manoeuvre. The slopes flanking both sides were steeper now too, as the lane curved into the mountains, the forestation denser. And as the rain changed to sleet she switched the wipers to rapid and flicked the headlights on. What if something was coming the other way?

Oh God, this road was freaking her out. Concentrating on the prospect of running headlong into an oncoming vehicle any second and knowing full well who would come off worse, she slowed the car to a crawl. This was really dangerous. There hadn't been a passing place in at least a mile now.

Suddenly the sound of a car horn blasted from behind.

She visibly jumped in her seat. Glanced in the rear view mirror.

What the fuck?

"Bloody hell, mate. Back off!"

A truck was tailgating right to the bumper. Lights on full beam.

For Christ's sake!

He wasn't a fast driver taken by surprise that someone else was on the road, either, because he hadn't braked. If anything he seemed determined to shunt her clean off the road.

The concentration was immense. She stared at the road ahead for fear of an oncoming vehicle. Checked the rear-view. Back to the road ahead. Jeez…how far to the village? This was horrible.

Now he honked the horn. Not once but repeatedly. Flashed the lights. Revved the engine. Banged on the horn again. At one point the fender touched the little

Mazda's bumper and she speeded up as much as she dared. Oh God, this was it. Any minute now something would be haring this way and life would be over.

In flash glances she checked the rear-view mirror. The truck was large, red, the driver wore dark glasses….a beard, long straggly grey hair, baseball cap… A bend was approaching and she slowed again. He flashed, blasted the horn and speeded up.

This was suicidal. On and on it went. What if a tractor or four by four was coming towards them? Was the man mad? Couldn't he see how dangerous this was? She broke a sweat, gripping the steering wheel, tearful. It was one bend after another…then suddenly there ahead lay a straight run with a narrow grass verge to one side.

Beginning to pull over to let him past, the car bumping wildly onto the turf…she shouted, "Go on, overtake then you fucking moron!"

But he didn't. Instead deciding to ram the back of her car into the hedge.

After the first shunt, as he was reversing for another, she slammed her foot flat to the floor, careering off the turf with wheels spinning and mud splattering the windows. The car's engine screamed in first as she crunched the gears into second and got it back onto the lane.

Fuck! He was a psycho.

The best thing to do was not to stop or confront him, but accelerate the hell out of here. It couldn't be much further now! *Oh God, help me…*. The tyres squealed around the bends, rear wheels skidding. Hedges were a blur. Her heart was banging. Yet he was still on her tail, never more than a few inches away.

Finally, at long last, the canopy of trees parted and the road widened on approach towards Blackmarsh. At the first possible moment she swerved over to the left and almost into the wall of someone's house. As the truck not only shot past but so fast it mounted the kerb on the other side and bounced off again before accelerating away in a cloud of exhaust fumes.

She pulled on the handbrake.

Shaking from head to foot.

The stupid, stupid pig!

Sitting in her car with rain needling onto the windscreen, it was looking more and more like she shouldn't have bothered getting up today - what with Lorna bloody Fortesque-Barrington-Smythe or whoever she was, giving her a ticking-off - and now being run off the road…Jeez, was there anyone round here going to make her welcome?

Trying to calm down, she started up the engine and continued the drive into Blackmarsh. It was so tiny as to be entirely centred around one corner - with The Drovers Inn on one side and the cobbled square on the other. Still shaking, she parked in the same place as last night. There were no other cars. And again there came the distinct feeling of being watched, of shadows hovering behind net curtains. Well, there were bound to be some oddballs in an isolated village like this, no doubt the angry male driver was one of them.

Still muttering to herself, she decided to walk down to the church to see if there was a number on the noticeboard for the local vicar. The urge to go straight home and lock the door was overwhelming, but something good had to come out of today, and having a chat with the vicar might be just what was needed. Hopefully he would be good enough to pop over – preferably this evening. It might be an idea to have the house blessed if she was going to start work as a medium.

The thought, frankly, was as terrifying as it was annoying because she really did not want to spend her life communing with the dead. Not that she'd be telling that to the vicar. They didn't like or trust mediums any more than most people did. Although it didn't stop people wanting their fortunes read – odd, she thought, our relationship with the other side.

The February sleet came straight off snow-capped mountains and like the night before, with it a thick rolling fog. It curled around the Victorian railings and hovered over the gravestones. Shivering inside her coat, the lichgate clanging shut behind her, she hurried down the church path. Considering graveyards and cemeteries had such a spooky reputation, she didn't find many spirits troubling her here. Quite the opposite – by and large these were deeply restful places. No doubt if she touched a headstone the story would be different but simply walking through during daylight hours, the atmosphere was of a serenity that defied the passage of time.

These places held so many secrets - family names, ages and illnesses immortalised in the stone for as long as they were legible. So many children too - the tiny burial plots and cherubic memorials always startling in this day and age. Still, all it took was an outbreak of scarlet fever or whooping cough in those days and a whole community was wiped out. It was the way. No wonder fireside tales and ancient superstitions held fast. They were dark times. Fraught with poverty too. The simple Celtic crosses and toppling headstones reflected this, the inscriptions bearing witness to early deaths and sudden departures. With one major and noticeable exception - that of a large, white marble vault, which had been maintained in pristine condition close to the entrance. Isobel peered at the engravings. Ah, the Fox-Whatelys! So they had been the gentry here for centuries, then? No wonder Lorna was so snooty about her land. No doubt her ancestors had employed the entire village and owned all the farms round here too?

Here was Edgar and his wife, Cecily...who died in 1942. And Edward and Cecily's beloved only daughter, Olivia who died in 1981, a spinster of this parish. How funny – wonder why she didn't marry? Oh well, no doubt it would all make sense one day. It was hardly her concern, anyway. There were, after all, far more important things on her mind, and happily it looked as though St Winifred's church was open – well at least the porch was – and it had a noticeboard. Gladly she stepped inside, glad to be out of the rain.

"Can I help you?"

In the stillness of the church porch, the voice was startling and she swung round. "Oh, sorry, you made me jump. I didn't hear the gate or footsteps—"

"No need to be sorry, I was just round the back locking up the vestry when I heard footsteps. I'm Mercy, the local vicar. You must be our newbie?"

Isobel held out her hand. A bright and breezy blond

of middling years, the woman had honest blue eyes, a beaky nose, and a handshake as wet as a dead fish.

"Yes, hi! Isobel Lee – I'm renting The Gatehouse up at–"

"Yes, I know," she said. "Small place. How are you settling in?"

"Fine, thank you. To be honest, though, I only arrived last night so–"

Mercy was bustling past her with the keys to the church door. "Fab. Well, I hope we'll see you at our service on Sunday? Ten-thirty and all welcome. It's only once a month now but we'd love to see you. Anyway, must crack on."

"Of course, but could I just ask you, well this is a bit embarrassing actually, but–"

Mercy stopped on the turn of the door handle and looked at her directly. "Yes?"

Darn it, why did she feel so awkward talking to a spiritual person about a spiritual matter? Or was it all about church fetes and children's groups? "Well, the thing is, I did wonder if you might be willing to come over and bless the house?"

What had she expected? That the vicar's face would light up? Further words escaped in an ill thought-out jumble from her mouth. "It's just that, well, I'm a little bit psychic and I tend to pick up things…and…"

Oh God, the woman's cheery face had crumpled along with the rest of her demeanour.

"Really? Gosh, I don't think I've ever been asked that here before. I mean, of course, if it makes you feel happier. Although, frankly I am rather busy at the moment."

Mercy seemed to be at pains now to find something else to do. She began to rifle through her bucket handbag. "Where's my diary? Oh no, I don't have it with me. No, no…it's not here. And after this I'm back over to Lampeter for a baby shower. Such fun. Look, tell you what – why don't you give me a ring when you're all settled in and we'll have a pot of tea? Ah, here's one of my cards. Must dash, lovely talking. Absolute pleasure."

Isobel stared after her.

In one instant the world felt like a bleak and lonely place again, and her eyes filled with tears. Clearly there was no help here unless she baked cakes or donated a raffle prize. She looked at the locked church door and turned away, her footsteps echoing dully on the damp path towards the lychgate.

Back in the courtyard, hers was still the only car there, and on a whim she decided to pop into the local shop before it closed for the day. Then that would be the tour of the village over and done with. The gloom of the day matched her mood.

Later she would recall walking through that jingling doorway and laying eyes for the first time on Branwen Morgan. The woman who was to take her to the very edge of sanity and make her question every belief she had ever had.

But in that moment, standing there on the threshold, she could do nothing but stare, aware on some deeper level that nothing would ever be quite the same again.

***

Chapter Ten

Branwen Morgan had the expectant air of someone who'd been waiting, a half smile playing on her lips, the light of a dance in her eyes.

Startlingly arresting in appearance she was of indeterminate age – although her complexion was that of a young woman, her jade eyes held the knowing expression of one far older. An abundance of chestnut hair waved past her shoulders, studs pierced her nose, ears and tongue, the make-up blackly dramatic around her eyes, blood red on the lips. Isobel took in the rest of her in what she hoped was not too obvious a sweeping glance – the Gothic corset topped with a black shrug, stiletto nails tapering at the end of every ring-adorned finger, crystals hanging around her neck…

"Can I help you?"

She recovered herself quickly. The woman was a Goth and why not? It had always been a look she admired but never had the nerve to try. "Hi, sorry, I'm a bit flustered – bit of a day. Sorry – were you closing soon?"

Branwen's Welsh accent was soft and lilting, surprisingly high and girlish. "No, you take your time my lovely, find your breath."

"Thanks."

"Something happened, is it?"

"Oh, just this bloke tried to run me off the road. You

know, road rage or something? I'm still a bit jittery–"

"Oh?"

"Yes, well it's nothing really. I was on the way back from Lampeter–"

"You staying here, are you? You the one at The Gatehouse, is it?"

"Yes." Isobel smiled. "I guess news really does travel fast round here?"

"That's right, small place, see?"

"I just bumped into the vicar and she knew who I was too–"

"What sort of car was it, did you say?"

"I didn't. Not sure, to be honest. Some sort of truck, a Toyota I think, red–"

"Was he wearing a peaked cap? Grey beard, cigarette hanging out of his mouth?"

"He might have done. Yes, I think so. To be honest it was all a bit of a blur, he was right up to the bumper – inches off–"

"Sounds like my friend from Copa Hill again."

Isobel's eyes widened. "Oh, you know him, then? Has he done that before?"

Branwen's eyes twinkled. "Bloody Rhys! There's some who don't like incomers, that's all."

"Oh God, so it was personal? But I'm only a lodger - I'm hardly planning to turn the place into a theme park."

"I know lovely, but for some reason, and it's always been the same, there are some who don't like anyone coming here, especially him. One or two wanted to open a B&B a few years back – you know, to make a bit of extra cash when the old mines started opening up to tourists? But no, we had a right to-do in the church hall about it. Anyhow, the business has gone elsewhere and we're left with just the scraps of passing trade. Makes my blood boil, it does."

"Well, hopefully word will get out I'm not a threat. Honestly, though, he was a menace – the situation was really dangerous." She looked around, just beginning to notice how different the shop was from every other grocery store she'd been in. "Anyway, that's why I was a bit, you know…and I thought I'd pop in to see what you sold so I won't have to drive into town every week. Not that I'll be using that particular road again."

"Of course, take your time. No rush, is it?"

The shop was bijou and abnormally dark for one of this nature. Chimes tinkled and fairy lights blinked. The walls were black. And it didn't smell like a village shop either…more…she tried not to make it obvious she was sniffing…herbal. Was that incense or joss sticks? Kind of like burning leaves.

"From London are you? England?"

"Um…" Transfixed by the selection of crystals, runes, incense, and beeswax candles – displayed on the same shelves as more mundane items, she tried to gather her wits enough to reply. The strangest feeling of being drugged was clouding her senses. "No, not London, although I was living there with my husband–"

"Ah! So where you actually from then? You, yourself?"

"Derbyshire."

"Oh yes? I can't say I've been, but I went to London once. Didn't like it much – too noisy and crowded for me. And I got lost on the underground."

She needed to leave. Immediately. The sudden nausea caught her off guard, as if she'd been reading on the back seat of a bus and just looked up. Heat fired into her cheeks. God, what could she buy? Maybe a newspaper or…anything…a magazine…She lurched towards the back of the shop to pick one up. Straightened. And stared.

Holy crap!

Branwen's voice floated on a woozy daydream, "Oh, you're looking at my pictures…?"

The intense horror of a nightmare began to take a hold, exactly as it had all those years ago – that sense of dropping into nothingness, the breeze of a tunnel whistling in her ears as she fell, and continued falling, into a black void.

It took a huge effort to turn and face Branwen, to offer a half smile, to nod, and act as normally as possible.

"Only I've more in the back if you like them. Come see - I'll take you through."

She did her best to follow, clutching at the walls like a drunk, as Branwen led the way through an archway of vertical ribbons into an unlit corridor. Here it narrowed like the entrance to a cave, the walls lumpen and slightly damp. She tottered and reeled. If she didn't get out of here soon she was going to be horribly sick.

Thankfully it branched into two ante-rooms, one a kitchen, the other an artist's gallery.

"This is my painting room. What do you think?"

The aroma of oil paint and candle wax was a powerful, heady mix, the room a candle-lit lair. Every inch of space was covered with paintings of the same little creatures adorning the walls of the pub. Some held walking sticks, necks craning around to see who was following them in the woods. Others peered out of the darkness with lanterns, quizzical faces as white as corpses, their tiny features out of kilter with the width of their skulls – the foreheads too broad, eyes too small and far apart – both different - mouths skewed to one side. All, however, wore the same expression of surprise - as if caught out, shocked to be seen, creatures existing in a parallel world that should have remained in the dark.

"You see them, don't you?"

"Yes, these are in the pub. So you're the artist?" Jeez, her words were slurring.

Branwen nodded. "I'll give you one if you like. To put on your bedroom wall."

"Thank you, but really, I can't afford and–"

"Oh no! No money changes hands for these, lovely. These are always gifts." She lifted one from its hook, a witchy looking creature in a long, full-skirted dress with a bustle on the back. The tiny poppet's face was creased and warped, its expression puzzled and unworldly, the eyes pinhead black.

"Oh no, really. I couldn't."

"Take her. She'll look after you. In the dark when you're all alone out there."

A huge wave of nausea surged in a tidal swell that was now unstoppable. She slammed a hand to her mouth, swallowing repeatedly.

As from another room a baby started to wail.

"Okay, well thank you very much. If you're sure? They're odd creatures, aren't they? I mean–"

"You see them, don't you? You see the Unseen?"

"I'm sorry but I think I'm going to be...I feel–"

"Excuse me a minute, the baby's crying. Come through while I change her."

In the kitchen an old-fashioned cradle had been placed near a cooking range, the cot piled with blankets. Branwen was still chatting away, but the minute she turned her back the words were lost amid the noise of a howling wind - like a storm blowing through an empty church. It filled her ears. She had to get out of here immediately. It was too hot. And getting hotter by the second. A pressure-cooker.

She rushed to the back door. "Sorry, got to–"

Branwen was leaning over the cradle, pulling something off ...the scene unfolding in slow motion as Isobel lunged for the door handle, the other hand clamped over her mouth. She yanked the door open, shot into the back yard and grabbed onto the stone wall, taking great gulps and gasps of fresh air.

Behind, in the doorway, Branwen stood with the child tucked under one arm, simultaneously turning to toss something back onto the cot. Something that clunked heavily.

"Are you all right?"

Her eyes were streaming. Nodding, still with her back turned, she held her hand to her stomach waiting for the nausea to subside, gratefully inhaling from the mist. *Mustn't be sick...mustn't be sick...Deep breaths...*

"You all right, lovely?" Branwen called again.

"Uh-huh...sorry, sorry–"

"No, no, you take your time. You did look a bit peaky – probably the shock you had earlier, is it? Being run off the road like that?"

After a minute or two, she recovered sufficiently to

consider making it back through the shop and out to the car. "I'm okay now. Honestly, I'll get straight back though, if you don't mind. I had a sleepless night and it's been quite a day. I haven't eaten much, either, it could be that."

Branwen nodded.

"And thank you for my picture. It's very artistic...very unusual..." she was saying as she picked it up again.

She'd put it down on the kitchen table in the rush for the back door, and as she did so, now noticed the object lying in the empty cot.

Branwen caught the direction of her stare. "Oh, you're looking at the iron scissors! We use them to protect our young from crimbils."

"Crimbils?"

"Changelings. We call them crimbils round here. You know, when your baby isn't yours anymore – when it's an imposter? You must have heard of changelings?"

"Well yes, but only in myths and fantasy stories."

Branwen smiled. "Ah, but they affect you so, Isobel...the pictures."

"I was just a bit hot that's all, and I've had nothing to eat since this morning and–"

Branwen smiled and laid a hand on her arm. "The fae. They affect you."

"I don't understand."

"Come back and have a chat some time, lovely. Come soon. You know where I am."

***

Chapter Eleven

Flora George
March 1893

After the stabbing incident there has been a change here. We no longer congregate for treatments, but are taken out one by one. For myself this entails being marched across the yard to an outbuilding in order to have freezing water tipped over my head - often as many as fifty bucketfuls.

They segregate us as much as possible too, the already nervous atmosphere now thick with resentment and fear. And gone the laughing and frolicking in the corridors at night. Doubtless, Dr Whately-Fox has put a stop to Gwilym's little business of bringing locals up here to view the mad people. I imagine watching someone scampering around on all fours or lying naked and prostrate on the floor would be hilarious fare, and well worth the few pennies Ivy and Gwilym charge for the entertainment. But that, as I say, has stopped. Perhaps Whately is nervous of gossip, of attention being drawn to his fine establishment?

And today there has been a visitation from someone on high. We watched through the bars on the windows, as the doctor and his wife shook hands with dignitaries before ushering them inside. The more outwardly insane have been removed entirely from view, the most docile positioned at work in the gardens or the laundry. The rest of us, those of us currently undergoing treatments, have been doped and left in the dormitory - too fuzzy headed to care about the shuffle of visitors' feet outside the door, or their hushed voices as they peer through.

After a couple of hours they depart with cheery waves, the spectre of Diane repeatedly banging her forehead against the window upstairs, going quite unnoticed.

This girl, Diane, is of recent interest to me. How, I wonder, has she become so fat in here? She sees me looking from time to time, smiles shyly, pats her stomach and explains she swallowed a snake. But deep behind her eyes I can see there dwells a private hell, as if the soul is trapped and struggling to reach out, to make contact. It is the faintest of human connections I have with her, one which waxes and wanes. Twice now she has extended a childlike hand and tentatively touched my arm or face, before slumping to her bed once more, rocking to and fro as if to console herself somehow. Nevertheless, she remains one of my few hopes. There is a kindred soul there, I know it.

For my part, not one of the letters sent to Amelia has elicited a response and now the year tips into spring. Evenings sink into a rosy amber glow that spreads across the walls, lambs bleat in the surrounding fields, and through the bars the distant lake shimmers and glints. Once or twice, at dawn or dusk, I swear there is a figure standing at the water's edge looking straight back, hand raised as if to wave…although it is probably just the way the shadows fall. Nonetheless it is an eerie sight and one which plays on my mind, for the figure is dressed in a long, hooded robe and holds a staff…before vanishing into the mist. Ghosts? No, I do not believe in ghosts. My mind is quite cured of wood sprites and creatures of the supernatural. A trick of the light, therefore…yes indeed, this magical landscape is quite the painter's dream.

With no clocks or calendars available to us, the only clue to the time of year is the length of day and hue of colour. Sometimes the beauty, as now in the late morning after our visitors have gone, causes such pain inside me as to be almost unbearable. This summer I will not feel the sun's warmth on my skin, or lie in the meadow amid the drone of bees and fragrance of honeysuckle. Not for me the cool rush of the brook over my toes, or the hypnotic sway of the great willows while I paint. Perhaps never again? Ever!

The panic at this prospect is immense. Daily I beg Nesta to see if there is mail for me – a note from my sister - but there never is. Not a word from the sister I grew up with, learned to ride with, shared a schoolroom and nursery with, sat alongside for many an hour, sewing, painting and discussing who we would marry. Not a single line. I cannot say how heavy my heart lies. It is as if I have been erased from her life. Left to decay until I am dead and buried in the ground.

But somehow each day is faced once more, and with each passing month there can surely not be more to go? He said six months, he did, pray to God I have not remembered incorrectly.

Again my mind has wandered into painful introspection. And our distinguished visitors have been gone not yet ten minutes when there is the quickening of footsteps outside the dormitory. Ivy and Myra.

They bustle in with purpose, Myra with keys jangling at her waist like a jailor. Both are dressed as usual in the dour uniform of long grey woollen dresses buttoned to the neck. They turn and lock the door behind them lest one of us bolts, faces grim, boots echoing on the floorboards.

There is a lull in the dormitory now, from the muttering, humming and fidgeting. Who is it they come for? Some chuckle nervously, convulse and twitch; others shake uncontrollably or continuously pull and snatch at imaginary irritations of clothing or hair. All scurry into the shadows, fleeing with squeals like alerted quarry in a jungle. Except for the silent old woman with blinded eyes, who seems to watch. And know. They call her Violet. And Violet nods in my direction.

Yes, I thought so.

With no words of preamble Ivy and Myra grab my arms and in one swift movement we are hurrying through the locked door and marching rapidly down the corridor. Not a word is spoken. I will not show my fear. I will not ask. I will not feed their pleasure. Where are we going? Outside to the yard now the visitors have gone? More freezing water? But no, it is not to the main staircase but to a wrought iron one at the back, which leads only one way. *Upstairs!*

I will not panic. I refuse to ask. I can and will endure whatever is coming.

Once onto the upper landing we hurry to the point

of running, towards a door at the very end.

The door is flung wide.

And once again that cold blade of fear plunges into my stomach.

Seated side by side, at the end of a large room devoid of any other furniture, are three women, each strapped to a chair in a leather straitjacket. And there at the end is one vacant chair.

Every nerve in my body fires - the instinct to scream, kick, buck and scratch my way out of here. But the hands gripping my arms are of iron. And besides, I can hear him coming – the loping, key-clanking power of an idle stride - the one who has turned up no doubt to enjoy the show. Gwilym Ash would delight in sending me spinning right back and worse.

Without a word of explanation, Ivy and Myra begin busying themselves with locks and clamps. What have I done to merit further punishment? Have I not taken week after week of near-drownings and freezing head baths? But there is nothing for it, nothing to do but acquiesce as with alarming speed they shove me into the fourth chair. And now there are four of us sitting side by side. Each positioned with our backs to the window, necks held rigid by leather straps, ankles bolted with chains to the floor.

Finally the two women retreat, joining Gwilym Ash who lounges in the doorway. The door is then locked. And the four of us are left to the throb of our own pulses, and the gentle fluttering of birds in the eaves.

One of the three laughs as their footsteps retreat down the corridor.

I can and will endure this. I survived the cold water

treatment when others did not. Many of the weak and the frail have disappeared, and not for the first time it begs the question - where did they take those shivering, waxen bodies when they collapsed? What happened to those who burned with fever and delirium in the night? Did they have funerals? Did relatives claim their bodies? Certainly, with the exception of the distinguished guests this morning, there has been no clatter of hooves in the courtyard. And I have been here night and day, lying awake in the hours of dawn especially - the only sounds those of screech owls in the forest, and tortured souls wailing and crying in the dark.

After a while I dare to speak. "How long are we here?"

No answer.

"My name is Flora. Please speak if you can."

Again there is no reply. One woman is quietly crying. Another is making harsh, violent movements, repeatedly she jerks her neck with full force against the leather clamp, determined it seems to break it. Another has quite obviously soiled herself, forced to sit in excreta for the rest of the day.

It is inhuman. Whatever we have done we do not deserve this. Tears blind me. *Oh God, please, please help us.*

But only when the light dims once more and the silhouettes of branches stretch across the walls, do Ivy and Myra return. Carrying gas lamps and chatting to each other over our heads, they unfasten the clamps and unlock the chains as if it is simply another annoying chore.

Once free it is hard to straighten up much less to walk. The relief, however, is enormous – to have survived that horrible day – it is like walking on air and I almost fall.

"Enjoy that, did you, Madam?" Myra whispers as we race back along the corridor.

I will not give her any satisfaction or cause to make my life worse. I will not.

"Better get used to it. You've got a month of that. Every…single…day."

No, no, no….

Nor is there supper. And it is dark in the dormitory after I have been taken to the bathroom and thrown back in. Gloomy with pacing spectres of people who had once been in the world, but who now scrabble on the floor like scavengers or pace, moan, cry or rage at things others cannot see. It is a kind of hell. Yet tonight I stretch out my legs and embrace it, wiggling my toes, stretching my fingers. I am still here.

The next day and every day thereafter, at mid-morning, the four of us are taken out for exercise - straitjackets concealed by great coats and flanked on each side by an attendant as we stumble along for the daily walk on weakened legs. It is brief and quick, a march along the driveway to the lane leading to the vil-lage and then back again. Perhaps a mile.

One day, a week or so later, there is a moment, only fleeting, when a smart carriage clatters by and without thinking I call out, my voice croaky and hoarse in the soft, early mist, "Hello! Hello! Stop - please, help me! I am just like you…"

It is, of course, a huge mistake.

"You are to be restrained at night too now," says My-ra when we reach the dormitory. "Perhaps one of these days you will learn to behave with respect, my girl. How dare you embarrass the doctor and his staff? How dare you!" Clamping one of my arms to a crib, she adds, "I'll be back for you in in the morning."

The words come to me from nowhere. Words I have never used and never heard except once from a coach-man. They explode inside my mind, the voice no longer mine. *Fuck you, vile bitch!*

***

There are angels, though. Here on earth – truly. And mine is called Diane. Diane's story is heart-breaking, the poor child more vulnerable than I could ever have thought possible. It transpires she is the very same age as myself - a farm girl from over the border in Shropshire. For years she said she had felt restless, aimless, as if her life was pointless and empty, and was often beaten by her father for staring into space instead of, say, milking the cows or churning butter. Increasingly she found her-self quite forgetting to wash or eat, would be seen stag-gering into the village not knowing for what purpose or how she got there. And soon people began to gossip, calling her simple or tapping their head when she walked by. She said she found it difficult to speak in a coherent manner, that the words came out all in a jum-ble, her hands working away with frenzied gesticula-tions.

Then one night there was an almighty racket and her father burst into her bedroom with a gaslight to find her repeatedly slamming her head on the floorboards having ripped the room apart, shouting, 'Get out of me, get out of me!"

"And do you remember that? The words?"

"Oh yes! I saw him you see? I saw the devil in the moonlight and he entered my soul." She pinpointed the nape of her neck. "He got in here. And he's still there. In my brain."

"You told your father this?"

She nodded. "Yes, that was when he got the doctor."

I think what is most sad of all is that her parents have never visited. It is quite as if she has been removed from their life and forgotten. "I'm inconvenient, Flora – an embarrassment. I don't know why no one will believe me."

How her words resonate.

"And I was with child."

She has no recollection of how she came to be with child, except to remain convinced that some foreign entity had crept into her brain while she slept and made her do unseemly things, turned her into a village harlot. And it was this entity which had set about slowly destroying her mind in order to take possession of it later.

"You see," she explained. "I know what caused it all. I have told them it is the devil's work and my mind is being destroyed in order for him to take it over and make me do unspeakable things. It is why I stood up in church and shouted at the vicar, why I slapped a boy in the street. The child was laughing at me, smirking – the devil's helper. Only if I try to explain it all comes out wrong."

"And yet you speak so eloquently now?"

"Yes. So you see it's true - they have to get him out of my brain, make him stop destroying it, or he'll take over."

"And you really believe this?"

"Yes, oh yes, of course. But Flora, he comes more often to me now too…I see him all the time - in the shadows waiting. I can smell him. He smells of sulphur and follows me everywhere. Just waiting… I've told Doctor Fox-Whately, but he won't believe me either, and now I fear no one will ever come for me. I will die here."

"Oh, Diane!"

Yet she is often rational too, explaining the secrets within this living tomb, and it is only when I see her drifting away into melancholy with that silent, vacant stare that I know her period of lucidity is coming to an end once more and I will not see my friend again for a while.

Through Diane I have also come to understand about the rooms upstairs. Often I have lain here puzzled, wondering where the blood-curdling screams are coming from, and the plaintive, almost inhuman level of sobbing. Perhaps now it makes a little more sense. Although, what she tells me is far more alarming than anything I could imagine.

She recalls waking up one day in a padded cell, filthy and manacled to the walls. There is a peep-hole in the iron door, which is bolted on the outside, and there was a pervasive smell of smoke, of fire. She had no idea how long she had been there or why her nightdress was smeared with blood, but she does recall a violent dream.

"I was gagged, retching with a rag in my mouth, and those bitches had me pinned down while a snake was pulled out of me. I was screaming and screaming, choking on the vomit and blood was pouring out, but they kept pulling it and pulling it…"

"You gave birth, Diane."

"To a snake."

"But you said you were with child when you were admitted? So you came in pregnant and then they delivered you in here?"

"Yes, but it was a snake." She shows me the stretch marks on her thighs, breasts and still protruding abdomen.

This is my worst fear. The very mention of the blood stained mattress and the pulling, dragging pain was enough to make me cry out and Diane slammed a hand across my mouth to stop me from attracting Myra's attention. "Shush. When will you learn to stop calling out? You have to stay quiet."

I do not always know whether to believe Diane but I do believe in her advice. To remain silent - do whatever it is they want or it will be so much worse.

Worse than you can ever imagine.

Up to that point I thought I had been chosen for the harshest punishments, but after listening to Diane, that is patently far from the truth.

A month later when they come to unstrap me at the end of the day I can no longer straighten up, the muscles utterly wasted and unable to support the bones. Bent as an old crone, my legs wobble and give way on the rush back along the corridor. Ivy and Myra almost carry me between them. I have reached the end. My heart flutters and dances as a leaf in the wind, most days blacked out with faints. Yet I draw breath.

I am still here.

Perhaps they know I am near death? This night there are to be no manacles in the crib, and one of the kitchen staff brings brandy and a slice of bread and butter. Have they done with me? Have they? Finally?

Lying in the dark, listening to the screech owls in the forest and the unearthly moans from hidden rooms upstairs, my breathing even to my own ears is rattling and heavy. Where is Diane? My guardian angel? I have come to love this girl, who held my hand during those long, lonely nights when I was manacled – a whole month - protecting me from Cora and Beatrice. At first I was surprised to feel the contact, but soon came to understand. Diane is ill only part of the time. Sometimes she is completely lucid, alas these periods are becoming more and more infrequent, but when she is free of torment I find her to be quick minded, observant and kind. Such a warm-hearted soul I have never had the pleasure to meet and I reach for her now.

It is because of Diane my fears regarding Gwilym Ash are validated. I was right to be fearful. Right to sense the danger and secrets within these walls. Alas, the reality is far worse than my imagination would allow and I feel his eyes on me constantly, sense him watching and waiting, almost slavering. I must escape from here before he can do me harm. The more weak and fragile I am the more concerned I become. I will endeavour to write to Amelia again, persuading her most pressingly of the imminent threat to both myself and Diane.

Two mornings come and go with no straitjacket. And two nights without a manacle.

Have they finished with me?

They must have.

Then on day three, not yet breakfast time and with Diane banging her head against the window - becoming ill again, descending rapidly into her terrifying world of torment and imaginary devils - the creak of the dormitory door causes us all to wing around. Ivy and Myra are walking towards me. For the briefest of moments Diane catches my eye. She is lost to me, almost, but the spirit in her reaches out. This time they mean to finish me. And she is saying goodbye.

The women grab my upper arms with vicious pinches and we march from the dormitory once more. No allowance is made for my weakened limbs and stumbling gait. Yet hurry we do, along the corridor towards the main stairwell, then along more corridors and down more sets of steps. Down and down. The air becomes markedly colder. Through another door now and into one of the turrets. The steps spiral further and further down, below ground level and still we descend.

To the basement? Underground? *Christ!*

"Nearly there, Madam," says Myra.

Ivy laughs. "That's about the size of it. Called the others an inferior class – didn't think she should have to share the same air! Well you're not so superior now, are you Madam? Not giving out orders now, is it?"

Their grips tighten as the hostility builds, fair shoving me through the last door into an unlit tunnel that drips with damp and smells of the sewer. Gritting my teeth to stop the screams coming out, I tell myself over and over that I can and will endure this. Whatever is coming, it can and will....pass.

One of them wraps a blindfold round my head and ties it tightly. They whirl me round and round until I don't know which way I'm facing, then tie my hands together.

"Now walk the plank," Ivy says.

I don't understand.

"Give her a shove."

"What's the matter with you? Deaf, is it? Get walking, Flora."

Stumbling, I put one foot tentatively in front of the other.

Cold as a crypt, underfoot is slippery and squeaking with rats. Slime coats the walls. There is nothing to grip.

Suddenly the rock underfoot becomes wood.

"Stop!"

A low groan now like that of an old door creaking open. Then the slamming of wood on stone.

"Now step back."

There is nothing there. A cavity opens and I plunge backwards into a freezing tank. Icy water rushes into my lungs in a frozen scream. An iron rod slams hard across my neck making it impossible to surface.

Lord Jesus Christ I am going to die. Lord Jesus please wash away my sins. Take away my pain. Whatever I've done…please… Lord Jesus, I will let it go, let go of this life, whatever I have done…

My lungs are full and bursting with pressure, the pain blackening and deafening…. My heart kicks out one solid thump…

Then fingers pinch into the flesh of my upper arms and yank me out, a sopping dead weight of teeth chattering and bones. And they are laughing. Laughing like hyenas.

"Enjoy your bath, did you, Madam?"

Afterwards they leave me in sopping clothing strapped to a chair in the basement. Hour upon hour, with the chill seeping through skin down to the marrow.

Will this be every day? A week? A month?

I will die of consumption.

They mean me to die. Of course they do.

But I am still here.

And I think the only reason I am is because of hatred. Such a hatred seethes in my veins as almost to claim my very soul. I have become it and it has become me. There will be no peaceful death into the hereafter, I can promise that. I will haunt these bitches and that sanctimonious creep upstairs in his comfortable office until the end of their days. And beyond.

***

Chapter Twelve

The comfort of Diane's small hand wakes me from the aftermath of fever. Has it been days or weeks?

"Shush, now." She lays her cool touch on my forehead, wipes my brow with a handkerchief and whispers low, "You are alive and through the worst, Flora. Shush, keep quiet, lie still."

Through fitful dreams come stories that make sense of the madness in here, the curios, and the demons. How Cora, who scrabbles around on all fours and eats grass and dirt in the outside yard, believes she is an animal. "She had fifteen children and her husband beat her black and blue, they say. I think she lost her mind altogether. You know how she searches, all the time searching and rummaging through drawers and cupboards?"

"Mmm…"

"She's looking for her children. Thinks she'll find babies in there. I swear it's true. That's why she keeps bits of bread in her apron from breakfast – it's to feed them with. Poor thing."

"Hit me–"

"Oh yes, she's very violent. Her old man hit her and she hit the children. She probably thought she'd found one of her children and hit them. Only it was you. Who can say?"

She tells of Ada, who paces constantly, repeatedly

dresses and undresses, jerks her neck in great spasms, and rips up the sheets. Before coming here she was frequently to be found in the town quite naked, performing the most bawdy, lewd songs imaginable. They say she was chained up in a local prison, left without clothes, filthy and out of her wits. No one knows where she's from or who her family are – she seems quite cast out, a woman of over forty. And then there is Beatrice. "She was too much, her mother had enough. One day Beatrice went and stuck her head in the fire. They had her swaddled in bandages and still she threw knives and scissors across the room. Her family couldn't cope. She's dangerous, like a demon. You have to watch out for that one."

"The old lady, the blind one, what of her?"

"Oh, you mean Violet? No, she's not blind. She can see everything although most of it's in her third eye. Violet's a witch, they say. A medium."

Somewhere in the fog of my brain I wonder how she knows all this because neither Cora nor Ada speak. And Beatrice reminds me of a little monkey the way she crouches, watches, sniggers and squawks. Certainly she would not have told anyone she was ill in any way, or what happened before she came here.

My voice sounds slurred, and my chest wheezes with every word. "Diane…how do you know all this?"

Her face is close to mine. Without opening my eyes I know she constantly glances at the door for any sign of a hovering shadow or the dim glow from a lamp. Small and slight, she moves quickly when there's trouble and in light of what she tells me next, I realise why. Indeed, the more I come to understand the more I too am alert to the hidden perils in this place. Cora and Ada, in their incontinent lunacy, are in many ways safe. Diane and myself, however, are not. Now, I must make best use of her lucid phase. She is about to tell me something.

There is a little intake of breath and when she finally speaks it is with whispered urgency. "I started to pick up some of the Welsh between Ivy and Nesta. I knew a little before because my village school was on the border with one foot in Wales, the other in England. Some of the local children spoke Welsh so you see I learned a bit. Anyway, listen to them chatter away because they think we're either mad or we don't understand, but soon enough you'll come to recognise some of the words and then you get the gist. Nesta's a gossip – you'll hear plenty from that one. Pretend you're asleep and let her prattle on."

"Llyn. What doess that mean?"

"Oh, that's easy. That's Lake. You'll hear that a lot. There's Llyn Mynachlog behind here – you can see it. That's Monastery Lake behind the church."

"So this was once a monastery?"

"No, I don't think so. I think there might have been druids, I'm not sure. But that's what they call the lake, anyway."

"What is gwynt?"

"Wind."

"And cwtch?"

"Cuddle."

"And twp?"

Diane giggled. "Daft! They point to their heads when they say that, don't they? That means they're talking about one of us."

"Thank you. I think I will understand a little more now. One hears a lot when lying still like this. Oh yes, and something else they have mentioned - tylwyth teg – what does that mean?"

"Ah, that means fairies. They all believe in fairies here – even the cook leaves a bowl of milk and some bread out each night to keep them happy."

"Really? The little creatures in fairy tales? And I thought we were supposed to be the mad ones?"

"It's folklore. Especially in this village. They believe the fae snatch new-born humans and replace them with changelings. Crimbils they call them."

She laughs and it's beautiful to hear, like a tinkling fountain on a hot day.

"So do you know enough Welsh to pick up anything about Ivy and Nesta?"

"It's a very fast and thick local dialect so I can't always make sense of it, but yes, enough. Nesta and Ivy were maids. Nesta was a scullery maid – lowest of the lot - and Ivy worked in a laundry. This is a really good job for both of them, a step up."

"What about him? Gwilym?"

She grimaced. "He's just a common thug with no brain. A workhouse officer from Cardiff. That's where people like Cora and Ada were kept in filth and chains. Separate pens they had like cattle – padlocked into leg locks and leather masks. That's what he's used to doing. They say Cora was chained into a crouched position for so long that's why she can't straighten her legs and has to crawl about on all fours."

"Oh, my Lord."

"I know. So it is better for them here, see? Better for

all of them. And the doctor even has Sunday sermon in the little church by the lake for those who are well enough."

"Really?"

"Not for you and me, mind. Only for the obedient ones, the silent, the deaf and dumb who shouldn't be here at all, and the staff. It's so they can say we all go to church every week."

I squeeze her hand. "You should have stayed home with your family and simply seen a good doctor."

"The thing is, Flora, I am quite sane but no one will believe I'm slowly being possessed. It's only when the demon gets a grip, usually when I'm sleeping or have taken drink, that I can't control him. When they tell me later what he made me do it's hard to believe. Don't you see? I don't need a doctor I need a priest?"

Sleep is claiming me again now. The fever has washed out of me, leaving this body wrung out and chilled. Diane pulls up the sheeting.

"Is it winter?"

"No, my lovely, it's the end of April. Nearly May."

Nearly May! "Go back to bed, Diane. You will catch your death - it is so chill in here."

"I wish that I would."

"Do not say that."

"Why would I want to live, Flora? What hope is there for me?"

"But you recover, do you not? Just as I?"

Again she presses her small, cool hand to my fore-head, as if sweeping away the fret. "You have indeed recovered your mind. Your ills have passed. But mine recur ever more swiftly, each time leaving me with little to distinguish between what I saw and what I dreamed. Don't you see? Flora, I will never leave."

Sweet Jesus, but she is just a child. "We must bear it. And one day–"

"No, maybe one day for you, my lady, but not for me. And besides – there is nowhere for me to go. My family would not wish me home again. I haven't received one single letter in reply–"

"But that is quite dreadful."

Her face crumples.

My mistake was to remind her of her family's desertion and I hope melancholy is not about to take its fateful grip of her again. It is as if she is a shadow continually trying to escape the pull of the dark, until finally her will is lost.

"Oh, but I am quite sure that is not the case. You see, I have not had a single reply either, so it may not be your family at fault but that our letters are unreceived? My sister, Amelia, would not allow this if only she were made aware of the conditions here. She would send for me immediately if she knew of Dr Fox-Whately and his wife's cruelty. I am sure she believes they are good Christian people and treat us well."

A spark of hope flickers in her eyes and she squeezes my hand. "He has a public commendation now. I overheard Ivy saying he has a special honour from Parliament for his work with the mentally infirm. A groundbreaker he is, for integrating all social classes into a successful regime."

"Successful? But people here – do they ever go home? I know they vanish but I thought…" Here I raise my gaze to the ceiling.

"Up there? Oh no, that's not for the dead. But Flora, that's where you do not want to go."

"Why? Tell me who resides up there. I hear the most fearful wailing."

"It's called the chronic block. You won't come out again. Not ever. No one gets out of there – once there your fate is sealed. The only way people leave that room is in a wooden box."

"And that is where all the howling noises come from?"

She shakes her head. "No, not from there."

"Then where?"

"I don't know. There is something none of them talk about."

"You said you were chained up in a padded room, that the mattress was soaked in blood?" My heart begins to race sickeningly at a return to this conversation, already the images that trigger panic surging forth. But the secrets of this house hold the key to everything. "You must know you gave birth? What happened to the baby?"

Her voice comes from far away, tiny like that of a lost child. "I told you it wasn't a baby," she insists. "It was a snake. I asked if it was a snake and they said of course it was a snake. And now I have another one growing, see?"

She is shaking, her hand weakening in mine.

"Diane, you had a baby not a snake."

Of course, I see now why she would say it was a snake - how very much easier to cope with the loss. I see too, that she is not fat. How could she be? She is pregnant.

Her eyes are limpid pools of sadness. Somewhere in the deeper recesses of her mind she knows she has given birth to a child and that she is heavy with another. Perhaps first time around one of the village louts raped her when she was half out of her wits with delusion, but in here…A cold shiver works its way up my spine. The girl is in care. In an asylum.

"All I can say is, I woke in the padded room on a blood-soaked mattress like I told you. And they said yes, I had swallowed a snake and they had taken it out of me."

"They?"

"Myra and Ivy. They clean up his mess."

"Whose mess?"

But now she has turned her face away, begun to mumble, to work her hands in that strange distracted fashion.

After a while I tell her in firmer tones to go to bed. That it is pitch dark now and cold in here. The damp gets into the fabric of these walls that never see the sun.

"Do you smell sulphur?" she asks.

"No. Diane, there is no devil. Listen to me, you must know the truth of that - deep in your heart? That there is no devil – only humans and the evil deeds they do."

Even as the words tumble from my mouth a horrible truth lodges into my brain. What happened to the child she gave birth to? And what will happen to this one?

"But Flora, there is. I can see him. Look, he's there now – just outside the door."

There is certainly a light there.

The small, red flare of a lit cigarette.

***

Chapter Thirteen

Isobel
Present Day, The Gatehouse

By the time Isobel arrived back at The Gatehouse, the fog had settled once more into the valley and was closing in quickly. A fresh belt of sleet blew against the windscreen as she parked, her face ghostly white in the reflection from the headlights. And as she switched off the engine, the same mounting sense of isolation crept up on her as it had the night before. It was so quiet out there, every sound of her own seemingly amplified – from the ping-ping of the seatbelt reminder, to the dull clunk of the car door.

She hurried around to the boot for her shopping.

Then stopped and turned around. There was a light on in the hall. Did she leave it on…in broad daylight?

She frowned. Well, she must have. Besides, it may be possible to see ghosts but they sure as heck couldn't switch lights on and off.

Could they?

Good God, what a nervous wreck and it had only been a day!

Snatching the carrier bags, keys between her teeth,

she slammed the boot shut and was about to press central locking when the painting on the passenger seat caught her eye. There it was, lying face down. Oh no, it seemed mean to just leave it there when it had been given as a present. Especially from the only person who had actually been kind.

She'll look after you. In the dark when you're all alone out there...

Why would Branwen think she needed protecting? Did something happen in The Gatehouse, after all? It was hard to believe when it was only a lodge. She'd checked. Or maybe Branwen knew differently?

Come back and have a chat....you know where I am...

Oh, for goodness sake. Girls like Branwen flirted with the dark side and enjoyed spooking people, was all.

The woman made you ill. She meddles and you know it.

The damp was soaking into her back now and she hurried to the front door, dumped the carriers and then, against all her instincts, turned back for the painting. It was, after all, just a bloody oil on canvas, but knowing her luck if she left it in the car then Branwen would come over and see it.

The creature in the painting was creepy though, and the more she looked the more its eyes seemed to glint and darken. Something else too... that strange feeling of standing in the woods with a storm brewing and the treetops swaying, the earthy smell of moss and decay so strong it was dizzying, nauseating...The darned thing was unnerving. She put it on the floor in the front parlour, facing the wall. Then shut the door. If Branwen did come round there was time to whip it out but no way was it hanging in the bedroom.

Enough, enough for today. And this house was freezing. It really would be stupid to get ill - not out here on her own, facing whatever was coming - a psychic onslaught could be draining and she was going to need every bit of strength going.

And so it was later, much later, after a hot bath and a rump steak washed down with the best part of a bottle of red, that she found herself sitting once more at the kitchen table in the harsh fluorescent light, listening to the silence. There wasn't so much as an owl hoot tonight, the night muffled by darkness and fog. God, the chill of this house was like a crypt. That was the problem with a house unlived in for so long - damp had seeped into the wood and the walls, even the fresh paint oozed with beads of moisture. The front rooms were the coldest, the grates empty and black with no supply of firewood to cheer them. She wandered into the parlour, which had been furnished with a single armchair positioned by the green-tiled hearth together with a standing lamp. It looked as joyless as a hospital waiting room, and she was about to turn away when a shimmering static over the armchair arrested her attention.

Please don't let anyone materialise. Please....Oh God...What was coming? Would it be the same woman as before...?

And yet it was impossible to look away.

Transfixed, with one hand on the door handle, she stood stone-still, her heart thumping in her ears. What appeared to be the shape of the old lady began to take form.

This wasn't happening. It couldn't. No!

Her hair was white and scraped back severely from a masculine, angular face; and as before, the long dress was black, funereal…but this time the image didn't fade. This time it was shockingly clear, and slowly the woman's head creaked around on its stem to look her straight in the eye. The old woman's features now stretched into one of incredulity and horror. She began, with difficulty, to stand…

No!

Isobel backed out of the room, frantically feeling for the door handle, then shot into the hall and clicked the door shut firmly behind her.

God, no. Just no!

That woman – she was the same one as last night. And she didn't like her being here one bit, did she? There was a horrible feeling about her, something truly menacing.

Her hands were shaking as she walked into the kitchen for the wine intended for tomorrow night.

Fuck it…I need it!

So someone had lived here then? But there were no records of anyone being a resident here. There had been gatekeepers apparently, during the time Lavinia House operated as an asylum, but only on short term work contracts. Importantly there had been no permanent residents or deaths recorded here. That's what she'd looked for. So who was the old woman? Perhaps one of the tenant's wives? Someone who'd been particularly partial to the place?

At the back of the house, overlooking the garden and adjoining the kitchen, a smaller, cosier room had been furnished with a cheap nylon carpet and a black faux leather sofa. It looked as though this was intended for the new lodger since an electric heater had been fitted. Old-fashioned as it was, it did the job, with two bars and a back light, of at least providing some comfort, so gratefully she opted for that, closing the curtains and regretting now the lack of a television.

The evening stretched out. As did the night ahead.

She took a sip of wine and flicked on her laptop. There had to be more information on this place, but first it would be interesting to google the Fox-Whatelys. It hadn't occurred to her to do so before, no doubt because he was the local doctor and nothing had seemed remotely odd. But following such hostility from Lorna this morning, a person had to wonder why. Maybe she had something to hide?

Her interest piqued, the first Fox-Whately to pop up was a famous one. Could she be related? The newspaper photograph was of a young woman snapped leaving a West end theatre with a rather serious looking older man. While he wore a business suit, the woman presented a far more outrageous spectacle. Her hair was extremely short, cut sharply around the ears like a fairy-tale pixie, and she was wearing an over-sized embroidered coat in shades of red, mustard and turquoise - the kind not found on the high street but in exclusive boutiques with no price labels. Her shoes too, were quirky - purple with pointed toes and a Peter Pan buckle. Awful taste, she decided. Probably the whole ensemble was top-end designer. In fact it definitely was. She read his name and raised an eyebrow. Ah, so it was the woman who was the Fox-Whately. An actress.

But was she Lorna's daughter or not, that was the

question?

The face shape did bear a passing resemblance, but caught in the flashlight smiling broadly with fridge white teeth it was difficult to tell. Worth digging around a bit more, anyway. And as it transpired there was plenty more about the publicity hungry actress who seemed to delight in shock tactics and nude stage performances. In fact, it seemed Ophelia was quite the celebrity while her husband was rising through the ranks of the parliamentary opposition. So then, there must be some wedding photos?

Yes, great – here - featured in one of the top glossy magazines. God, there were loads.

And there, standing proudly either side of their daughter on her wedding day, were Mervyn and Lorna Fox-Whately - she in a flowery frock with feathers speared onto her head, and he by comparison, considerably smaller - wiry and somewhat ferrety in looks, wearing top hat and tails. *Hmmm…little doubt who wore the trousers in that relationship!*

Isobel scanned the catalogue of glossy photos. Clearly the wedding had not been hosted at the family home. The shots were taken at a hotel in Surrey. It was definitely them, though. Ophelia and her parents – just the three of them representing her side of the family. No more relatives? So was Ophelia an only child? For another hour she scrolled through google, gleaning information.

Hang on a minute! Now that was interesting. There was nothing up to date…All of these articles and photographs were before 2016. After that Ophelia vanished. Was it one of those celebrity cases of going off the rails, or into rehab? Something to keep quiet? All social media trails ended just as abruptly. There were a few articles on her husband and one or two interviews, where he was asked about his wife and he politely declined to comment.

Was it true, one journalist asked, that his wife had post-natal depression following the birth of their first child?

Again he declined to answer.

Was his wife planning to work again as an actress? the reporter probed. Was the child being cared for at home?

Slightly less politely now, he told the journalist his private life was just that, private, and asked him to respect that.

Isobel frowned. Hmmm…why were there no photos of this baby? Ophelia was famous for her celebrity magazine shoots…

Call it intuition but she'd lay money down this family had something to hide. There were so many questions, though. Like, why did the doctor and his wife live in pretty shabby quarters here in the middle of nowhere? Why, if they hailed from such a grand family, did he need to go on working as a backwater GP, when surely he would be well connected enough to own a private practice on Harley Street. And why was this house, The Gatehouse, being rented out at all? Were they hard up? Surely not!

It was odd, all very odd…Her imagination careered in all directions. Perhaps they had to stay here to keep guard of something, which was why he couldn't leave to work in London? But the house cost a fortune to upkeep, hence the need for the rent? Oh, it was far-fetched. Intriguing, though. And not impossible. Did Ophelia live here too? Is that why Lorna hadn't wanted her around?

Ah, no. It was none of her business and quite frankly she had problems of her own.

Even so…

Her thoughts constantly flitted back to Lorna's determination to march her off the premises that morning. Could it be to do with the tiny church, then? Was there something about that? Or perhaps the graffiti in the house itself? No, that could easily be painted over. Unless it was under constant attack…Certainly there had been something Lorna was protective of. And then there was that bizarre road rage incident this afternoon and …

Holy crap, what was that?

While her mind had been otherwise occupied, a frantic unintelligible whispering that had been present for some time, was escalating, and now came to her full attention. Coming from the hallway, it ceased the second she tuned in.

Silence hissed over the cranking electric fire.

Swallowing the last dregs of the wine and refusing point blank to be annoyed with herself for drinking – anyone in these circumstances after a day like that would down a bottle, probably more than one – she took a deep breath and turned to face the closed door leading to the hall.

Her voice came out in a warble, weak and trembling even to her own ears. "Hello? Is anyone there?"

***

Chapter Fourteen

Perhaps there was a draft in the hall, but the door seemed to waver in response.

Her heart crashed in her chest. The room all at once suffocating.

She had forgotten to protect herself. Forgotten everything. It did exist, the other side…it did…that had to be accepted…had to be…

"Who's there? Sh…show yourself…"

Again the door seemed to wobble on its hinges.

Fuck - what if someone answered? Oh, God…

She pictured running outside into the fog. But to where? Down the long, dark drive to a half-derelict house with hostile owners? Or the unlit lanes towards Blackmarsh, which would be battened down for the night…? She could call someone? Who? Nina? Yes, Nina.

Or better still, take a few deep breaths and handle this – have the confrontation she'd been trying to avoid since her teens.

Okay then, here goes. As an adult armed with more insight and knowledge…here goes…let's believe in this, that I am a medium, that spirits exist but cannot hurt me. Others cope with it and so can I. Come on, Isobel – bloody well face up to it!

She closed her eyes and offered a prayer, asking for God's protection with what she was about to do. As a Christian she knew of no other way.

Then opened her eyes.

Standing right in front of her was a corpse-pale young woman in a blood-soaked nightdress.

Her heart jumped so violently she nearly passed out.

Then she blinked and the image faded.

Christ!

All courage deserted her. With wildly shaking fingers she picked up her glass and shut the computer down. All the lights in the house were now on and staying on, even if from the outside it did look like a galleon on the high seas. This was no good. She must get busy. How to get through the night here on her own? *Bloody hell...*

She did the washing up, then dragged her suitcase out of the cupboard under the stairs and took it up to the bedroom to unpack, making sure to note every drawer was fully closed and the wardrobe door clicked shut. The upstairs seemed even chillier, her breath steamed on the air, and the image of the blood-soaked girl would not disappear; nor the ghost of the old woman - both in a house that had no record of official dwellers.

Frowning, she was closing the now empty suitcase ready to take it back down, when the frantic gibberish of a whispered conversation struck her once more. She stopped to listen. What were the secrets of this house?

And again it ceased, just as she tuned in.

She hurried downstairs with the case, just reaching the bottom step when what sounded like an impish giggle floated down the stairs from behind.

Fuck! No doubt about it this house was bloody haunted. Oh great, just bloody fantastic – these weren't nice ghosts either, these ghosts had malice, an agenda.

Screwing up her eyes she forced back the tears. Tears mixed with disbelief and rage. This was supposed to be a respite, a place of peace to come to terms with the massive cock-up that was her life. She was supposed to be learning to meditate and take steps towards being a spiritual being, go to church, discuss it with the local vicar, take long country walks and finally decide what to do next. Not this…more hauntings and angry dead people waking her up in the night, distorting her face in the mirror to get attention, flashing images into her head or inflicting pain …

"No!" she shouted into the empty house. "No! I will not have this. Do you hear? I will not have this."

Her words echoed into the stillness.

Overhead the lightbulb flickered in its paper lantern.

"No, I will not be frightened. I will not. I will sleep. I will get well. I will–"

The door to the lounge wafted back and forth.

Isobel lunged for it, swung it wide and glared into the brightly lit room. "If you have a message for me, tell me what it is."

Nothing.

"Is anyone here?"

The electric fire was cranking out heat, the light swaying slightly on the flex.

She switched both off. Then filled a hot water bottle and popped a couple of paracetamol. That should send her into oblivion for a while.

Another bad habit.

126

Yeah, well….

She stomped upstairs, determined to be normal and keep sane, to assert her right to live a peaceful life. Other mediums controlled this and so could she. Fear bred fear and even caused illusions in its image. That was all. *That was all!*

God, she was tired. She brushed her teeth and cleansed her face, resolutely not looking in the bathroom mirror; before climbing into bed under the full glare of the light, relishing the warmth of the hot water bottle.

Dear Lord, please protect me this night, please let me sleep through safely to morning. I promise to address the gift you have given me and to raise the courage to use it, but right now I really need to sleep because I'm exhausted. Please God, please keep the spirits away tonight. Thank you and amen.

They came to her in dreams.

The bed was soaked in blood. It poured out, draining her life force, staining the white sheets, spreading to the edge of the mattress and dripping onto the floor. It frothed and foamed, rippling in a tide towards the top of the stairs.

Oh, there were visitors down there…she had forgotten… people in fine clothing…people standing in the hallway clutching drinks, expressions filled with horror as looking up, they saw her crawling on her hands and knees towards the bannisters, peering through the gaps with her nightdress drenched crimson.

A baby screamed.

And Isobel jump-started awake.

Coated in sweat, her hair was matted against her forehead and her lower body ached badly. Frantically she reached for the bedside lamp and pushed back the covers to check for blood, initially relieved and then appalled. There wasn't any blood, of course there wasn't...but the stopper was no longer in the hot water bottle and the eiderdown was drenched. Fortunately the hot water hadn't leaked onto her skin but...Puzzled she stared at what lay on the brown nylon carpet in a pool of lamplight. How the hell did the stopper get into the middle of the floor?

And on the back of that came the second thought. *I had to switch on the lamp. But I left the lights on...Didn't I?*

Someone giggled, the sound ricocheting around the bedroom, and in the corner of her eye a shape – was it human – growled as it scampered across the floor. At the half way point, in the penumbra of the shadow, the creature paused and sat on its haunches, turning its head to look at her.

Then it broke a crooked smile, cracking a face withered to bone as it urinated all over the floor, the stink of hot uric acid cloying in the frigid air.

Isobel stared, near paralysed, her breath caught mid inhalation.

Then the image dissolved.

Christ! That was horrible. Evil.

Her breath was coming in rapid pants, tears burning her eyes. That was no spirit wanting to pass to the light, but the blank stare of pure malevolence and insanity.

Flopping back against the pillows she glanced at the time: 05:00 hours and still dark. There was something of a solemn sadness about the ashen-faced girl who had appeared in the lounge, though. Not all of this was evil. A girl drained of blood? Perhaps she had less strength to show herself and had come through dreams instead?

If only she wasn't so alone with this. Mercy hadn't been too keen to come here either, had she? Perhaps her belief wasn't strong enough? Well, it was her darned job so it bloody well should be. Still, it wasn't.

Branwen? What about Branwen?

Instantly she dismissed the thought. No, Branwen was a silly girl who liked dressing up and burning incense, fancied herself as a weird kind of artist. And besides, she was dangerous. She dabbled. More than that, she raised dark spirits.

Does she raise dark spirits? Why would you think that? You know she does.

And who the fuck was speaking inside her head? Oh God, she could go mad out here on her own.

For a while, propped up with the lamp on, Isobel's thoughts trailed along a myriad of different courses, eventually slipping into a fitful doze. Only to be re-awakened moments later by the sound of steady banging. Like that of a joiner nailing a coffin.

She flung the covers back.

Time for breakfast and a hot shower, then it would be a good idea to get out of this house for a while. Maybe the answers would come as she walked? It was often the way – pieces of the puzzle slotting in almost unawares, so that on coming home things that previously hadn't made sense now did. One thing was certain though, she was here for a reason and everything endured to date – being ostracised, not fitting in, bordering insanity with terror – had led to this.

The only question was what? Because it seemed one hell of a preparation.

***

Chapter Fifteen

Flora
April, 1893

I am next. He is coming for me…But waiting, biding his time.

The danger grows insidiously, a living thing beginning to take form with each passing day. Of course, how could I have thought Diane was overweight when she either runs around in a state of great agitation or is so melancholy as to be rendered completely inert, unable even to lift a spoon to her mouth? That they loosened her dress to cover the bump is now obvious. Why had I not noticed? How could I have been so blind? Or perhaps the thought, being so utterly repugnant and unlikely, was never thought at all?

And so he waits. But on some instruction, perhaps for the right time? And they – all three – are complicit…A knot of deep unease twists into my stomach. Why have my letters not reached Amelia? What keeps her? Have, and dear God I hope this is not the case, our letters been intervened? Has she perhaps written but received no reply? Does she think me well? Why then would she not visit? It must be nearly May!

Dawn rises now in shades of silvery grey, the chatter of birds incongruously wild and merry beneath the eaves; and Diane drifts away to the shadows, muttering to herself about seeing the devil. Time and again my thoughts return to this devil of hers – the one with the lit cigarette at the peephole in the door. Is Gwilym Ash the father of her second child? Is it he or some other? And why would the women help him to conceal such acts? *They clean up his mess...*

Is the doctor aware? It beggars belief a woman can be delivered of child and him not know!

Round and round the questions swirl until quite suddenly it is light. I must have drifted off. How strangely the unconscious mind works. Stark and cold as always, the room is today, however, bright with the tilting axis of summer promise, woolly clouds scooting freely beyond the bars. By ill contrast, the wailing and screeching of fetid madness wakes the dormitory to its dreary routine. Ada, now blinded in one eye, and still bandaged from the attack, is being held down while the wadding to her oozing sores is changed. Her screams pierce the ear drums, while Nesta and Ivy curse her to keep still. The stench of pus, soiled beds and fear is rancid; the hopeless imprisonment deeply depressing.

When God's earth is so disturbingly beautiful, the stark juxtaposition of human filth and degradation is both painful and sickening. How can it be so ugly, so badly wrong, with these poor souls left to suffer as they do?

Diane lies atop her bed, cold as waxwork, staring at silhouettes of shivery boughs and iron slats stealing across the walls. Her eyes are doll wide and fixed, lips working silently, as if these sliding shapes have arrived just for her this morning. She is lost to me now, for a while. I only hope she can be persuaded to come with me when I find a way out of here, and that it will be in time, before her next child is taken.

Thus, to all intents, I must remain of calm countenance in order to convince Dr Edgar to assess me with favour, to see I am quite well and must now be allowed home. Surely I have endured enough harsh treatments? That I am still alive is testament only to my will power and nothing to do with his care. This has gone on for long enough and whatever qualms my family have regarding my mental health, they must surely see I am quite recovered.

Ada's squeals are finally abating to the pathetic whimpers of a whipped dog. Nesta and Ivy are moving onto another of the women, one who was pushed out of bed during the night, doubtless by Cora. Of course, she likes nothing better than to scamper across the darkened floor in the dead of night, leap onto a bed and shove the occupant out. Or violently assault them with the leather of her shoe. This particular lady has just been discovered lying comatose on the floor between the metal frame and the wall, with a swelling the size of a lemon on her temple. Some of the women are shrieking, others hiding, one laughing hysterically. Amid the pandemonium Myra is called for and soon other attendants hurry in to help remove the victim by stretcher. I wonder if she will be taken to the chronic block upstairs, and if we will see her again, poor soul.

As the entourage passes it is clear she is close to death. Her eyes are closed, the lids bruised and swollen, and a trickle of blood congeals at the corner of her mouth. As frail as a bag of bird bones, she was a blue-toned woman who blended into the walls unnoticed - quite it seemed, without the power of speech.

Many have clamoured to watch her departure, huddling in a babbling group of concern. And it is among these that the silent watcher now stands – raising her eyes to meet mine with a steady somewhat disconcerting stare. I say disconcerting because her eyes are blinded with cataracts and yet she sees. I recall her quietly watching me in the early days and weeks, very gently shaking her head when I shouted or questioned what was happening. Diane said her daughter-in-law had her admitted because she held séances, that Violet is a spiritual medium able to stream voices of the dead through her body. Well now, she and I exchange a look, and there is indeed something of the darkness about her, some secret knowledge. Something which causes me to quickly turn away, cheeks aflame. It is as if she sees deep inside…as if she knows…

Around us the morning routine has fallen into disarray, the shrieking panic of Bedlam as the London madhouse has come to be known. And for once I am heartily glad when Ivy Payne finally yanks me to my feet for the washroom.

"Come on, look sharp and get dressed, Madam. You're seeing the doctor this morning, so be on your best behaviour, is it?"

***

They keep me waiting for such a long time as to be

unnatural. Indeed hours pass, the metronome tick of the carriage clock on the mantelpiece the only sound in this, the room referred to as the admissions room. On and on the click-clock-click-clock...until eventually the light dips to that of forthcoming rain, another day is spent, and evening shadows lengthen over the fields.

Within the rest of the house, however, the atmosphere seems fractious and has done so all day. Screams echo from high in the house, ghostly wails floating down chimney flues and along pipes. And all the while pounding footsteps rush up and down stairs, keys jangle and doors click open and shut. Perhaps this is some kind of test for the nerves? To see how long it takes me to start hammering on the door pleading to get out.

At one point my pulse quickens. Is that the sound of horses and carriage outside? Are my family here at long last to collect me? Am I, in fact, waiting to be taken home? Oh, God please let it be so!

But how could that be - still dressed as I am in the disgrace of an asylum uniform with identity tags sewn clearly on the outside? They would most certainly have made me presentable and covered my scalp with a bonnet. No, no... they would not permit a patient to be discharged like this. And after a while my poor heart squeezes with disappointment at the knowledge others possessed all along...that no one is coming...and the horses now clatter away, having only perhaps brought the mailman or some such delivery.

And now the gloom of impending rain collects in balls of angry clouds, spitting against the window and gusting down the chimney. There is not a sound in this house save my own breathing and the fluttering of a bird's wings against the leaded pane. Poor thing, he has flown into the glass. And soon enough, predictably, his small body plummets to the ground with a soft thud.

A death omen.

Still no one comes. Are they to leave me here all night?

Then it occurs to me. I have been placed firmly out of the way – left on chair inside a locked room. All day…

Diane!

This makes sense. All at once I see this is the case. Something is happening today and they wanted me out of the way. Yes, he saw Diane and I last night, observed us talking, reported back…So they know about our friendship! Despite the fact we kept it secret in the shadows and hushes of pre-dawn. They know.

Gwilym. The puppet…the tell-tale…

Suddenly footsteps clatter down the corridor and the door flings wide.

Ivy Payne and Nesta Winters walk smartly in with towels, a bowl of hot water and a razor.

My eyes must be wide as a frightened pony's. Immediately I shut them tight. No one will see my fear. No one. Especially not these two.

The towel goes around my shoulders with ne'er a word, and one of them sets to work scrubbing my scalp with detergent. Then without any explanation but plenty of chat between themselves, what remains of my cropped hair is shaved to the bone with little care taken not to nick the skin.

I am trying not to cry. Truly - not so much as a whimper. I will not ask. I will endure this. I will endure it but make no mistake, when I die I will haunt these bitches to the end of their damn days, so help me God.

"Be quick now," says Ivy, quite deliberately in English. "Bend her head down, get the neck done."

"Why don't we leave a strand of it, you know – just to remind her of what she had?"

And so they do – an odd length of curl an inch or so behind the left ear, just to make me look even more peculiar.

Back to their local tongue, the chatter quickens now along with their fingers. They want to leave as soon as possible, their urgency palpable. I wish I could understand. It is a difficult language to learn and they talk rapidly in heavy dialect. Thanks to Diane and the habit of listening to their morning gossip though, a few words stick. Enough, as Diane would say, to fathom the gist.

They speak of a child…and a lake – specifically Llyn Mynachlog – the one behind the house. So much is flying over my head at such speed and with such an unusual level of vehemence it is clear they want the working day to be done. 'Nos,' 'nos calan,' and other words I do not understand but which are oft repeated, must be committed to memory - 'coelcerth,' 'calan mai,' 'mochyn' and, 'eglwys.' That last word, I am sure, is 'church'. And 'nos' means 'night'. So something to do with a child at the lake at night? In a church?

It makes little sense and is most frustrating. Diane would know, but Diane might not be lucid by the time I return to the dormitory, and I have a feeling that what is being said is about tonight - that something is going to happen imminently. If only there was someone else who understood both Welsh and English. Maybe Violet, the one who is spiritual? I wonder if she does? Alas, she seems quite mute.

The towel is now whipped away.

"There's lovely," says Ivy Payne. "All ready for your treatment."

"She having it done in here, is she?"

"The doctor said to leave her here. Anyhow, we'll be off now, M' Lady. Important day tomorrow - you're going to the village church."

Nesta laughs. "She's going to look lovely in the photographs, is it?"

Treatment? What treatment?

***

Chapter Sixteen

It is dusk when he arrives. The room remains unlit, swaying boughs brushstroke the walls with shadows, and leaves scratch at the window. Occasionally soot blows down the flue and spews across the hearth. The whole house is most curiously silent.

He does not bring with him a gaslight or candle, but instead sets on the table beside me a small glass jar. And in the semi-dark it is clear what lurks inside.

Two black leeches are probing their surroundings, and the very sight of their shimmering, pulsating bodies with suckers shortly to bury into my veins, sets within me a lurch of sickly panic. Perhaps he hopes to bleed out my madness? But why shave my hair? Not...oh, not... please God in heaven, no...he cannot mean to place them to my head?

I must urgently persuade him of my sanity, yet without giving cause to diagnose hysteria - hold his gaze quite steadily and inform him that...

"And how are you this evening, Flora?"

I should dearly like to say I would feel better had I not been starved, attacked by fellow patients, repeatedly drowned to the point of death, manacled and strapped into a straitjacket. I would also feel happier were I not facing two black slugs ready to drink my blood. Alas, I am lightheaded, faint with hunger and eager for this rare interview to produce my release.

"I am well, sir."

"I am glad to hear it. Perhaps then, a little tea and beef would be in order this evening?"

"Thank you, sir."

He nods, observing me in a most disquieting manner, the eyes so without colour as to be made of glass. "We must first assess your fitness for church tomorrow. It is an important day in the village and we at Lavinia House must show our support."

"I have no calendar, sir. Is it Easter?"

"Easter has passed. No, tomorrow is the first of May, and whilst we do not condone or participate in the unseemly revelry, the erm…festival…the villagers request our presence and there are few well enough to attend."

"Yes sir."

"You will be presentable enough I think, if you are able to convince me you will not go about screaming or becoming violent, which you are wont to do."

I hold my tongue. Would he not be violent if he had been stripped of his liberty and subjected to such torture?

"I can assure you sir, that I will in no way be vociferous or violent."

"Good. Now please remove your clothing."

"Sir?"

"Take off your dress. And underwear."

My face blazes. Of course, he is a doctor and wishes to examine my physical fitness for a trip into society, but there is something about the way his tongue licks those worm red lips, something about the dilation of his pupils, the slackening of his jaw.

What choice do I have? And besides, what cause does

my poor, beaten body give any man for lust? Thus it is with shame and misery that I let the grey serge dress slip from my shoulders, exposing a carcass of jutting ribs and protruding hip bones.

He nods at my underwear – this must come off too - and as it slides to the floor I can hardly bear to look at my reflection in the window behind his head – at the cadaver that stands before him.

"Walk around the room."

No, no, no….

His voice is now thick and syrupy. "I said walk around. Let me see all of you."

There is no fight left in me. The hags who normally torment me but whose presence would be preferable at this moment, are absent. The house is quiet as a tomb. What does he want to see? What he has reduced me to, as a woman, as a human being?

"Good. Now get dressed."

Scrambling into my clothes in a blur of shock and confusion, it occurs to me that he is not writing any-thing down. Nor is he reaching for the glass jar. Fear lumps solidly inside my chest. He is the puppet master. He is the one. This is the danger which has at last fully taken form. And it is the doctor himself.

Fumbling with shaking fingers to fasten my dress, I feel his eyes upon me, willing me to look up.

I do not wish to, but the pull is magnetic and our eyes lock.

Recognition passes between us. And in that instant the veneer of his pious respectability falls away.

Without doubt, this is Diane's devil.

***

Chapter Seventeen

Isobel
Present Day, Blackmarsh

The morning was still dark when she locked the door and stepped onto the drive. The Black Mountains were obscured by cloud, the lane which led towards them damp with drizzle and mist. From what she could remember it divided into three - the most direct route through the mountains being Drovers Pass, a gorge frequently flooded and shrouded on both sides by forest. The lane to the left was spookily named The Hill of Loss, which was rather off-putting considering the state of mind she was in today. No, it would be best to stick to the one on the right – the track rutted with tyre tracks and signs of human life, which led to the mines and had a clear public right of way.

As she tramped along in the mist, the fields either side squelched and squeaked as if populated by a thousand mud skippers. It seemed strange for the deserted countryside to be so active, yet also comforting. It was good to be in life again.

Soon the lane began to steepen sharply however, and it wasn't long before, despite a nip of snow in the air, she was out of breath and getting hot. Enveloped in wet cloud it was no longer possible to see more than a few inches ahead and with each step she began to question the wisdom of climbing further. But she'd come this far and the place was so magical and intriguing, it was worth at least giving it a go. Besides, the weather might clear up. She stopped for a breather and another look at the map. Copa Hill should lead up to the old copper mine, and although it had long since been abandoned there were photographs on Wikipedia of a tiny chapel clinging to the side of a precipice, which she had to see.

The incline was tough going though, far more than anticipated, the track becoming narrower, the edge crumbling away on one side into a deep ravine. The sound of her own panting sounded loud in the muffled morning air. Her hair was matted and it was sweaty underneath the waxed jacket, especially with all the thick woollens layered underneath.

It took an hour. But just as her hamstrings were about to give out, the path began to level and a weather-beaten footpath sign loomed out of the fog, beneath it a large boulder etched with, 'Copa Hill Farm.' The arrow pointed to an overgrown stile leading across boggy fields. She narrowed her eyes. In the distance the faint outline of a farm building squatted darkly, the open path exposed to the elements.

She frowned. The map showed a track circumventing two farms – one Copa Hill, the other Redmoor, which if the public right of way was followed, should skirt the edge of one and pass straight through the yard of the other, before looping back to the mine and where she was heading anyway.

Sounds like my friend from Copa Hill....No one likes an incomer round here...

Now that was a thought! Wasn't that where Branwen said Rhys the-bearded-road-hog lived? Well, if there was a red pick-up truck parked in the yard it definitely was. Perhaps it would be as well to know? No one was going to see her on a morning like this and besides, it was only ten minutes out of her way...

At the far end of the field lay a dry-stone wall. But with no further signs, boulders or styles it was hard to see how the path continued. She scanned the entire length but there was nothing. Right, so they'd blocked off the right of way, then? What to do? She looked around. Visibility was still little more than a few feet and every foothold sank ankle deep into the mud. From somewhere in the distance the sound of lambs bleating travelled across the valley. Oh, what the hell? The place was pretty deserted.

She made the decision and clambered over.

Not that she need have worried - Copa Hill Farm looked as if it had been uninhabited for a very long time. Foggy drizzle and relentlessly damp weather had rendered the slate roof and stone walls to a miserable skeleton coated with moss and lichen, the splintered bones of its tinder framework jutting through the stones. No one, it seemed, had lived here in quite a while.

So it was not the owners of Copa Hill Farm who had opposed tourism in the village or tried to scare her the other day. She glanced over her shoulder at the way she'd come, at the sodden fields swallowed in fog, then back to the other farm. The footpath was marked as passing through their yard before looping around to a track leading back to Copa Hill mine. That would be on firmer ground. And not above a few minutes.

The outline of Redmoor Farm appeared moments after scrambling over the next wall. And this one was definitely lived in. Tentatively she crept forwards, peering through the fog, looking for the yard, when suddenly shouts went up.

She stopped dead, breath caught in her chest.

Someone was running out of the house towards her...a woman...An engine fired up...and headlights flashed into her eyes.

***

Chapter Eighteen

For a split second Isobel stood dazzled in the lights, before quickly realising she was in the middle of the farmyard. About to hold up her hands to indicate she was harmless, the driver, however, began to accelerate towards her at speed.

Flaming hell! Was that a gun shot?

She plunged almost headlong into the woodland at the side of the driveway, stumbled over a wire-topped fence and scrambled up the hill.

"Get off our property!" A woman yelled. "Clear off or I'll set the dogs on you!"

The vehicle with its headlights on was roaring down the lane full throttle and another gunshot cracked out, propelling a flock of screeching crows into the air.

Terror kicked her in the ribs, as with feet slipping and sliding in the mud she grabbed at branches to get up the bank. *For God's sake, she was just a woman on her own, unarmed and in retreat.*

Another shot fired, the sound ricocheting around the trees. Blind with panic now and utterly without bearings, instinctively she kept climbing. Dense undergrowth twisted round her feet, thorns ripped her palms and twigs snapped into her face as sharp as elastic bands. Pray to God the men weren't in pursuit because they would rapidly close the gap, knowing the terrain so much better than she. Maybe Rhys, whatever his name was, had sons? And what if there were animal traps? There wasn't time to feel the way carefully...*Fuck, fuck, fuck*...and she hadn't told a single person where she was going. No one would know she was missing...and these people were nasty, on the edge...

Time blurred. On and on she ran. Stitch burned her side and her lungs were fit to burst. Any moment now a hand would grab her shoulder and slam her to the ground. What then? A basement? Slow torture or a clean shot? Oh God, this was horrible...

Then quite suddenly the forest came to an abrupt end, giving way to a sheer drop of several hundred feet - the quarry, and the very top of it too. There was nothing beyond this but wilderness.

So this was it, then? She could run no more. Sinking to her knees she glanced around, defeated and miserable, flinching with the expectation of there being at least one assailant, probably more.

There was, however, no one there.

Instead, the woods were eerily still, soft mist curling around the tree trunks in a blue haze.

Doubled over and gasping for every breath, she checked her watch. That had been full pelt for the best part of fifteen minutes - most of it uphill with a rucksack on her back. She'd never been one for keep-fit or strenuous exercise. The pain in her legs and chest was off the scale. Nor would it be wise to assume safety yet. They would know of short cuts and likely had quad bikes. Oh yes...bikes...motorbikes or off-roaders...

She strained her ears, but the morning was absolutely

silent. Just the steady drip-drip-drip of sopping trees.

Still, it would not be wise to linger.

The track back down Copa Hill was not an option. And the disused quarry had no way across. The weak morning light had lifted the mist a little, and on the opposite side of the ravine the outline of a tiny chapel had emerged. Clinging to the side of the rock face, several hundred tiny steps led up to it from the bottom with as many again to the top. It looked, she thought, like a ghost town, and sounded like one too with the wind moaning through it. Why build a chapel there? Were the miners not allowed to use the one in the village? Perhaps they lived up here as well as worked? She closed her eyes, seeing at once a scene resembling a refugee camp - hundreds of wooden huts, of lanterns in the mine and the chapel windows in the dark…this was a place of grief and loss…and rage too. There had been a lot of deaths here, explosions, men with blackened faces, stretchers being carried up those steep, narrow steps to the chapel. The smell of fires, the sound of children crying, of…yes a kind of camp situated where she was sitting now…

A full range of emotions passed through her. That tiny building held the pain of trapped souls. Little wonder local people didn't want the place opening up for tourism if their relatives met their deaths here. Who owned it? Or had owned it? There was a residue of deep anger, of despair and bitterness. Again came that feeling of layers…layers and layers of lies.

She shivered as the sweat dried on her skin. Time to get moving. At least they weren't coming after her, thank God. Hurriedly she unfastened her rucksack and drank half a flask of coffee while scanning the map. Not yet lunchtime but already fatigue was setting in, and the weather up here could change in a heartbeat. The problem was avoiding Copa Hill. So that left one option - crossing the moor in order to circumvent the mine, and track back down the forest on the other side, the path she'd originally shunned because of its name – The Hill of Loss.

Acutely aware of the cold seeping into her back, she swung the rucksack on and forced herself to stand up again. It was going to be a long day with miles to go yet. This had been a stupid idea, although to be fair no one could have predicted being shot at. At least, she consoled herself, it had taken her mind off the bloody ghosts for a while.

The rest of the climb was rocky and steep. And the higher the altitude the denser the cloud, until eventually sparse woodland gave way to a blast of barren heathland. A veil of rain was slanting across a boggy plateau rippling with pools of water as black as tar, and resolutely she put her head down against the freezing onslaught. As she walked, eerie creaks and moans carried on the wind, echoing like the dinosaur groans of collapsing metal and whinnying horses...It must be, she rationalised, just the whistling wind - how it swept off the mountains and whipped around the plain. Yes, just the wind...

All the same, it would be good to get off the mountain.

It wasn't easy to quicken the pace. Underfoot the mud squelched and pulled at her boots and the further in she ventured, the harder it became to extract each foot. The imprints were now several inches deep and her legs ached with the effort. Exhausted, and still only a third of the way across, she stopped to look back at the path she'd left, to what now seemed like a distant shore of comparative safety. But the cloud had closed in so completely there was nothing to be seen, and on turning back again it was with a stab of alarm she realised she could no longer see ahead either. Had in fact, no idea in which direction she was now facing. Indeed it could be straight for the ebony lake, to where folklore had it many a man and his horse had been lured to a terrifying death.

That brief pause had been a mistake for another reason too – her feet had sunk by at least six maybe seven inches and it was now impossible to lift them out again.

Oh, God…

A fresh blast of wind lashed at her face and tears burned her eyes. How many others had met their fate out here? Caught out by fog rolling in so thick and fast they found themselves going around in circles until the quagmire took its prey…or the lake did.

In the distance, a tiny light hovered over the bog and now it came to her notice there were more and more of them…dancing fairy lights…the strange electric charges often glimpsed over marshland, known as willo' the wisp or corpse candles. Easy to see why local people would think of them as the villainous fae luring a weary traveller to their death. Nevertheless it gave her direction – in that she should take the opposite one.

The rain had set in now and gasping at its ferocity, she sank to her knees and pulled out her wellies, put them back on and resumed the trek, praying it was in the right direction this time. Albeit covered in mud.

It took another hour. But at long last the shape of a forest loomed out of the drizzle, exactly where the map said it would be. She almost cried with relief. This then, would be The Hill of Loss.

The Hill of Loss. What a strange and desolate name for a mountain pass.

Strange and desolate indeed.

The entrance to the forest was through a five-barred gate, once used for horses and carts, but now hanging from its hinges. Either side of the gate standing as guardians, were two ancient thorns, and thus it was with a sense of awe that she passed into the silent balm of the woods. Instantly the wind dropped and fire flamed into her cheeks. God, what a morning! She could have died. Twice.

Okay, well the thing to do now was to get back in one piece. After drinking the rest of the coffee she hurried downhill, almost running. The path had long since become overgrown but there was running water nearby, rushing downstream, so all she had to do was follow it. According to the map this should come out at the fields behind Lavinia House. Oh, who cared if she ran into bloody Lorna snooty boots, as long as it was nowhere near those bloody savages with guns.

Half an hour of rapid stumbling downhill and the path began to level out, quite suddenly opening up to a wide track ahead, with a T-junction and a large boulder. She squinted at the etching. Lavinia House was indicated with an arrow - one and a half miles to the right. This at least resembled a proper track, one that had probably been used for carriages taking people to the house, and gladly, she took it. On the flat and on the way back. Hurray. It had stopped raining too, mist hovering among spiky winter branches in skeins of soft white silk. Occasionally the wintry light picked out the glint of a silvery cobweb or the dazzle of a raindrop, the smell of fresh earth and budding foliage pungent with new growth. A buoyant mood lifted her heart and it felt, for the most fleeting of moments, like coming home. As if she had been here before and taken this path many times.

That elation however, was swiftly followed by the same oddly familiar sensation first felt on seeing Branwen's creepy paintings...dank moss, dripping stones, and the sickly sensation of vertigo. And without any warning there came another vision - the image of a smart carriage led by three horses trotting by, and a small white face at the window. Then, just as quickly as it had arisen, it was gone.

She grabbed the nearest tree trunk and swallowed down the nausea until the feeling passed.

These visions were becoming more frequent – several times a day now. They didn't mean anything though, so what was the use? Perhaps it was a footprint of emotions, of energy, from long ago? Something that for some reason she could tap into? But how to control it or make sense of it? Better still to not have it at all! Every time it left her drained, a little more depleted, as if her life force was ebbing away.

Desperate now to get back to the house, she walked briskly along the path in the surety it would soon lead to the estate drive, when it came to an abrupt end, a drystone wall covered in ivy barring the way. How odd for it just to stop like that! She scanned the length of the wall in both directions looking for a way through. Maybe this was the boundary to the estate and they'd decided to block off the legal right of way, just like the thugs up at Redmoor Farm?

Oh, sod it. She was climbing over. There wasn't a chance of backtracking – she was tired, muddy and starving. *So suck it up, Lorna Snotty-Drawers!*

One or two stones dislodged and toppled as she scrambled over but once on the other side there was no longer a path of any description. In fact it looked as though someone had gone to great pains to destroy all evidence of there ever having been one.

For a second or two she hesitated. Something had changed. The whole atmosphere...It was impossible at first to say what it was but the forest here was so hushed as to seem devoid of all life. It seemed to hum with static. Not a single rustling creature or ruffle of leaves. And the longer she stood there the more it seemed as if time had stopped.

Gradually there came the sound of murmuring.

Someone was meditating or chanting. Soft and low.

Unsure if this was real or another vision, she carried on walking as inconspicuously as possible, when a twig snapped under one of her feet. Wincing, she inched away from whoever might be there, one eye on the perimeter fence and the fields now in view; when a flicker of movement caught her attention. And once she'd seen it, she couldn't look away.

Through a tunnel of tree trunks in a circular glade of grass, a woman dressed in long black skirts and a cape, sat cross-legged with her face held up to the sky and palms outstretched.

Isobel's mouth dropped open.

Branwen Morgan was deep in trance, swaying with the movement of treetops that blew one way and then the other despite the icy stillness of the forest down here in the valley. There was not a breath of air save for that within the circle.

Hanging from a nearby branch was a pyramid of hemp and sticks; and the more she looked the more she saw…bracelets of rosehips and stones had been strewn like fairy lights…offerings of elderberries and sprigs of thyme lay presented on a small altar,,, and scenting the air was the heady aroma of burning henbane, pine and ferns. This was a very private ritual and she had to leave. It felt like prying. All the same it was a spooky sight and utterly entranced she found herself swaying to a sickly, rushing feeling, the sound of wind soughing through the bare branches.

This girl was real. Branwen was summoning something.

A prickle of fear gripped her and backing away she prayed another twig wouldn't snap and break Branwen's concentration.

With enormous care she retreated several yards before deeming it safe to run downhill towards the fields. Anywhere this came out would do. This was the weirdest place she'd ever been to in her life, and right now a crippling bank loan and a seventy hour week working in Asda to pay for a bedsit seemed like nirvana. Carry on like this and the risk was total insanity. Why had she come here? Why the fuck couldn't she just be an ordinary person without this freaking scary shit jumping out at her all the time?

Bursting out of the trees, it was to emerge precisely where the owners would not want anyone to be - behind the house. At the lake. Not far off where Lorna had marched her from just the day before.

It was, however, a breath-taking view. Unlike the lakes on top of the heath, this one glistened with light and rippled with life. Beyond it lay the great house with its extensive lawns and ancient oaks, and to the fore, the fascinating little church and walled garden. Yes, it would have done well in this valley as a monastery, she could picture that. Those guys got all the best places. That lake though, it looked as though someone was there.

Squinting into the white glare of the rising mist, she tried to see who it was. Someone in a long cloak...looking directly this way...lifting his or her hand...

The sound of a soft voice from behind almost stopped her heart. "You can see him, can't you, Isobel?" Branwen drew level. "First time I've seen him in a long time."

On the far shore of the lake stood a man in a white cowled robe, staring across the water.

"They say when you see the druids it's an ill omen. That danger's coming. A warning."

"Druid? Warn us of what? Why?"

"I don't know, lovely. But I do know you're in danger. Terrible danger."

She turned to look at her. "I'm sorry I disturbed you. I got lost and–"

Branwen brushed the words away. "Listen, I had a nasty feeling about you yesterday - you know, after what happened with Rhys Payne? Really nasty. I don't often conjure the fae unless I have to – they can be pure evil if you don't play it right. But I'll tell you this, they'll show you the dark side all right… Isobel, something bad's coming. We don't have much time - you've got to let me help you."

***

Chapter Nineteen

Flora. Lavinia House
1893

He motions me to sit down again, and though his stare burns into the side of my face I will not meet his eyes, forced instead to stare at the leeches - sweaty and pulsating in their glass jar. I wish he'd get it over with.

"I think," he says after a while. "That you are too weak and feeble to be bled tonight. That is the cure for you, Flora – to drain the illness from your blood, do you understand?"

"Yes sir."

Of course I do not understand. I burst to ask the fool what he thinks bleeding an emaciated, undernourished woman could possibly accomplish. But it would be an act of folly to provoke him or give any reason for further detainment. I must leave this room as soon as possible and escape this intense and most unnatural scrutiny. But where are the housemaids, the attendants, his wife even, in this oh-so-silent house? Why are we alone?

Since this morning not a morsel, even a drop of water, has passed my lips and such sickly dizziness overwhelms me that I must grip the edges of the chair to keep from fainting.

Yet still he says nothing, does nothing.

On and on the metronome ticking of the clock.

The leeches fade in and out of my dulling sight, the jar blurring with the wallpaper. From somewhere outside a waft of wood smoke filters into the darkness.

"All right," he says, eventually. "I will call Miss Strickland to accompany you back to the dormitory. You may be brought brandy and beef. We will try again in a week or two with the leech application."

"Yes sir."

He stands to pull the bell rope and this time it is I who become the watcher. He is of short stature with a slight, bird-like chest, the nose aquiline in profile, chin receding beneath the grey beard.

In an instant he swings around.

A glimpse of inner rage sparks from him – a palpable, malevolent fury of indignation. And oh, how quickly it rises from the depths, how he suffers to keep that hidden. I see that now. See it, despite staring at the floor, praying Myra Strickland will hurry up.

She takes an age.

And all the while the good doctor stares. What does he want from me? Why so much hatred when surely I have done him no wrong? It seems he is a man born with a violence of the soul and it begs the question why he elected to become a man of pious religion. Perhaps his vocation is a shield for the monster inside, for it is an effective one at that. Or has he become this way due to some ill-fate or perceived injustice? Yet with all that he has, how could that be so? What would a man of property and power need with such anger?

A plume of fiery smoke gusts down the chimney once more. Indeed there is a haze to the evening. A charge in the air.

But before he is able to challenge my inspection of him, footsteps at long last click along the hallway and the door opens.

"Good evening, Doctor."

"Good evening, Myra. Take Mrs George back to the dormitory and see to it she has bread and beef, with some brandy."

"Yes, Doctor."

Mutely we retreat along the corridor. Shadows lurch around the tiled walls from her gas lamp, our footsteps a hollow echo. The smell in this establishment is like nothing else could ever be... the air trapped and stale with human decay. It permeates the skin and mind alike, an earthly hell.

In a fanfare of rattling keys Myra unlocks the dormitory door and ushers me inside. "Your supper will be brought."

It is pointless to ask when or even by whom, and besides, by the time she has locked it again all thoughts of supper immediately evaporate. The room is thick with smoke. It billows down the chimney and chokes the air in a crackling, amber glow. Several of the women are standing at the window in their nightdresses, peering through the bars. Some are clapping, their eyes alight and excited like children at a travelling fairground. I thought so. Fire!

From up here the view is a panoramic landscape of fields, forests and mountains. And tonight the sky is aglow with not one or even two, but dozens and dozens of bonfires dotted all over the hills in every direction. Although the grounds of the estate are grimly chill by comparison, the surrounding countryside is ablaze, the night sparking with flames, and carrying on the breeze are faint cries of excitement along with the low beating of a drum.

There must be a local festival of some sort, something I now vaguely recall being referred to earlier...*of course, we do not condone or participate in the unseemly revelry*...Perhaps they celebrate a pagan event here and that is why he does not agree with it? Certainly it would explain Ivy and Nesta's keenness to leave early. What is not explained however, is why I was kept in the room downstairs all day. Purely to assess my fitness to attend church tomorrow? Or because something has happened to Diane...It strikes me as odd.

And she is not here.

Most of the women are at the window, their backs to the darkened room. Along the far wall, bodies of the inert shift and groan beneath white sheets and it is to these I hurry, checking the occupants one by one. An occasional claw hand reaches out with surprising strength – the grip of madness – but no, she is not here, not in her bed lying disorientated and rambling...but absent. And her bed is not merely empty but stripped to the bare mattress.

My heart bounces sickeningly, suspicions confirmed.

"Yes, they have taken her," says a voice, softly spoken and unknown to me.

Standing behind me is the one who never speaks yet watches with eyes that cannot see. The one Diane said

held séances. Violet. I must confess her appearance causes me great consternation. With hooded eyes misted and
opaque, the skin and mouth quite shrivelled, she resembles an ancient soothsayer in storybooks. But her appearance is deceptive, her clutch cool and gentle on my
arm.

"Sit awhile."

It is a risk. What if Myra comes back?

As if reading my thoughts she says, "We have little
time and I will come to the point. The meanings you
seek are, coelcerth, nos calan, and mochyn, are they not?
Llyn? Nos?" Her voice is startling, low and urgent.

"I beg your pardon, Madam?"

"You wish to know what the words mean. It is Beltane, my dear. They celebrate with bonfires and another
word you have heard tonight – the crogi gwr gwynt?"

My mouth must have dropped open and I sink to
the bed next to her, clasping her hands in mine. So she
reads my mind. What is she? I had derisibly thought a
parlour room séance holder but am quite caught off
guard.

There is a smile behind those unnerving eyes. "Don't
be afraid, dear. I watch for a long time before I speak
these days."

"But how do you know? I mean, that I wanted to
understand those particular words?"

"If I trust you I will speak what comes to me. They
mean bonfire, and Beltane or May Day; and llyn is lake,
mochyn - pig."

"Pig? Why pig I wonder?"

She nods, lowering her voice ever further despite the
distraction at the window, clearly listening for the door

too.

"It is an ancient custom similar to All Hallow's Eve. Twice a year the veil between the living and the dead thins, and fires are lit all over the hills and valleys, horns blown, bells rung, fiddles played and songs sung while the people play games and generally have a merry old time getting drunk. But you see, when the ashes die down around midnight and turn into a smouldering mass, they believe the black sow will make its appearance. The black sow is an embodiment of evil, which arises from out of the blackened debris to chase terrified revellers home. The churchyard is where it's at its most dangerous. If they get past that safely all should be well, but it has been known to pursue people to their very door. If it catches one of them, legend has it they will be possessed of evil and their souls taken straight to hell."

"And the local people believe this?"

"Oh yes, I've spent many a happy hour listening to Ivy and Nesta tell me all I need to know about what they believe. They have no idea I can understand every word."

"How did you learn Welsh? I'm trying desperately to–"

She puts her fingers to my lips. "Shh, my child. All in good time. I have digressed. There are things you must know and soon. Here in this village some believe the veil thins enough to allow the fae to cross the threshold."

"Fae?"

"The fae are thought to be both the most wicked and powerful of the supernatural elements. Anyone with a young child must cross their crib with iron for fear of it being exchanged for a crimbil as they call them here - a changeling. They say the village is plagued with those not really human, those who are in fact, really the fae. They've been seen in the forests and along the edges of the fields - smaller than us, about three feet or so, and older, wiser and infinitely more evil. A mother will be convinced the baby is no longer her own almost immediately, but no one else will see it until later when the child is around eighteen months or even two years old...by which time it is all too late. The tragedy is that no one will believe her, you see."

A prickly chill clings damply to my back, the old woman's words a distant tinkling, disembodied, echoing...*a mother will be convinced the baby is no longer her own*... It is a huge effort to concentrate on the message she is trying to convey. "So tonight, Beltane, and again at Halloween, they make fires to keep them away? To prevent the fae from—?"

"Not to stop them coming dear, no one can do that. No, tonight is the night they offer them sacrifices of bribery and appeasement - in order to get their children back."

"Oh, dear God – sacrifices? Not live animals? Cattle and such? I have heard of that in medieval times but—"

Again she cuts me short, this time with a hiss and glance sharp towards the door. "Not animals dear - humans. The crogi gwy gwyllt or the hanging straw man would often be a village idiot or a diseased person encased in a straw cage, but here in this village it is a human baby."

All words fail me. Partly it is disbelief and partly a horror so great it is paralysing.

The old lady appears spent, the light behind her eyes abruptly snuffed out, leaving once more that opaque blindness which shields her so well.

What nonsense she has imparted. It is, of course, superstitious and ridiculous gossip overheard from Nesta and Ivy. The villagers would surely never throw a human baby onto a fire – what mother would allow it?

Diane, Diane…Diane…they took me out of the way so I wouldn't hear your screams, didn't they? All day…

The old lady nods. Squeezes my hand.

"Go to your bed now, dear," she whispers. "They are coming…"

***

Chapter Twenty

What could have happened to Diane?

Tonight the plaintive wails sighing through the walls, mingle with cries of a most unnatural sort – it is ungodly the howling in those woods, and quite makes the hair stand on end. The twilight too is strangely surreal, being of a smoky lavender hue with clouds too white and too bright. Here and there the strain of a flute carries from far away, as if in lament for the dowsed bonfires... a pied piper departing for another year.

Until soon there are no sounds at all.

Nothing now but the hissing whispers of the house, and the onset of darkness. It is indeed, most unusually quiet – not even the pacing, fidgeting and mumbling of its disturbed inhabitants. No striking of the clock in the hallway far below, none from the distant church tower or the stable yard.

Occasionally a shrill scream from the rooms above kick starts my heart. Could that be Diane? Have they taken her to the padded cell? Is she still alive? I cannot bear not knowing. I wish it was myself instead of her, I truly do. The humiliation and embarrassment with the doctor all is as nothing now. I would suffer it all again and gladly, a thousand times over, if only they would not harm Diane and her child.

Tonight is the night they offer them sacrifices of bribery and appeasement…no, not animals dear, humans…

No!

My dreams are at once vivid and horrific, and I would rather stay awake. Perhaps it is the suggestion of veils thinning between worlds and spirits passing through, but terror has crept into my heart and shrouds me in its chill. The night now is at its darkest, with only the sliver of a crescent moon glinting on the glass. And something woke me I fear…

There…again… "Eeeiu!" Loud enough to raise the entire house and immediately outside the window, "Eeeiu, Eeeiu!" A peacock.

But there are no peacocks at Lavinia House.

I must check myself for dreaming. Count the bars at the window. Touch my raw, tender scalp. I am here. This is real. And that is a peacock.

For a Christian man, Doctor Fox-Whately does not care for animals in the least, and as such there are none. In truth, with the exception of birds fluttering in the eaves, even the wildlife chooses not to dwell here. Owls screech and hoot from within the forest and the haunting cries of vixens sound from far away, but none reside close to the house. And that peacock is outside this very window. Besides, even were the place overrun with them, it would be far, far too early…

The others here lie oddly still, slumbering on. Even Cora is asleep, and the impish child, Beatrice. So much so I wonder if they have been sedated. And tomorrow there is church. Why tomorrow? Why church on what is a pagan celebration?

My mind is tired now…

The call of a peacock at dawn… is it not another ill omen…? Drifting into exhausted dreams once more, a feeling of profound grief and dread weighs down my heart. And in that slip between sleep and consciousness her face appears. And I know, just know for certain, that she is dead.

***

In a sharp lance of cruelty, the morning brings forth a day bright with sunlight and the sweet scent of spring. Yet death clouds my spirit. She is gone, I feel it.

They took her, and I will never know where to, or why, or what happened. Even to her body. There will, I am sure, be no marking of her passing, no remembrance, no funeral. Worse still, I cannot even ask.

The knowledge is there in the tight smiles of Ivy Payne and Myra Strickland. There too, in the smirk on Gwilym Ash's face. I can smell it on them - the salty tang of fresh foetal blood. Oh, death is too good for these abominations of nature. For them I wish eternal hell, in this life and the next and for every vermin they spawn from their poisonous loins. Loathing for them blackens my heart until I am twisted and sick with it inside, and must keep my eyes downcast lest they see it festering there.

And now for church. *God, dear God, are you there? Are you there for Diane, for me? Indeed, for any of these poor wretches?*

They have us walk to the village in a troupe while Doctor Fox-Whately and his wife ride inside a horse-drawn carriage at the helm. There are but twelve of us, and astonishingly half are men. All this time I have never seen a male person here, such is the skill at keeping us apart. These men though, are hardly a threat to womankind, walking ahead in a motley pack, two so hunched and warped they cannot properly see the lane ahead. Behind them, trailing by several feet in order to continuously glance back at the women is Gwilym. Another reason to keep my head down and eyes averted.

It is a tragedy to be so stricken with despair on a morning such as this. Yet all this burgeoning life serves only to deepen my misery, a reminder that this world full of beauty is not for me; and never was or will be again for Diane. Somewhere other people are laughing or falling in love or dipping their toes in a fresh, cool mountain stream…maybe watching sunshine glint on a harbour bobbing with fishing boats. Somewhere, somewhere….people have joy in their hearts.

And the walk is both long and painful, my legs unused to such a distance buckling at intervals. Ivy Payne shoves me in the back. "Get a move on, Madam!"

She and Nesta are white about the gills today, their breath rank with alcohol. Out here in the stark light Ivy looks more sallow and gaunt than ever, the gouged rivulets around her lips and eyes deeply etched. She catches my swift assessment and her eyes harden to flint. That was a mistake. A big one. It is she who metes out the treatments, who sees fit to take us to the edge of existence each day. Casualties are many and only to be expected. And I must not forget the leech application is due when the good doctor deems me well enough, and it would be easy for her to extract the leeches with suckers still in the veins, or worse - leave them to burrow inside my nose or mouth. She would do so too, without a qualm.

At last the village comes into view, such that it is - a dank, overshadowed cluster of cottages either side of a cobbled square. But to my horror a crowd has gathered. Clearly in excitable spirits already, the jostling, jeering mob begins to clap and shout. We are the carnival of fools, the idiots on display for entertainment, and one or two of the more vacuous in our troupe appear to enjoy the attention, grinning and witless.

Taunts and insults are levied, the bravest leaping into our faces with ghastly screeches. Alas, in such a dialect it is difficult to, as dear Diane would have said, fathom the gist. I am in no doubt they are calling us dumb and im-becilic or cursed with demons, and what a good thing it is we are kept locked up so they can sleep safely in their beds.

I am glad for the hat hiding my face, and the fear I know will be marked for all to see. This public parading of the asylum inmates is perhaps the most galling of all - the most utterly humiliating experience imaginable, and a great swell of tears drop down my cheeks. For now. For this moment. And for Diane, who will never again hold my hand in the darkest hours and tell me to keep living, keep fighting. For what though, Diane? For what? For this? Or even to be a free woman again and return to life as it was? For that can never be so. This will forever scar my soul. I am much changed and will never again be Flora George. I am losing hope now. All that she instilled...I am losing.

Help me God, please, for I am losing my will...

The church service at least, save for those constantly

turning around to nudge each other and snigger, is a time and place of peaceful respite. Sunshine streams through the stained glass windows, illuminating the vaulted building with what can only be described as exalting divinity. It strikes such an intense emotion within me that the sermon passes in a blur of words; the only ones I actually recall being so paradoxical the irony almost makes me cry.

For behold, the winter is past; the rain is over and gone. The flowers appear on the earth, the time of singing has come.

The time of singing. I hardly think so. I doubt I will ever sing again. If I open my mouth to do so absolutely nothing comes forth, and the pious explanation of the Bible lesson serves only to sour my heart further. What God do they worship? What crippling messages of servitude! We are all sinners. Yes indeed, except for the sanctimonious self-righteous persons in the front pews.

Afterwards, Doctor Fox-Whately shakes hands with the minister, and as the congregation spills outside into hazy sunshine, local men doff their caps to him and his wife. What good work they are doing. The people shake their heads in wonder, admiring all they do for people like us. Truly, they are Christians carrying out God's work.

During the hour we have been in the church, however, much has awakened in the village – the other half of the village, that is. These are the wild folk, and as such have arrived from far and wide for the festivity. A birch maypole takes centre stage on the village green. Girls in white dresses with flowers adorning their hair are preparing to thread the ribbons in a merry dance, and musicians tune fiddles and flutes in readiness.

Screeching cockerels have been packed in adjacent cages close enough to bait and taunt, and the square has filled with throngs of peasants already tanked with ale, their faces ruddy, spirits bawdy and high. These people are of the honest and straight forward ilk but are raw and brittle with it, raucous humour perilously close to cracking into blood lust at any given moment. And in the ensuing chaos, our group becomes separated, a huddle of us suddenly several yards behind the others.

The mob now pushes and swells, rearing into our faces with garish masks, hurling abuse, goading each other. A prancing jester leaps around us like a mischievous collie herding sheep as we struggle to make our way across the square. Panic grips each one of us in a contagion as we struggle to hold onto our hats and keep our clothes about us. Ahead the doctor's carriage has stopped at the inn on the corner, and the male patients are being lined up for a camera man. The photographer gesticulates with instructions, neck craning over the crowd for the female contingent.

Lord in Heaven we are to be photographed. Pray this will be the final indignity of the day. At least there will always be the memory of the light in the church - the way the rays shone in a prism of colour for the spirit of my one true friend – a treasure to hold onto. Besides, I suppose this is one last thing. We are almost done here, soon away and forgotten.

This is what I am fixed upon, this thought that the whole ordeal is nearly over. Which is why what happens next takes me so badly by surprise.

It happens all at once. A feast is being prepared, a

spit roast, a fire lit beneath it. Sparks from the dry wood crack and spit. A little parade of ponies and carts arrives carrying the May Queen, turning the corner in a blare of trumpets and drums. The crowd roars forwards. And a hobby horse covered in a sheet jumps into the throng with a troupe of jingling dancers and merrymakers, its head that of a real horse's skull, the eyes made of glass, a mane of ribbons and a mechanical jaw that snaps and neighs. Children scream. And then quite without warning it turns its mischievous attentions to me, trying to nudge the hat from my head.

"No, no, please!"

The children are laughing, urging the horrible thing to get the hat, to force me to walk through the village as a bald freak. Perhaps they don't know I have no hair? I have to assume it is innocent, a joke. Alas, their determination is escalating alarmingly.

And then above all the shouting and high jinks, Ivy Payne hisses behind her hand, "Grab her arms, Nesta, so they can get it off her!"

At the same moment, a cockerel breaks loose from its cage and a sudden high-pitched squealing has everyone swinging around. A huge bloated sow is being led into the square. Bound in ropes she is screaming for her life but in less than a second is wrestled to the floor and her throat is slashed.

Blood sprays the cobbles, instantly pooling into a dark lake that ripples outwards in a crimson tide - an ocean of thick, hot syrup.

The world stutters and stops.

The chamber is dark.

A heavy sash window slams shut. A hollow-eyed

woman looks into the shadows of her bedroom mirror at what she has done. And there is not a drop of air. Only the sensation of blood draining away, saturating the mattress, dripping onto the floorboards and flowing under the door...

"Grab her arms, Ivy, I can't..."

"Hold her, will you? Shout for the doctor...why you little bitch..."

"Get a hold of her! Hold her!"

***

Chapter Twenty-One

Isobel
Present Day

Isobel waited for the rest of the day and into the evening, busying herself with hanging clothes and then answering emails. Once again the fog lay heavily in the valley, and through windows blurred with drizzle the ghost of her reflection stared back. Why hadn't Branwen come? It was she who had insisted.

It didn't make sense - why would she not turn up after all she'd said? There were things she should know apparently, and people to watch out for. Terrible danger, she was in…Presumably she was referring to Rhys Payne and his wife, Cath? Well, they were just aggressive types, weren't they? The human equivalent of guard dogs trained to snarl and chase, especially if the quarry was on its own and defenceless.

With another cup of coffee to hand and the little electric fire on full pelt, she scrolled through her inbox. Ah, finally here was one from Nina. Brilliant.

'Hi Issy! It sounds amazing where you are – just what you needed – there's nothing like the beauty of nature to

recharge your batteries, is there? And that village! You had me in stitches. I was thinking about the League of Gentlemen. Any isolated place and there are always some odd reactions to strangers, it's age old psychology so don't take it too personally. I am sure you'll soon be accepted and settle in. And at least The Gatehouse was just the lodge and not the actual asylum – somehow I don't think that would have worked out for you too well. On that subject, though, I was having a look at the history of Victorian asylums, which you're probably already au fait with because you worked in one once, didn't you? But there really are some nightmare stories of people wrongly incarcerated because family members wanted them out of the way; or they were simply deaf or had epilepsy. I imagine that Lavinia House has some tales to tell? Didn't you say one of your patients had been institutionalised her whole life because she got pregnant out of wedlock? Honestly, it beggars belief. And it really wasn't that long ago!

Anyway, all is well here and I hope you'll keep in touch and tell me how things are going? Remember what I said – I will be there at the drop of a hat if you need me.

Love Nina x'

Nina, bless her, always made her feel that bit less alone in the world - that bit less abnormal. She'd reply straight away...

The vision came with startling clarity - a gloved hand reaching for a door bell.

Someone was here.

She gasped, but no sooner had the image appeared than an old-fashioned clang resounded through the house and she nearly jumped clean off of the chair.

Bloody hell, that was loud enough to wake the dead. An unfortunate phrase, she thought, having spilled coffee everywhere. Still, hopefully this would be Branwen? In fact, yes, she knew it was Branwen. Part of her gift was to accept it and have confidence. It was pretty helpful, after all, to know who would be on the other side of the door.

Swinging the door open however, the smile died on her face.

"Right, one thing we need to get straight," said Lorna Fox-Whately. "Mrs Lee, isn't it?"

Behind her a Volvo estate had been left with the engine running, two dogs barking themselves into a frenzy on the back seat. With the light behind her, it was impossible to be sure, but it did look as if there was another person in the car. Was that her husband, the GP?

Trying to recover her composure, Isobel spluttered, "Yes–"

"You were seen again, for the second time in as many days, walking across our grounds at Lavinia House. Now I thought I'd made myself quite clear? We do not permit trespassing. Your rights as a tenant here are categorically restricted to this house and the immediate garden. That is all. Do you understand? Quite frankly, if you don't stick to the agreement we will have no option but to terminate the contract and you jolly well won't be getting a refund, either. I really am astonished, quite frankly, that I should have to tell you twice!"

Isobel's heart was beating so fast it almost tripped into fibrillation. Her entire neck and face flushed deep red and her legs began to shake. "I'm sorry, I didn't realise how close to the border I was. I'd become lost in the woods and–"

Lorna's eyes lasered into hers. "I don't give a tinker's cuss about excuses, just don't let it happen again or I will - and make no mistake I will do it - contact the agent and issue a formal complaint."

"Right."

After she'd closed the door, she slumped onto the bottom stair and found she could do nothing but stare blankly. *Jeez, what was her problem? What a fucking mare!*

She'd been badly wrong-footed there as well. Bloody woman! If she'd known it was her she wouldn't have answered. It was hardly a heinous crime anyway was it – a ten minute walk across the far border of a field? What was it with her? She hadn't hurt anyone, hadn't been anywhere near the house or…

Frantic rapping on the front door interrupted her thoughts.

God, I feel sick. If that isn't Branwen this time, I… She opened it an inch, keeping the chain on.

"Fuck me, I'm bloody soaked – it's rank out there," said Branwen, throwing back a long hooded cape. "I see you had a visit from the village bitch, then?"

"I'm still shaking actually. Come in. I don't suppose you've brought any wine, have you? Or anything – I'm not fussy. I'm trying not to drink but I really could do with one, and I don't fancy going to Delyth's–"

"Oh, Delyth's not that bad. It's not her you've got to watch." She pulled a dark brown glass bottle from a pocket inside the cape. "Here we go – how about a lovely bit of mead to warm us up?"

"Brilliant, you're a life saver. Come through to the back room, Branwen, I've got the fire on in there. I'll fetch some glasses and–"

"Bloody hell, it's freezing in here. Hey, hang on a minute – stop a second, will you?"

"What? What is it?"

Branwen was standing by the parlour door.

"What is it?"

"Well, I didn't know that! And I was born and bred in this village too. I've never been in this house before, though."

"What? What didn't you–"

Branwen held up her hand. With her head cocked slightly to one side she seemed to have tranced out. Then suddenly snapped to. "Did you know this house was used as a morgue?"

***

Chapter Twenty-Two

Branwen unscrewed the bottle of mead and poured them both a glass. "Here's to a new friendship! Knock it back, lovely."

Isobel didn't need telling twice. The impact, mind, was a powerful one - the after-burn a furnace that took her breath. She gripped the mantelpiece. "Fuck me! What's in it?"

"Best not to ask. Here, have a top up."

"Thanks. Take a seat, Branwen."

Was it her imagination or was she a bit drunk? She plonked onto the opposite chair rather too abruptly. Surely not! It would take a lot more than a glass of mead to do that. Even so, her face was aflame and not a single coherent thought would form. And after a second glass her voice sounded as loud as a party bore and she couldn't stop talking.

She slumped against the back of the chair, dazed.

"Good bit of stuff, isn't it? Thing is, you'll see more clearly now–"

"See what more clearly? But I don't want to…"

"Hold on now and let me do some grounding work. There are dark spirits in here as I think you know" Branwen closed her eyes. "Just relax, lovely."

Her reply came out slurred. "Yesh…I don't want to

see, though…"

She must have dozed. Then suddenly jolted awake. Had she slept? Had time passed? She looked at the clock. A couple of minutes at most….Yet the atmosphere was different, the furniture leaping out as if from a 3D picture, Branwen's eyes a startlingly vivid green, and there was the strangest feeling of being outdoors, of smoke in the air.

"There, that's done. You know it's funny none of us have been in this house before. I know they had Gwyn do the cleaning, but according to Delyth she was keen to finish, said she felt someone hovering behind her all the time… And even then I never guessed it had been a morgue. Well I never…Mind you, one or two things make a bit more sense come to think of it."

"How do you mean?"

"Well, Lorna and Mervyn hired all the contractors from out of town and I can tell you they were glad to leave. Some of them had funny turns, got ill and went home sick - wouldn't come back here again, either. To be honest, I'm not surprised you've had it bad."

"How do yer know I've 'ad it bad?" Her empty glass slipped softly from her fingers, landing on the carpet with a dull thud, the hollow feeling inside expanding with the shock of being outed. Branwen could see right through her… what she was, who she was…

"The fear clings to you, to be honest, like swirling black shapes that sometimes take form. Imagine a candle smoking with herbs and all those dark tendrils coiling into the air… kind of like that."

"Really?"

"You know when I was a kid I remember the old

lady who lived here, the one who went into a nursing home. She was the asylum doctor's daughter – Edgar Fox-Whately's. I suppose she would have been in her nineties by then. I only saw her once or twice, mind, if I was cycling past the garden or something and she'd be tending the roses. They were proper ones, you know, scented-?"

"Oh, yes…I thought I smelled roses–"

"They pulled them all up to build that pebbly bit round the back, but yeah, you will have had that…Olivia, that was her name. Olivia."

"That Lorna was ever so, ever so, blurry rude–"

"She's such a jumped-up cow! We're not all like that, you know? Anyone would think she was royalty the way she carries on. And she's only from the village same as the rest. Lorna Strickland she was before she married him - went to school with Gwyn and Delyth until they sent her private, then when she came back she started working as his receptionist - still does mind, guards him like a snappy terrier."

"Whassee like? Sorry slurry words…the cotdor…I mean docra–?"

"Keeps quiet, that bastard. His surgery's in a back room in one of those little cottages on the square. Only the local's know it's there. I've heard, and it's only a rumour mind, but I've heard there's pressure on him to close it down and join a medical centre over in town. Only he won't. They're a bit screwed though, because there's got to be an out-of-hours service for people in rural parts and there aren't many who want to do it these days. Anyhow, take it from me – you're better off registering in town because he's a proper nasty piece of work. Just like his grandfather. I wouldn't go there if I was dying. And…" here she leaned forwards, "…he does abortions."

"What? Inish shurgery?"

"Oh yes. Did you think backroom abortions weren't done anymore? Well, they are here - he does them I'm telling you, and not only that but there's an unnatural amount of still births in this village…They should come to me but oh no, why not go to Doctor Death over there instead? Ooh, it's bloody freezing in here, Isobel - like a morgue, I nearly said. You know I can't get over that! A morgue. No one ever told me that and I've been nosy enough."

"No one knew." The words flew out of her mouth of their own accord.

"Yes, you're right. Good, it's taking effect now, is it?"

"What?"

"You're channelling messages better. You've got to be able to still the mind and focus properly, you see. Sometimes you need a bit of a relaxant, is all. And you must know how to protect yourself or you'll attract the wrong sort, which is why I've done it for you. If you get dark spirits you'll get liars and tricksters. They'll pretend to be people you know who passed over, move stuff around in the house - my God they can fuck up your head."

"Oh, they have, they really have."

"Oh my God, you were in hospital with this, weren't you? I can see you running through a park at night…"

"Oh, don't. Stop. I can't relive it."

"I think whatever attached itself to you is still there,

Isobel. And that's why you have to do this – why you have to address it. Honestly though, I had no idea how bad it was in here. Mind you, it would be wouldn't it, if they were using this place to store the bodies?"

"Bodies? What bodies?"

"All this time I've been looking in the wrong direction–"

"Branwen! What bodies? I don't understand any of this."

"Sorry, I run away with my thoughts. Listen, there are no asylum patients buried in the churchyard, okay? And the thing is, in this village there's some who get all uppity if you ask too many questions about Lavinia House - try to shut you up - and then there's others who hate the Fox-Whatelys for what happened with the mine. But I knew there was–"

"The mine? But I thought they ran the asylum – that the family came here to open that?"

"No, no, they've been here forever. They owned the mine first - made a fortune from skipping safety measures and refusing to pay the miners. A lot of those men got sick and just died up there, that's why they call it the Hill of Loss. They say Annwyn is buried in the forest, the Lord of the Dead, and the whole area is cursed, but if you ask me that's just to keep folk away because the forest is the most peaceful place on earth. It's what happened at the mine that's evil. Anyhow, there's folk welded to the Fox-Whateleys at the hip and then there's those who hate them. You can probably tell which camp I'm in? Anyhow, like I say, there are no graves for those patients."

"There's a little church in the grounds with graves."

"A few. But ask yourself how many hundreds of patients they had?"

"Wouldn't the bodies have been claimed by the families?"

Branwen shook her head. "Rumour has it no one ever left Lavinia House or Pond Hall as it's fondly known. There was stigma, you see, shame to being an imbecile or lunatic – that's what they called them."

"Pond Hall?"

"It's got a lake out back but I don't think that's the reason. They say it stank to high Heaven in the old days, that Edgar and Cecily wouldn't allow people to come and drain the sewage tank. Some of the families from round here had people work there, see? They'd go to the pub, get drunk and tell stories about it. Still, you've got me thinking now…I bet they're buried underneath this house. Is there a cellar?"

"Not that I know of. There isn't a door to one anyway."

"Odd that. Everyone I know's got a cellar. That's where the coal used to be delivered."

"No, I checked. And you mention Olivia, the doctor's daughter, but no one was officially registered as living here. It was only used to accommodate gatekeepers for the asylum when required - apparently temporary residents – there were no births or deaths recorded - it was one of my, um… pre-requisites."

"Bloody liars the lot - and you've been caught out, my lovely. Mind you, so have they. I bet Olivia was kept here to protect the place, then after she left they had it bricked up."

As Branwen was chatting Isobel's sense of surrealism

began to sharpen dramatically, and was now at such an intense degree as to affect all the other senses too. The room appeared so bright as to be backlit by a brilliant harvest moon. Every sound was amplified, and the scent of fragrant roses was alternating periodically with that of something rotting and foul.

Her own voice echoed unnaturally around the room. "There should be registers for the asylum, though – for admissions and discharges, but I don't know how to get hold of them."

"The only thing the local authorities have is the license for Lavinia House to operate as a private madhouse, as they were called back in the day. They have no patient documents, not even the censor with a list of numbers, which was the basic legal requirement. Apparently it was all destroyed in a fire."

"Convenient."

"Yes, that's what I thought - plenty of arsonists in a lunatic asylum, eh? Anyhow, I don't think we'll ever know names or–"

"Papers. Parchment and pen. In a shabby leather suitcase. I can smell mouldy paper. A dark place, crushed against a wall."

Branwen narrowed her eyes. "You see that, do you?"

"Just a flash like a camera still. It's gone now. Could it be inside the church in the estate grounds? Lorna was very uneasy about me being there yesterday."

"Nah, we've ransacked it. I mean…whoever was up to no good ransacked it."

"What about in the crypt? The vestry? Underneath floorboards?"

"Yup. And the main house."

"You're brave, I mean whoever was doing the ransacking was brave - going into the house with Lorna there."

"Well, a girl gets married and the parents have to go to her wedding, don't they? Call it a once in a lifetime golden opportunity."

"Oh, yes I read about Ophelia." Despite her earlier reservations, Isobel started to laugh. "You're evil."

"True. Okay look, I'll come straight to the point – why I'm here and why I said what I said to you this morning. I need to know what happened here, you see. There's been conflict in this village for as long as I can remember and it's got everything to do with the doctor. I don't know why folk protect him either, because there've been that many babes he's let die. Plays God he does. And then there's Rhys Payne going out of his way to stop people asking questions, and he's really bloody aggressive with it – threatening. There's something to hide here – something terrible - and it won't stop bugging me. But now you're here the truth's going to come out. I knew as soon as I saw you…you're a catalyst."

"I don't follow. I really don't – I mean why did you say something bad was coming? Because Rhys-whoever-he-is thinks I'll find bodies under the house? But the doctor rented it out. It's the estate they don't want anyone going near, and I'm guessing that's because of all the graffiti and the mess it's in."

"It's funny really. I mean, there they are grabbing your few hundred quid because he might have to close his back parlour down and they won't leave that house, and all the time they've leased it out to a spiritual medium. Who invites me in! Bloody funny, is that. Here, pick up your glass and let's finish this off. That pair would go ballistic and have you thrown out immediately if they knew. Mind, there's none so paranoid as the guilty. Here – hold out the glass lovely."

"Not sure I should."

"Ach, knock it back. Anyhow, that old guy in the pub the night you arrived?"

Isobel saw the one she meant, instantly recalling his eyes boring into her back while she looked at the paintings. "The one with ferrety teeth - not very pretty?"

"Hywl Ash. Right. Don't let him trick you into thinking he's a nice bloke because he isn't. He's got a good social act but I'm telling you he's one to watch. His cousin's Cath Payne, married to Rhys up at Redmoor farm. I bet he's the one told him what kind of car you drive."

"They fired shots at me this morning as well."

"They really do want to run you out of town then." She drained her glass. "Do you know I couldn't have asked for more – I mean, you coming here. The fae – they've delivered in spades this time - this is epic."

"Well I'm glad you're happy about it but there's no way I'm staying. I've been scared half to death and it's only been two days. Frankly I'm prepared to say, 'fuck the money' and go camp on the streets."

Branwen's demeanour darkened. Her pale jade eyes flashed jet. "Spirit wants this out."

"Well I don't. I'm terrified here, Branwen. I can't even do another night. Honestly – I'm going to sleep in the car."

"No! You've got to see this through – please. Here

me out – this isn't just a village dispute or something that happened a long time ago. There's been a terrible injustice. And if I don't honour my part in the pact I made with the fae then some nasty shit is going to happen to me. Or my child. They have given me huge insight but in return-"

"Branwen, I can't possibly-"

"I'll try to explain something to you. I practice the dark arts. I'm a hedge-rider, a necromancer."

"I knew you meddled."

"I don't meddle, I work with the Dark Lord, Lord of the Dead, and have done since I was thirteen. I envoke the fae, but if I don't keep my part of the bargain it gets wild, nasty and could potentially be fatal."

"What do you mean by the fae? Like fairies?"

"I suppose I mean wood spirits - kind of a parallel world to ours but with more vibrancy, energy, colour and poignancy. It isn't remotely like seeing ghosts or having Spirit send you visions – it's more of a rushing feeling right where you're sitting. So you're not moving but you feel as though you're running like hell, breathless, the trees speeding by...And then there's a flash of insight, a revelation that's often intensely painful. Everything is amped up. Your heart's pounding so hard you think it's going to give out, and your deepest emotions are flung in your face – all the terrible things you thought, said, did, had forgotten were there... all slam into you. It stays with you too, leaves you reeling for days after. And I'll tell you something else – if you cross them or you don't give them gifts or play by their rules they can be evil. Evil, malicious and cruel. So don't work with them unless you're prepared for that because they're wild and unpredictable. But this morning at their sidhe–"

"Sidhe?"

There's only one in those woods and it was where you saw me – in a circular grove of pine surrounded by ferns and if you're lucky you'll see a few fly agarics too–"

"Ah! So that's what's in this bloody mead?"

"It's just to aid flight, that and a bit of mugwort. Now listen - only my great grandmother knew where that place was. Then me. And now you. And I've been told something important that you have to know."

"I doubt I'll go there again. I probably couldn't find it, anyway."

Branwen nodded but by then the lights were flickering and the door to the hallway was tapping on its hinges. "You should by rights have more preparation for this and that's what I intended, but we have to start work right away or you'll be driven out, or worse. And yes since you ask, the threat is real and you are in danger. Now this is what I'm trying to say to you – the revelation I had this morning left its mark. Fear. Fear and insanity. Terrible madness. That is the price you will pay if you don't right this wrong. And my price is my child."

"What? So there's no choice is what you're saying? I can't just leave?"

"No, you can't just leave. And you know how bad it can get. You have seen into the abyss, haven't you? You know I speak the truth, that the Unseen exist. You know it!" Her voice had risen, her agitation crackling like static. "So far it's been someone pulling open drawers and cupboards, moving objects around, watching you through the bannisters, yes? Those are human ghosts. But this is far, far worse. And I worry for Immie – really, really worry."

"Your child?"

Branwen's eyes were now pools of very human tears. "They'll take her."

A cot in front of a range. An older woman rocking it to and fro, singing something softly in Welsh.

"Your mother has her tonight?"

"My mother's been dead ten years but you're probably right. No, she's with her father, dopey twat that he is, but he loves her and won't take his eyes off her til I'm back."

"Is that what you paint in the pictures? The fae?"

She nodded. "There's only me who sees them but everyone in this village and beyond knows they're here. There's been that many stories of sightings in the woods and fields over the years."

Isobel nodded, frowning. Ghosts and spirits, even dark entities she got. But this was bonkers in the extreme.

"I know you don't believe, but that's okay – just please help me find out what happened here and then the job's done, all right? You will feel well again and be free if you do. And I am tasked to do it or the consequences will be unthinkable."

"I'm sorry, I can see you're upset - I didn't mean to deride what you do. And you're right – I have seen into the abyss. It was a very long time ago and everyone thought it was depression, well depression with psychosis, but truth be told I've always seen spirits and just about everything I've been told or shown has come to fruition. I'm prepared to help is what I'm saying. I get that something happened here."

"Thank you. Okay, let's get to work."

"What – now?"

A prickle of profound unease jabbed her chest as the room was plunged into darkness and Branwen busied herself lighting candles, undoing packets and phials, and sprinkling powder into an incense burner.

"What's that?"

"It's for the third eye - a nice blend for calling on spirits."

The aroma filled the room, transforming it from a hollow shell of new paint and old wood to one alive with sound, touch, taste and colour. Isobel lay back against the armchair breathing deeply to try and calm herself.

"Just relax and let your mind go completely blank."

It wasn't difficult. Tiredness and intoxication swept her away.

After a while a voice came from far, far away. "Have you done that, lovely? All nice and empty?"

"Mmmm."

"Hold still now, I'm going to dab a touch of oil on the back of your neck – it's just a bit of frankincense… breathe normally…in and out, relax, in and out…in and out…Let the fear go, loosen that knot in your stomach…good, visualise it unravelling…and now imagine a series of trapdoors inside, a kind of ladder starting with the lowest point down in the sacrum. Picture opening that up. Now move up to the stomach…now the heart…up and up to the throat…the third eye….and finally the top of your head…See now… an open channel letting the light flow all the way through you."

"Yes."

"You are a beacon in the darkness now, Isobel, and they can see you."

"Okay."

"But if you feel a tingle or an itch at the back of your neck you have to stop."

"Why?"

"Entry."

A tiny stab of alarm. "What? You mean like possession?"

"Don't worry, if it happens it's only mild, not like that Roman Catholic shit people get fed, but you don't want to lose control or be a passenger. Just stop if that happens, okay?"

Fucking hell…

"It's all right. If you stop they stop. You are stronger."

"Branwen, I don't—"

"Shush, just breathe calmly, deeply. It's too late now anyway, there's someone here."

The candles quivered and flared as if a door had opened.

A gossamer light touch brushed her hair.

"Who is with us?" said Branwen.

***

Chapter Twenty-Three

Flora
Lavinia House, Summer 1893

So here I find myself in the place no one leaves. This is where I thought I would never be - the Chronic Ward. These souls are lost to the world and tonight I am one of them.

Since first arriving at Lavinia House I have always assumed the eerie moans and screams wailing through the house emanate from here - that this is where the most deranged creatures of all are kept, perhaps even chained. But that is not the case. Indeed, it appears there are further rooms above this one. An attic, perhaps? And the pitiful cries are coming from there. What kind of person could be more insane, more violent or sicker than here in this terrible ward? What wretched creatures reside up there, I wonder?

It is a question, at least, which keeps my mind alert now that the blur of morphine is wearing off. I will die now, I think. This is where it will end.

Eventually the blackness of night gives way to the ethereal blue of early dawn, and with it comes the emergence of my new companions...ash-skinned cadavers with hollow eyes and flesh rotted to the bone…their bare skulls and malignant sores a sickly sight to behold. Occasionally a macabre chuckling sounds from a wheezing chest, an occurrence quite disturbing from a creature dying in a pool of their own waste. One of these unfortunates has pushed back her covers to begin a perilous journey across the room, balancing on the tips of her toes, claw hands grasping at thin air like a spider feeling its way. She will fall, I am sure, as she stands swaying and twitching, arms flailing wildly.

"You must go back to your bed, you will fall!"

The poor creature turns, alarmed, and too late I realise she is blind, the retinas eaten away by disease, along with most of her nose and mouth. Feeling her way towards the sound of my voice she holds out her arms, quietly cackling to herself. And I realise my mistake.

"No, no!"

She is a bundle of sticks, the stench from her foul, but I rise and steer her back to her bed. I must. Even as she fingers my bare skin and breathes the rank, fetid stink of malignant lungs into my face.

If only I had not done what I did back there in the village. If only I had closed my eyes and nose to the blood…

How long will they leave me here - surrounded not only by those who are diseased, violent and insane, but contagious with consumption? These are the weak ones who did not survive the hard moral discipline and cold water treatments, those who now have the pallor of ghosts and cough blood. Spittoons sit on every cabinet, full, no doubt, of the warm, globular expulsions. Enough. Or I will surely retch.

The air in here is cold and clammy. It is also utterly dark. Unlike the dormitory below there is no light in the centre of the ceiling and the windows, sealed shut, are considerably smaller. It is here we come to die, then? I wonder if my sister will ever know I passed? Will there be a grave? And of what will I die - smallpox or consumption? There are some here covered in pustules and scabs, the smell of carbolic lingering in the air. I think, perhaps, I would rather consumption. And yet I am alive still. My heart beats. My breath draws.

How long? How long here?

Til death?

How long?

They have a new plan for me, I feel it.

Thumps and the pitter-patter of running feet sound from above. Another day is rising now, streaks of rose across the sky, a cacophony of birds in the eaves…God, how I envy them their freedom.

Why did I do it? Oh God, the despair, the stupidity…And the only answer I can give myself is I don't know. There was blood…blood spilling everywhere…splashing onto the cobbles, the sanguine tang of it…people shouting and laughing and grabbing at my hat, manhandling me…And then what… a flash, yes…the camera clicked to take a picture…

Oh God, yes. It was then. In that single blinding flare that I saw what happened in the chamber…a curtain flung wide to reveal the scene…

Alas, only to drop back once more.

***

Chapter Twenty-Four

"Morning, Madam." Gwilym's rude gaze travels the length of my nightdress all the way down to the ankles and back up again. "Get up. The Master wants to see you."

How badly I need to ask why. A punishment is coming, but what?

"First we'll go to the bathroom, is it?"

Humiliation and rage boil in my blood. What happened to the female attendants? How come this disgusting foul pig is allowed to witness my personal needs?

And stand over me he does - while I use the pot and pull the nightdress off - leering at this naked body made wretched by starvation. And then come buckets of freezing water. It is to cool the temper, says he, tipping one after the other over my head. After that he hands over a new uniform for the summer, that of a long, flowery smocked dress. It goes on a wet, shivering body. No hat, no gloves. Just the attire of an asylum idiot for the lighter months.

I will not meet his eyes and I will not speak, even as he turns me around, straps my arms to the sides with a bandage of cotton sheeting, and lets his hands wander all over me while he does it. Every muscle freezes rigid. I will not tremble. I will not show how repulsed I am. I will not say a word. But I will...oh, I will...see him in Hell for this.

When he is done we walk unspeaking along another grim corridor that echoes with hollow laughter and the screams of madness; through locked double doors, down flights of stairs, more corridors, more doors... and finally into the central atrium and wood-panelled, carpeted hallway to Doctor Fox-Whately's office.

Gwilym raps on the door.

It is strange how the knots in the wood hold no fascination for me now. I wonder, in fact, how they ever could have done, yet I recall it so vividly. How it was.

"Come!"

Seated at his desk, the doctor is again busy scribbling.

Must Gwilym maintain a hold of my arm? I can hardly bolt for freedom. But I will not give him the satisfaction of a struggle he will win. Nor will I glance at the bald-headed, wild-eyed girl in the monstrous flowery dress reflected in the mirror.

A dress was made for me when I turned eighteen...I can see it now...of white silk with stays tied in bows of violet blue. People said the ribbons matched my eyes. Another lifetime, another world, another person. Whatever did I do? It must have been a heinous thing for it to be buried so deeply, to flare and die, flare and die. Yet it hovers with such frustrating glints of clarity...Would it kill me to recall it? I must know. I must. It would make this punishment so much easier to bear.

"So then, what a spectacle yesterday, Flora!"

The man is speaking. I suppose I must respond.

He nods to Gwilym, who finally relinquishes the squeeze on my arm. That pinch will bruise badly and ache for days.

"We were preparing to allow you more freedom, but it seems you repaid our trust with one of your usual acts of violence. What say you?"

I say nothing, you fool. I have nothing inside of me to say.

His lopsided mouth glistens with the flicking of his tongue, the wiry whiskers on his face curling like those on pigskin.

"I see. You are mute. In that case we must administer a course of isolation, a time for you to reflect on your behaviour. Nothing else, it seems, has had an effect on your temper."

My jaw is set so tight in its socket I can barely speak, and when I do it is with enormous effort. "Why have I had no letters from my sister?"

"Perhaps she has chosen not to write?"

"I know my own sister. I have written her. She would have written back."

Having picked up his infernal pen once more he puts it aside and sighs. "Had she written, you would have had the letters, would you not?"

"I do not believe so."

His stare radiates that ill-kept fury. Oh, how close it is to the surface. "What fresh delusion is this?" says he. "That someone has perhaps stolen your letters?"

"Yes."

"Flora, has it occurred to you that your family are perhaps a little disgraced by your conduct? That perhaps they are awaiting your full recovery before corresponding? We advise families that people who are very disturbed, such as yourself, often deteriorate with outside contact and in fact, regain their health more quickly without it. I would therefore put it to you that it is in your best interest to cooperate more fully with the regime here. That it would benefit you most greatly were you to do so."

Hatred consumes me. "You have them? You have her letters addressed to me?"

He nods to Gwilym to remove me, and it is all I can do to affect meek acquiescence. His paper knife lies on the desk. How satisfying to rip it across his jugular. But as Gwilym lumbers over a look passes between them, an understanding. My friend was right. There is indeed some collaboration.

"You will consider your conduct most carefully whilst in isolation," he is saying. "You will eat what you are given and you will think deeply about what you have done. And then we will talk again. Good day."

Isolation.

Back we go to the second floor, through to the bottle green corridor once more – this time, however, passing the Chronic Ward, stopping at the very end by an iron door. A prison. This is a prison cell.

"In here you little bitch."

No window. Padded walls. A stained mattress on the floorboards.

I was screaming and screaming, choking on the vomit and blood was pouring out, but they kept pulling it and pulling it...

Wait! I cannot see the outside. I cannot see daylight

or night time or trees or sky. And as this realisation is sinking in, he wings me around and fastens on a leather straitjacket. I cannot see, cannot move, cannot get out. Oh, God, no... for how long? My throat constricts in a soundless scream as pushing me down onto the mattress, he then walks smartly out, shoots a series of bolts into place and turns the key.

Christ! I cannot survive this. I cannot...

His receding footsteps click along the corridor, the double doors clatter open, slam shut...and then they too are locked.

Silence. Utter silence. Not even the inhuman wailing from the attic rooms. There is nothing.

Hours pass in a blur of white noise, with no way of telling the time of day, or week, or season. I could refuse the tray of food left at the door but they would only force it down by tube. I could bang my head against the wall in the hope my neck will break, as I have seen others do, but there burns inside of me still the faintest flicker of hope. This will end. They feed me, so this will end.

Meals are delivered by a gruff, heavy-set woman, who is also the one who takes me to the bathroom. And the food is much improved – there is tea and beef, bread with butter, suet pudding and fruit. First strawberries, now cherries. So then, it must be June? Or July? Months are passing...months...still with no sign of release. Yet they nourish me well.

On one trip to the bathroom, an indigo sky glitters through a gap in the stones and there is an itch on my upper palate from the sting of pollen. This female attendant - a coarse, red-faced woman clearly employed to manhandle the more difficult patients - stands with her arms folded. She has been a farm or laundry worker perhaps, her hands calloused and rough.

"Summer?" I say, feeling the strange roll of words form on my tongue.

She nods. "Lammas."

It is the first time anyone has spoken to me other than to snap orders in three months. I thank God she understands English.

"First of August?"

"Aye."

I'm not sure why my pulse quickens but it does. There is a charge to the atmosphere as at Beltane, a feeling the staff are off to merriment of some sort...And this woman is alone up here. Yes, she is quite alone. And that makes her nervous.

Although decidedly weighty of stature with forearms as thick as trees and legs just as stout, her countenance suggests one who has fallen on hard times, and therefore she has little choice but to carry out instructions without question. I would hazard a guess she is not as shrewd as Ivy Payne or Myra Strickland either, and has few wits about her.

"What is your name?"

She has been my attendant for many months and I have not spoken before. Perhaps she will trust me a little? All the same there is fear in her simple face. Checking over her shoulder repeatedly, which is patently ridiculous since anyone following her would have to jangle keys and therefore could not creep up silently behind, she mutters, "Never you mind about that. Have you finished washing?"

She has a strong Shropshire burr to her accent. Yes, I'd hazard a guess she was in farming but lost her job, or the family lost their farm.

"Sorry, I have not spoken in so long. I simply wished to speak, to form words–"

She nods. "You don't tell them nothing mind, or we'll both be for it?"

"No, of course not. Do you think I trust any of them?"

An expression of confusion passes over her features. "My name's Mary but you'll keep that to yourself. Have you done now?"

It is the time of year when dusk lingers, and each time Mary checks over her shoulder it's possible to flick another glance around the walls. There is another door at the end and it stands ajar. A cupboard. Stacked with towels and linen. An oblong of milky light falls across the floor. From a window. Most probably the window needs to be opened in order to be aired. So not bolted! I must keep this pulse of excitement in check.

After a while Mary and I walk back to the cell in silence. My thoughts are scattering in all directions. Some duping of this woman will be necessary - something to distract her on a night when the other, more cunning ones, are not in Lavinia House. Pagans all, they honour the four cornerstones of traditional celebrations it seems - but how are they to be known when I cannot count the days?

Later, when staring sightlessly into the dark, the unmistakeable smell of sulphur stifles the air and Diane appears to me as clear as if it were yesterday. Prickles goose up and down my spine. Her presence is all around. Her face is vividly in my mind and will not fade, quite as if she is imprinted there. Something is amiss or about to happen.

The attendants were off celebrating and you were removed...I was alone...

With him! Of course, she was here in this very room...on the eve of Beltane... Nos Calan...

There is such a silence in this house tonight. No thudding of feet or clanking of keys. It is quite different. And the conviction grows and grows that something is to happen...

How long ago that flare of a lit cigarette at the dormitory door and the feeling I was next?

Beltane?

And now it is Lammas...

Nor did they want me dead when the chance came.

Hours pass...hours and hours...Until quite suddenly the jangle of keys on an iron ring followed by the heavy stomp of boots signals his arrival. He has been waiting. Waiting and waiting...for tonight.

The iron door clunks open and there stands a man.

"Now it's your turn," he says. "Open your legs."

What? Him? No! I thought...

Instinctively I shrink into a ball, head between my knees, holding onto both ankles.

He has to unfurl my limbs with such force they must surely snap as twigs. "I said lie on your back and open your legs, you stuck up little bitch!"

Something cracks - a bone - as he rams back my head and unstraps himself.

It happens fast now, seconds, and in a shockwave of

disbelief. His knees weight the insides of my thighs, and both arms are pinned over my head with one great hand. His breath makes me retch, then great shards of white pain sear through my body. And all thoughts black out.

Sulphur chokes the air. Blood flows into the mattress, flooding over the sides, draining away in a froth of crimson. The sash window slams down…Slam! Slam! Slam!

Flora, look - look at the door…I saw the devil, Flora, I saw the devil at dawn…look…

A tiny pinprick of red light flares into the darkness.

Keep awake, Flora! There is a peephole in the door. The red light is in the peephole….look at it, Flora, look at it.

Diane's devil. There watching. Just watching. So, the puppet master and the puppet…

Alas, I can think no more. In the dark swirl of semi-consciousness, Diane is holding something out to me – a bundle of blood-sodden towels - but her face has changed, its countenance darkened now with confusion and distress… there is something badly wrong with this baby, she is saying.

And he is mine.

***

Chapter Twenty-Five

Isobel
Present Day, The Gatehouse

Isobel kept her eyes firmly closed, resolutely picturing a column of white light streaming through her body, breathing in and out, in and out, just concentrating on that. It was extremely important not to feel or show fear…but something menacing was creeping into the room…like an oil slick under the door… and it was so hard not to. *Oh God, dear Lord protect us. Dear Lord, I can't go through this again, I just can't…*

"Who is with us?" Branwen asked again. "I know you're here. Speak to me. Show yourself."

Upstairs the banging noises resumed, the same thud-thud- thud that had woken her on the first night.

"All right," Branwen said. "We have more than one presence in the house. But whoever you are – you're in this room with us. We haven't come to hurt or alarm you but to ask why you're still here - why you're earthbound and what message you have for us."

The candle flames flickered wildly, sending shadows leaping around the walls, and what sounded like a large dog pitter-pattered across the floorboards.

"Fuck!" said Branwen. "That's not supposed to happen."

Isobel's heart nearly catapulted into her throat. For Christ's sake, wasn't Branwen in control of this?

"Oh, I see, okay. You had me going then. I thought for a minute… Okay, why are you taking the form of a dog? Why do you show yourself like a beast? Are you trying to scare us?"

The scampering stopped, but instead of a panting dog the creature began to cackle and chuckle.

"I know you're human. Who are you? Tell me your name."

No reply.

"Tell me who you are!"

There was no answer but the shape of a four legged creature now skittered sideways, blending seamlessly into the darkest part of the room.

And upstairs a baby started to cry.

This was horrible. A terrible reminder of dark times she had no intention of revisiting.

"No, Branwen, I have to stop–"

Isobel tried repeatedly to pull down the trapdoors she had only just imagined opening, but instead of a channel of white light with a ladder, there was nothing but a long, dark corridor that whistled like a tunnel in the wind.

"Branwen!"

Unintelligible chatter suddenly filled the room - an emphatic one-way conversation – that of a woman confiding infectious gossip, yet not a word made sense. Greatly agitated, the woman seemed to be becoming increasingly desperate to be understood, until she was shouting.

Isobel had her hands over her ears. "No, no…"

Then to her horror her body became not her own. Her face began to twitch with tics, the jaw work and neck jerk as if she had a terrible affliction.

Again she attempted to call out to Branwen, but now the words wouldn't form at all, and instead she found herself hurtling through a darkened corridor towards somewhere she didn't want to go. A feeling of impending dread was escalating rapidly.

A baby was screaming.

Then suddenly - slam! Slam! Slam!

Upstairs! A sash window upstairs was being repeatedly crashed onto the sill. So hard the wall shuddered.

Drunkenly, dizzily, she tried to stand, but appeared to be riveted to the chair. She tried again but her ankles felt as if they were strapped together and back she fell. Now she tried to wrench free her hands but it was exactly as if invisible clamps held them fast. A silent scream formed in her throat, her heart rate accelerating into full panic, breathing coming in great gulps.

Then all at once it stopped - the banging, the baby crying, the window crashing and the whispering.

Her eyes snapped open.

Branwen was no longer there. And the room she now found herself in was small, without windows, and completely dark. This was a vision – that was all it was. She was being shown something. God this was horrible. *Keep calm, keep calm. What can I see? Do the job…what can I see?*

After a couple of seconds her eyes adjusted to the subterranean blackness, and a projected stream of hazy grey light as fine as a spider's thread caught her attention.

I see you.

And I see you.

The chink of grey now began to change, to expand into the shape of a keyhole. And the red ember of a cigarette tip glowed and flared. A man was standing on the outside of what appeared to be a prison cell.

Who are you?

All was now utterly silent. So silent it seemed the darkness was a living, pulsing thing. By way of response a tremendous feeling of dread began to assimilate, creeping up her back, pressing inwards, suffocating and choking the chill air with a distinct and powerful smell of sulphur.

This man, this man…it was all to do with him…

Who are you? Show me…

A flash of revelation raced towards her and she reared back…but just at the point where a face began to emerge, the scene cut - almost as if a thick, wet blanket had been thrown over a fire. And the sense of menace drained away as surely as an ebbing tide.

She opened her eyes. Blinked. The air now was clear and cold, her arms and legs quite free to move around; the electric fire was cranking out heat and Branwen was leaning forwards watching her.

"What happened? The candles went out and I saw your lips moving. Are you all right?"

"I'm not sure, it was a bit of a blur and happened really fast. I heard knocking and banging noises upstairs and a baby crying. Then it all went black and I was physically trapped - couldn't move - and then suddenly this room wasn't this room anymore, it was a prison cell and there was a man outside it smoking, looking through a peep hole. I thought I was going to pass out with the fear of him... Then I asked who he was, for him to show himself....but just as I was about to see, it all fell away. The whole scene just cut off. But the funny thing was I was accepting it, ready to see what I was being shown. Did you stop it? I could smell sulphur, so I assumed–?

Branwen shook her head. "No, of course not."

"I thought you were shutting it down because of what you said earlier, about being possessed, and I kept trying to call out."

"Okay, I'll tell you what I've got. There are a lot of spirits here trying to tell us something and we were getting close, but someone, a stronger personality, shut it down. It all just stopped, didn't it?"

"Yes, Like a blanket on flames."

"Were you frightened?"

"Yes, but not as much as I thought I would be. Not until that feeling of dread came. It was something to do with the man who was smoking."

"But you didn't see his face and you weren't given a name or a clue?"

"No, like I said it all happened really fast. Seconds. Just a flash."

"I'm going to take a punt and say the personality stopping the others showing us anything is the only person who lived here and that's Olivia Whately-Fox, Edgar's daughter."

"The old lady? I wonder why?"

"So do I. And you know what? We need to raise

her."

"How do you mean?"

"Necromancy. I'm going to find out. Blimey, we've come a long way tonight. I really feel like we've broken through a barrier now."

"Branwen, who are you? I mean, why is this so important to you? And what's necromancy if it isn't what we're doing already? How does that work?"

Branwen turned her face to the fire. "I'm a traditional witch. Like my great-grandmother, Riana."

"Yes but – necromancy!"

"All I'm saying is I am going to find out what happened and I'll use any way I can. You coming here is the best thing that's happened in years. A real breakthrough. They've given it to me…"

Isobel frowned. Shook her head. "I won't pretend to understand but I do agree that there are ghosts here, spirits who need to tell their story. What's your personal interest though, I mean apart from natural justice and an unsettled village, because you seem…well…obsessive…?"

Branwen shot her a look and Isobel winced with the force of it. Jeez, she'd hate to get on the wrong side of her.

"You asked what necromancy was. You're a medium, right? So your frequency is tuned into those who've passed and you're sent messages, visions or thoughts? Necromancy is conjuring or evoking someone who didn't necessarily want to be."

"Oh my God. Isn't it bad enough? Branwen, that freaks me out. I'm terrified of the demonic, of evil and insanity. We humans don't know what's out there or

210

what we're dealing with–"

"Humans don't, you're right, and they don't want to know either - most of them. That's why it's been so damn easy for the church to manipulate people, because of all that fear. But there's the beauty of witchcraft, you see – we're free of all that bullshit and they know it. That's why they had us rooted out and burned at the stake – because there is no fear to control us with.

Think about it, Isobel. There is light and there is dark. Positive and negative. And if you can face the dark side, if you see what lies beyond, then there is so much less fear, don't you see? You have to ride with it and take control – you are stronger than the spirits – your energy is more powerful. I'm not saying there aren't tricks or risks - you have to know what you're doing - but we can get incredible insight once we accept it's there. You'll never want to be the same again once you know–"

"What about the devil?"

"What devil?"

"Branwen, I could smell sulphur and you said to protect myself from possession. For pity's sake, this is scary shit."

"I'll tell you what I think – I think you've got to undo everything you've ever been brainwashed into thinking, then you'll be free of your fear and your terror of the gift you've been given. If you let magick into your life and cut the chains of dogma, you will, like I said – never want to be mundane again."

"I don't know what you mean. Are you saying I shouldn't believe in God?"

"No, I'm saying you shouldn't believe everything you've been taught by people who run the Church. Find your own way and then you'll truly be free. Everything you want is on the other side of fear. I really believe that. Just remember there's always a balance and a price to pay. Always."

"But necromancy! That's conjuring the dead, actually raising dark spirits. Aren't there risks?"

"Yes. But I do take precautions to minimise them. I make offerings – alcohol works very well I find – and in return I may be shown something I need to see. I have to be honest, I haven't done much in the way of necromancy except at the asylum that one night when Ophelia was getting hitched. I wanted to raise Doctor Edgar but I got thrown around the room. Angry man he was - a very, very angry man. I never thought about his daughter, but you know I bet she was here all her life and no one ever knew. Off the radar, she was. .."

"I wonder why. Perhaps she was ill? Or just a spinster? Or–"

"Or guarding something?"

"So we're back to bodies under the floorboards?"

"You don't believe it, do you?"

"I don't get why you are so personally desperate to know. I'll level you with you, since we're heading fast down this dangerous route together – I just find it hard to believe there is no other reason you're doing all this other than an argumentative village and a lack of graves from the old asylum. Curiosity in other words!"

"Do you really want me to tell you?"

"Yes."

"All right, well it's been simmering a hell of a long time...over a century...but they hanged her, Isobel. Those fucking heathens in that fucking village hanged my lovely great-grandmother for being a witch. They came for her in the cottage I live in now and strung her up in the woods, left her rotting on the end of a rope for all to see. She was beautiful, she was with child, and she never hurt a hair on anyone's head."

"Oh, my God! Oh Christ, I'm so sorry. That was late in history too - what, Victorian times?"

"Exactly. Yes, the bloody witch hunting was long over but any excuse. They say she brought crimbils to the village, worked with the fae and helped them kill and steal babies in return for magick. But the order to hang her came from him – from the good Christian doctor in Lavinia House and I'll tell you something else, I know who dragged her into the street and put the rope around her neck, too. And I'll see him in Hell for it."

"Why would a doctor, a learned man, go along with such a ridiculous notion?"

"People said they saw these changelings, crimbils, in the forest and in the fields – and they lived in fear of their children being snatched, and make no bones about it there were a lot of infant deaths in the village. Maybe he took it upon himself to appease them and call Riana out for being a witch? Or maybe something else was going on and she was onto him."

Isobel shook her head. "So he played on the villagers' superstitions and whipped them up enough to make them murder her? But what would he have been up to? Killing his patients, do you think? Why would he do that?"

Branwen shrugged. "I've spent decades digging away at this. I'll never stop. And now I've seen the hooded boatman by the lake I know it's building up - whatever revelation is coming, it's coming soon."

"The druid?"

"They were here for centuries until the Romans drove them out - this has always been a sacred place full of magick. The island in the middle of the lake was where they buried their dead, and if ever the boatman is sighted it means it's time for another death. You were brought here, it's what was needed – a conduit – for the truth to come, for the revelation. I can't do it on my own, I need you. Will you help me, Isobel? Please?"

She reached over and gave the other woman's hand a squeeze. "Yes, I will. I'll try not to let spirits scare me too much and–"

"I'd worry more about Rhys and Cath Payne if I were you. And the rest."

"Why? I mean, I know they're aggressive but why are they so angry?"

"Not sure. But Rhys Payne's great grandmother worked at Lavinia House. As did his wife, Cath's. Cath Winters as was. Oh, and Lorna Strickland's great-grandmother was the housekeeper. I imagine it has something to do with palms being greased back in the day. They're keeping the family secret as it were. Think about it – the graves and records for all those people who were kept in that asylum are missing. And when a few too many beers go down their necks, people talk and those secrets slip out. Those secrets then reach the ears of people whose ancestors were left to die up in that mine. You've seen the graffiti? Think about it…why daub 'pigs' across the walls? I didn't do it if that's what you thought."

"I thought it was to slander the patients, that locals

may not have wanted them here–"

"No, not at all. Those people were ill, some of them epileptics or with Downs Syndrome – you've only to look at the photos on the pub wall. But no one ever saw a single funeral there, is what I'm saying. And no relatives ever stayed at the inn or took them home again as far as anyone knows. This is a small place and all roads lead through that village or up through the woods past the farms. Every coming and going was noted and I'm telling you no one ever left that asylum. So ask yourself, where are the graves, Isobel? It's not just me and what I'm shown by the underworld. It's practical and in our faces to this day in the form of some very hostile neighbours. No, I reckon these restless spirits are trying to get your attention but Olivia is stopping them. So I'm going to raise the old bitch."

"Right. God, Branwen, I get it now. I need a drink."

"Me too. Good thing I happened to bring along a few more bottles of my lovely mead–"

The sound of a tumbling rock thudding onto the ground outside caused them both to swing towards the window.

"Shit, we left the curtains open."

"Who the hell's that?"

"I don't know," said Branwen, "but it isn't good."

***

Chapter Twenty-Six

Isobel

01:00 hours.
Email:

'Hi Nina!

I cannot begin to describe how rapidly things have changed here. All is not well. In fact, it's downright weird. No - more than weird - frightening. I know I should have told you the truth yesterday instead of pretending everything was fine, but please don't be too upset with me - I didn't want to worry you, that's all. The thing is, far from the house being only a gatehouse for various employees; it was actually lived in by the asylum doctor's daughter – for decades! She's a spirit I've seen a couple of times already, and believe me she does not want me here. There's a really bad atmosphere.

And yesterday one of the locals fired a gun at me. So my presence is more than just a tad unwelcome from both the living and the dead. Add to that, I've met a lady called Branwen - a practising witch, who instantly knew I was a medium and says this place was used as a morgue. She's convinced something sinister happened at the asylum over a

century ago, and it seems my new friend may not be too
wide of the mark because there isn't just one ghost here –
there are loads. And they're all trying to tell me something.
Nina, I think she's right. I've been getting visions thick and
fast, and a lot of hostility from local people who I don't
think want the truth uncovering. Anyway the thing is, it's
come to a bit of a head and very quickly because...'

She stopped typing. What was that? Hissing whispers
seemed to be coming from the hallway again. Always
the hall...

She stood and walked to the door, peering into the
white glare of a fully lit house.

Is someone here?

Walking to the foot of the stairs she stood with her
hand on the newel post and repeated the question in her
mind. Fear would not get to her, it would not!

"Is someone here? Do you want to talk to me?"

Instantly the temperature dropped from cold and
damp to an Arctic freeze. And this time it wasn't fear
that came to punch her in the gut, but a terrible, heart-
rending compassion. Tears burned her eyes and the
hopelessness of black depression was overwhelming. *Oh,*
God...the grief...the raw pain...

And then the girl appeared - the same one briefly
glimpsed on her first night here, but now standing at
the top of the stairs just where Branwen had said.
Watching. A young woman dressed in a hideous flowery
smock. Her bare feet were badly scratched and ingrained
with dirt, scalp shaved and covered in sores. At first
glance the apparition was terrifying – a mad woman
with eyes that radiated anger, fear and mistrust. Perhaps,

Isobel thought later, it was the terror the girl emitted that overrode her own, enabling a longer look rather than shutting down immediately. It had taken this spirit girl a great deal of energy and courage to reach out. It was her job to help her….

Who are you? What is your name? Mine's Isobel.

She had once been extraordinarily pretty - more than that, beautiful - her eyes feline and of the deepest violet blue. Tall and spindly, she appeared to totter on colt legs, her frame cadaverous with bones jutting through bruised flesh, the skull incongruously large. For several seconds the air was electric as the girl, clutching hold of the bannisters, began to walk downstairs.

Isobel stood her ground.

I can help you. I am a spiritual medium. Please tell me your name.

A reply buzzed in her ears but it didn't make sense, akin to a telephone not properly connected. All she could do was keep on trying.

I'm Isobel. Please tell me who you are.

After a couple of steps the young woman stopped and looked down at her dress with a puzzled expression. A dark stain had appeared. And it was spreading, beginning to soak through the flowers. Then a couple of drops plopped onto the carpet. And then it poured from her, gushing over the steps to the hall below.

Isobel's hand flew to her mouth as she watched the scene unfold. In a matter of seconds the girl's body had crumpled into a pool of bloody rags, and the silhouette of a man loomed large across the wall. The smell of sulphur filled the air, and from one of the rooms off the landing the disembodied sound of a baby began to cry.

Again a baby…

She looked up. Blinked. Looked down again.

The vision faded.

She took a few deep breaths and steadied her breathing. Well, it seemed there was little doubt now. And if she didn't do her best to find out what happened and wrong a right, she would never forgive herself.

Or be forgiven…

***

My God, my God, my God….

Boy was she wide awake. Wired, in fact. And tomorrow could not come soon enough.

Hopefully Branwen had got home all right. They'd waited a good hour since hearing the stone dislodge outside, and after that Branwen had pulled on her boots and fled through the back door, over the fields to the village.

Time for yet another coffee. There was so much to think about, especially all the fairy tales about crimbils or changelings. Everything else made a kind of sense but not that. In fact the scariest thing about it was people here believing in all that nonsense - apparently even committing murder because of it. Now that was scary. Being shot at was scary. Being frightened half to death by angry spirits was scary. But fairies… not really.

So why is that painting in the front room with its face to the wall?

She smiled to herself. This nagging inner voice, now she'd started to take notice of it, was annoying. Besides, it was right. Why was the picture in the other room?

Her friend had painted it and given it to her, after all. With that thought she brought it into the lounge and propped it against the mantelpiece over the electric fire.

"There, now," she said to the little creature. "So you are who Branwen talks to, are you? All right, well I don't believe a painting is going to hurt me and I'm fed up of being scared of everything anyway, so I'll hang you there."

After signing off the email to Nina, she closed the laptop and settled into the armchair, trying not to look at the painting. Jeez, there was something about it, though... Still, it was only that – a painting. And it would be good to try and get a few hours rest. It wouldn't help anyone if she was weakened, tired and hungover, would it?

Her thoughts drifted, hovering between overload and exhaustion. Tomorrow she'd walk in the woods Branwen used. It was miles away from the Payne's farm, and by the sound of it the locals were terrified of the place, believing it to be haunted by Annwyn, Lord of the Dead. For herself it should be the most private and quiet place to think and re-charge before the night to come...For now she would think only of good things...of memories that brought joy, of people who had given their love, of the beauty of everything in nature.

Please let me sleep... I will do what you ask...I will, I promise...

And when morning came the world was a different place, in a way she could not describe without sounding as if she'd taken a few magic mushrooms. Except the colours were as vibrant as if backlit, and the air was photographically sharp. The birds in the eaves clamoured in a cacophony of excitement, their feet hopping on the tiles. And above all that, her heart had lifted and exhilaration fizzed in her veins.

"Hello!" she said to the crinkled hunchback staring back at her from over the mantelpiece. "I've decided to call you Immie, after Branwen's little girl."

And now I'm ready. I think this is me. Where I'm supposed to be. My God, after all these years…I feel like I've come home. So show me! Show me my tasks and I'll do this.

It didn't feel unnatural to think and talk in this way. In fact it was the most normal, wonderful, life-affirming mind-set she'd ever had, everything leading up to this tailing away in a sepia blur of mistakes and confusion. She ran a hot bath, had breakfast, made up her face and washed her hair. .

And the mood continued during the walk towards The Hill of Loss, a name no longer laced with foreboding. This was a place where battles had been fought to hold onto a much loved land. Druids had worshipped in this haven of beauty and tranquillity, and little had changed over hundreds of years. It seemed to no longer be a brooding, remote forest overshadowed by the Black Mountains, but a gateway to something glittering and compelling. She gave no thought to running into Lorna or her husband, instead slipping into the misty woods under cover of the blue-grey dawn as if it was the most natural thing in the world.

Almost immediately the ground became muddy underfoot, branches dripping steadily into the long grass. And other than the soft fall of her own footsteps there were no sounds at all, the muted forest veiled with skeins of ethereal blue. There was a feeling of letting go here, of floating almost, stepping away from the world at large. Little wonder people through the ages had found this part of the world, put down their roots, and called it magickal.

Hoping to find the path from yesterday and the fairy ring Branwen used in order to meditate, it soon became clear however, that there wasn't one. There were no paths at all. In fact, the further she ventured the more the trees became densely packed, and no matter which direction she chose, the undergrowth prevented entry. Puzzled, she stopped to listen for the fresh tinkle of the mountain spring. Yesterday she had crossed the water so it stood to reason if she followed that either up or down she would come to the same crossroads with the etched boulder.

Alas, the stream proved totally elusive, and very quickly the morning mist thickened once more with rain. Out of breath now, she paused on the crook of a bend, leaned against an old oak and closed her eyes, face up to the mizzle, absorbed in the silence of the forest. Okay, she was lost. Totally lost. And suddenly incredibly tired.

Then she opened her eyes and saw her.

Real or a vision?

A small, wizened creature with parchment-white, crinkly skin, was standing on the path in front. Having turned to look over her shoulder, the tiny woman was squinting as if she couldn't see well, leaning heavily on a forked stick. Oddly, she was dressed in the long black garb of a Victorian lady in mourning, but even more bizarrely she was less than three feet tall.

The two stared at each other as if each had stepped out of another world. The little creature faded and loomed, faded and loomed. Then the ground rose in a soft swell as if it had turned into water, and the rich aroma of moss and damp wood filled the air. An icy coldness permeated her back and a crowd of voices echoed in the treetops, which rocked and swayed as if a storm was brewing. And then, from far away, a long, low whistle began like an express train hurtling through a tunnel towards her. Suddenly the trees were rushing by at great speed, and the voices were no longer voices but high pitched screams.

She fell to her knees with hands pressed over her ears.

But there was no stopping it.

The vision. A full reminder of the darkest moment in her life - the man in black leaning against the church railings, waiting…was now standing before her with his arms folded.

The image flashed.

Followed immediately by the face of the man at the cell door.

Flash. Flash.

Like resuming a film it had picked up exactly where it had stopped the night before - this time running on in graphic detail. Less than a hundredth of a second but she would never forget the face shown. The thin twist of razor-wire for a mouth, the pointed tongue flicking across wet, glistening lips, and a hard glassy stare emitting the most malignant hatred she had ever witnessed from another human being.

And just like the man in black, he was dressed in the harsh Victorian attire of one in mourning, his skin bleached of life. And he too was smoking.

She had also seen him before. Very recently.

***

Chapter Twenty-Seven

Flora
All Hallows Eve, 1893

In order to become physically fit enough to escape, I have taken to walking around and around this prison cell, stretching my limbs, using dance steps I once learned. And to keep my mind alert I practice arithmetic, French, spelling and general knowledge – testing my own learning as if tutor and pupil.

The layout of the upper floor and exterior of the house are now as a map inside my head and staff routine provides a clock of sorts. Locating a sharp implement has been the most difficult of tasks, but eventually it came to me. These walls are padded but underneath there is stone and mortar. It took a long, long time…weeks…of feeling along the cracks in the wall in the dark, but finally a loose shard came away and it is this I have taken care to hone to the sharpness of a blade. I have it now. And if ever that pig assaults me again, I will have his eye like a pickle on a fork.

Now to the staff routine. Myra Strickland replenishes the laundry cupboard and it is her footsteps which click along the corridor last thing at night and first thing in the morning, checking the doors are locked, rattling the windows for steadfastness. It is also she whose footsteps clang on the metal staircase to the attic. Three times a day Myra Strickland goes up, unlocks a door, and a few minutes later comes down again. No one else ever goes up there. Not ever. And I know because my prison is adjacent to that stairwell.

I wonder who lives up there. Some poor disfigured soul who whines and laments, occasionally screaming and pounding on the walls? I swear sometimes there is the pitter-patter of more than one set of feet. Perhaps that is where they confine the maddest of the mad? It is difficult to imagine one more insane than Cora, or more dangerous than Beatrice, but it must be so. I hope only never to be further punished and find out.

I feel it unlikely however, that they will subject me to further danger. The soft swell in my tummy is growing and the doctor's probing has ceased. It seems they leave me to harvest the progeny. And as autumn deepens, with no glimpse of the outside world, my other senses have become more acute to change - the wind blows more ferociously, rain lashes the stone walls more harshly and the birds have ceased to chatter in the eaves. A flock of geese flew noisily across the fields a while ago, and the owls screech and call less often. Yes, the days shorten and the year turns, bringing with it the smell of decay and wood smoke, and a crisp chill to the air – such a magical time for the artist with its smoky mists and apple-red leaves. How I miss it, how I ache…

The depression is the worst. The utter despair whenever I dare to think this will not work, that I will fail to escape and be subjected to whatever horror lies ahead.

And riding on its wave, sharp pangs of memory cut into those wounds. There was the wedding, a brief flare of golden light when I thought in my young heart that I would be the lady of my late parents' house and bear a family of my own; that I would paint and sketch, sit by the fire in gentle companionship with my husband and sister. And so it transpired for a while. Samuel was the local schoolmaster and without material wealth, but Amelia had most taken to him and insisted he and I marry at once – that he would be perfect. The elder of two sisters, I had been bequeathed the house and woodland on marriage, and he was a good, principled man with an education – so entirely different to the pompous fops I had previously met. The three of us, she said, could be so happy, and thus my guardian agreed. I was eighteen.

I did not look, for I suppose I did not wish to see. Those recollections visit me now though, and how! Perhaps I did not like him as well as I ought. The pain on the night of our wedding was unbearable, and once I had conceived we took to our separate rooms. I bled. Constantly I bled, all the way through the pregnancy and confinement ran almost the whole term. Oh, I saw them both in the garden and I noticed the touch of hands, the lingering looks, but then they had much to bear tending to my needs…

Slam! Slam! Slam!

The scene, to a point, replays in the deadness of dreams, yet never quite to the end. The baby was screaming in his cot by the window. The blinds were shut and I reached out but he would not stop. And then it occurred to me that the screams were not the child at all but myself – still enduring hour after hour of labour...with morning turning into evening...night to dawn...until finally the child was ripped from my womb.

I drifted in and out of a laudanum induced sleep, the doctor in attendance, but I know not how long I lay there. I know only that my heavy eyes lifted for long enough. To see the sash slam down across the child's head. Over and over and over. And to watch her turn to face me with the headless baby in her arms.

I wake up now bathed in cold sweat.

Amelia. The screaming was hers.

The child shoved into my arms a bundle of blood-soaked rags.

Samuel at the doorway. The look on his face...

Yet who would believe me? Who? When both of them swore to the local doctor it was I. And when the doctor himself heard me talk of spirits in the wood and faces in the walls...

Amelia, Amelia...what happened? Is that why you never wrote me in all these months?

***

Well now, I believe it is All Hallows Eve. And the time has at last arrived. Mary, dear pudding-brained Mary, tells me the 'carryings-on' will be tonight, shakes her head at the tom-foolery. She chats a little to me these days, believing there is no harm seeing as I won't be going anywhere or speaking to anyone. That I have not a friend in the world.

And thus the house tonight is quiet as a crypt, the

season turns once more, and I am ready. If I wait until the winter solstice it will be too late.

Mary is lumbering down the corridor…clomp-clomp-clomp…keys bouncing against her rump. Methodically she locks the heavy double doors behind her. Clomp-clomp-clomp…almost here…and my heart is thumping so hard I swear a craftier soul would hear it.

I must keep my demeanour absolutely deadpan. She will not pick up a nuance or change in me as long as nothing is said, no agitation shown. Mary is their plodding, reliable simpleton – a woman in need of bed and board who can be relied on to restrain an imbecile should they thrash around. That is all.

Her breathing now is laboured outside the door, rattling one key after another until she happens on the right one. I am her last chore this evening. There will be no other up here until Myra Strickland takes a tray up to the attic and checks the locks. An hour. For weeks I have counted every last minute that passes between these two visits. And there is one hour precisely.

As usual Mary nods pleasantly enough, before her great washerwoman's hands grab my upper arm for the short trip to the bathroom. She is tired, the weight of it bearing on her – it is in her wheezing chest and plodding gait. She dreams of sitting by the fire tonight with a bottle or two of beer before an early rise again tomorrow. Still there must be nothing out of the ordinary to alert her, and thus as always I feign weakness, leaning against her, stumbling once or twice. She hauls me along as a dead weight, sighing while I use the lavatory; turning now to gaze outside… and how could she not? The night is ablaze with dozens of bonfires lit as beacons across the landscape. Sparks fly into the air, and from high on the hills voices carry on the wind.

Diane's death.

"Halloween tonight, is it? I forget." My words are cotton wool inside my mouth, sounding peculiar to my ears.

Distracted, she nods. "Aye, it's a strange carry-on - burning things, drinking, dancing and the like."

"Burning?"

"Everything diseased goes on those fires - from bad harvest to sick livestock, while they get merry and cavort about like animals. You've never seen the like! Then once the fires die back they run home screaming fast as they can before the black sow rises. Ask me it's all an excuse to get up to mischief..."

There are eleven keys on that ring. The largest fits the door to the stairs and the small one's for the laundry cupboard. The ring is tied to her pocket with string, and although there would never be enough time to undo the knot, there is enough to slash through the cord with my knife.

I stare at it til my eyes burn. *I must do this. I can do this. That key is mine. I am holding it...that key is mine.....*

Now or never. One chance.

Still talking she is caught off-guard. One split second and the ring of keys plops into my hand. Another second to the laundry cupboard. Another and the door is locked behind me. I'm in!

Mary's screams fair raise the roof, her fists pummelling the door. But who will hear her? Who?

And she is locked in – alone on the top floor - until Myra Strickland comes around in one hour's time. And round about now, Myra will be taking supper in the kitchen on the ground floor.

So who will hear Mary?

I must keep calm. Think. I have time but not much. And from here on in I have no plan.

The sash window is jammed and will not lift above a few inches, but there is just enough of a gap to peer out. The grounds roll out towards the moonlit lake, a droopy willow shadowing the lawns. Alas, below lies a stone terrace which will shatter my bones on impact. This is thirty or forty feet high with nothing to break the fall.

Dear God though…what heaven is this…Soft mist mixes with bonfire smoke and the smell of fresh, clean pines. I have to get out.

Mary's fists are pounding what is only a flimsy wooden door. Pray it doesn't splinter and crack. She will be terrified of the recriminations and desperate to re-claim her escapee. Poor woman. Poor, stupid Mary. If I were her I would push straight past Myra when she ar-rives and just keep running. But I cannot afford to think of her fate at this moment. The minutes are ticking and the window will not open wide enough. Nor is there a drainpipe or anything at all to latch on to.

There must be another way out.

Oh no, oh God in heaven…something, anything…

Every shelf is densely packed with regulation sheets, towelling and clothing. With the moon behind and the amber glow from a myriad of bonfires, a weak light is cast around the room. Frantically I run my fingers around the walls, stand on the shelves, throwing off the linen, scrambling upward… yes, here is a small vent in the ceiling. A trapdoor of sorts.

One of Mary's big ham fists smashes through one of the wooden panels.

No time.

A wooden rod they use to reach the top shelves is propped up in the corner of the room. Scrabbling back down, I grab it and climb back up monkey-quick. Jab at the trapdoor standing on my tiptoes. It shifts slightly. Jab it again harder, then again and again. Finally it dislodges.

Mary's shoulder is through the door.

Christ help me! I am no match for her.

I cannot pull up my own body weight. A pile of horsehair blankets lies next to me. Standing on those provides another precious few inches. Every bit of kicking fight goes into this…I am clinging on with my nails.

And in.

Slam the door shut and swing around.

There's little here to weight it down – a portmanteau, a small suitcase, several heavy tomes. They will hopefully suffice for the time being.

What next? Where to? Think…think…

It is a small room – some sort of cupboard - completely dark save for a sliver of moonlight glancing through a hole in the roof. A cold breeze whines through the rafters.

There must be a door through to the attic rooms then, if this is a storage cupboard. If whoever resides in there is sleeping I could take what would be a softer fall onto one of the first floor bay windows, hopefully without them ever knowing. Maybe they keep the person sedated? But is it locked? And who lives in there? All is dark and quiet. I have an image of monsters leering lasciviously on the other side.

From below, Mary has started to shout, "There's no way out, Flora! You'd better get back down or you know what'll happen. You don't know what they do…."

Her voice fades away.

A key is slotting into the lock. A chink of candle light. And two small faces peer around the door.

Faces such as I have never seen the like in all my days.

***

Chapter Twenty-Eight

They cling to each other with tiny rodent hands. Identical in size, at a guess they stand at three, maybe four feet tall. But it is not their diminutive stature which shocks, rather the fact they appear to be very old - more than old- ancient. Both of these creatures have skins as wizened as walnut shells and are completely bald...as hairless as skinned rabbits.

Through huge pale eyes they stare at where I sit cowering on the floor, initial fear quickly giving way to fascination. The one with the lantern now takes a step forward, revealing herself to be a tiny lady wearing a long dress of crinoline, complete with miniature bustle at the back and fussy ruffles at the neck. Fingering a locket with one hand, holding the lamp with the other, she creeps closer, those enormous, protruding eyes growing ever wider.

Perhaps sensing my nerves, she stops a couple of feet away and stoops so that her face is level with mine. Concern crosses the startling little face. It's quite as if she is a miniature person but without hair. The skin is stretched to a sheen over doll like bones, the bridge of the nose arête thin and beaked at the tip, chin almost non-existent. And when she opens her tiny mouth the teeth are sparse and pointed. Again she fingers the locket.

Oh, the poor dear thing. I see now the skin is pulled tight to such a degree it is cracked and sore.

"Hello!"

"Are you English? Do you live here? I…please would you help me…?"

Suddenly she brings up her hand and, flinching to protect my head from what is coming, I feel only the stroke of tiny fingers on my cheek. "Ah," says a childlike voice. "Soft."

The other one comes forward now too, this one dressed in a suit, a miniature gentleman. He seems to hobble, leaning on a stick, and he too now crouches to peer in my face.

"Please…I have been wrongly imprisoned. I will not hurt you - please do not scream, I beg of you. I do not have much time and must escape."

They step back to confer, chattering away in high infant-like voices.

Who are they? What are they? I don't understand…"Please. Myra will be here soon. Do the windows at the front open?"

"We do not know who she is. She could be dangerous," the little gentleman is saying.

"No, no, I am not dangerous. I was ill following childbirth and lost my reason. I have been locked up ever since and subjected to terrible cruelty. I do not have time to explain, but I will die in here and so will my child. I must impress on you the urgency."

"You do not have much time, that is true," he agrees. "What is your name? Who are you?"

"Flora. I am nineteen. I have a child and another one

on the way. I have to leave here tonight. Please, please…"

From below the thump- thump- thump of Mary banging a broom on the ceiling makes the floor judder, her shouts and threats muffled but obvious enough.

Again their eyes lock with each other's, seemingly conveying thoughts without words.

I have to get through to them, make them trust me and quickly. What if they suddenly become alarmed and decide to shout for Myra? They are well dressed. Perhaps they have much money and influence? Perhaps these are private quarters?

"Why do you live up here? What are your names? Are you married or…?"

The woman shakes her head. "Oh no, we are still children. I am Leonora, I am only eleven. And this is James, my brother, who is twelve."

"Twelve and three quarters."

The information will not lodge in my mind as correct. "Pardon?"

Leonora pushes up a sleeve and shows me the thick plates of skin that have separated with deep, reptilian cracks. "It is something that we have, a complaint. But we are children."

"Oh, my Lord! But who are your parents? Have they abandoned you?"

"No, our parents are here. We are Doctor Whately's children."

It is barely possible to comprehend.

"And you are the only ones up here? Is it you I have heard howling and crying?"

Again they look at each other. "No, no, we have

books and games."

"Then who is it who screams? I have heard such wailing, like a wounded animal - it carries through the building–"

"Ah, that could be the babies, or the mothers."

"Babies?"

"They are along the corridor at the end. We think it is a nursery. Or maybe they are sick. We hear them too. Our father is a doctor, you know?"

"Yes, yes, of course. Goodness, you really are his children? I often wondered if he and your mother had any."

"It is most unfortunate we are the way we are and cannot attend school. We must take our walks at midnight in the forest - on this side of the wall lest anyone see us. I'm afraid we are a grave and terrible disappointment."

"Oh, but it is not your fault. Not at all."

I wish I could talk for longer. I am coming to the opinion that perhaps these children have a congenital defect and the good doctor keeps them hidden for the shame of it. How I loathe him all the more. However, time is pressing and I have no option but to implore them for help, remembering that they are indeed only children, and extremely sheltered ones at that.

"Leonora and James, I must leave before Myra returns. I know you are young but I implore you to understand that I am not a lunatic, that I am with child, and that my punishment if caught will be a most heinous one. Please help me, I beg you. You will not be in trouble, but I must return to my family forthwith."

They hesitate, again looking at each other with those

great searching eyes.

Finally Leonora nods. "Yes, Flora. We think you are nice. We are sure you are not mad like some of the others we have observed."

To my enormous relief they now begin to totter towards the doorway, beckoning me to follow.

The attic room is expansive with a lit fire, paintings on the wall and furnished with a couple of couches and a good deal of books and toys, including a magnificent dolls house in sugary pink. But it is to the windows I hurry. Sash windows that overlook an orangery at the side of the house.

"There is no one here tonight," says James. "They are all at the church."

"The church? Oh, I thought perhaps the fire – I mean, I saw flames from within the grounds at the back–?"

"Yes, it is by the lake."

I am confused. Do they mean their family is at the church or a bonfire? But not to dwell, the only people to worry about now are Myra Strickland and Mary. Between them they are strong enough to overpower me and time is of the essence.

Panic surges anew at the thought of Myra suddenly dashing up the stairs and throwing open the doors; and my hands visibly tremor trying to lift up the window.

James peers over the sill. "The drop is not too far. But should we knot sheets together? We have seen this done, haven't we, Leonora, in our storybooks?"

A cold blast of smoky night air wafts into the room. I'd say twenty feet or more down to the glass roof. Freedom is so close I can taste it.

"Yes please. Good thinking, James - the glass might break."

They busy themselves excitedly, fetching sheets from the cupboard, but oh so slowly, hobbling with difficulty. And time ticks steadily on. Everything takes the twins, as I now refer to them in my head, an age. At least I can reach for sheets from the shelves and stretch them out to be tied together. My whole body is now shaking from head to foot. I keep glancing at the clock on the mantelpiece. Another ten minutes gone.

"You are cold," says Lenora. "I have scarves for your head but I rather fear nothing else would fit you."

"Oh, thank you, how very kind." I had forgotten until the window was opened, how chill a night in late October can be, especially up here in the mountains. And here I am in a flimsy cotton dress with my hair shorn clean off and no shoes. She hands over a long, woollen scarf, reaching up to wrap it around my head and neck in a cowl before fastening the whole with a brooch, then fetches a shawl and ties it around my shoulders, shaking her head at the sight of my bare feet.

"Do not worry. I will–"

A door bangs from far below. All three of us freeze. Soon Myra will hear Mary's shouts and the pair will be up here in minutes.

"I have to go."

"But we have not made enough rope for you, Flora," says James.

"It is enough, I must take what we have. Thank you. Thank you both with all my heart."

My last view of the twins is of their astonished, quizzical faces as I tie the sheet rope to the dining table leg, then toss it out of the open window. It dangles half-mast but is better than none at all and besides, there is not a moment more to think.

A shout has gone up but it's too late for Myra and Mary – they cannot leave the house tonight with all those charges, not to mention the doctor's children. Thus I fall badly onto the glasshouse and tumble down the lead pipes to the gravel below, to the sound of one of the harridans screeching herself hoarse, another banging on the glass…

Spitting shards of rain and pitch dark, the flight is uphill and through long grass. Ahead lies the forest but a long way yet, and the exertion is a strain on my weakened heart and lungs. Stumbling every other step on legs that constantly buckle, with inhalations sounding like one diseased and desperate, there is nevertheless a glorious misty dampness on my face, the fresh rush of night air, and the earth's mud caking between my toes. This is life, if only for the briefest moment, and if I die now – still far better than in filth and despair.

The nearby bonfire crackles more loudly up here, the heat of it reaching the left side of my face, wood smoke curling around the tree trunks. But it is when at the perimeter rim of the forest that I dare look back, gasping for every breath.

Lavinia House stands as a dark mansion with only the faintest glow of lamplight coming from the uppermost windows. And perhaps it is my imagination, but I am sure there are two small faces looking out of their prison into the night.

"Poor things."

The voice behind is low, almost a whisper.

Whirling around, my heart almost gives out with the shock.

"Oh!"

***

Chapter Twenty-Nine

Isobel
Present Day

The vision left her badly disorientated. Overhead, the spidery canopy was spinning and she clutched the nearest tree trunk in an effort to stand. Her head pounded and exhaustion threatened to pull her back to the ground. The forest now seemed an alien place, threatening, dark and oppressive. An icy wind whined along hidden pathways.

Backing out, she turned and hurried towards the light. Clouds had swooped in low across the fields and a couple of raindrops spotted her cheeks. She quickened her pace, resisting the urge to turn around. What or who was watching her go? Forests had only ever been places of deep serenity and natural beauty, a refuge in which to recharge and think things over – never before had they felt menacing. But there was something about the Hill of Loss that held onto its secrets. Dark ones.

Instilled with a sense of urgency, she began to march towards Blackmarsh in search of Branwen. If Lorna Fox-Whately loomed large now she'd tell her to get stuffed. Something far more pressing was taking shape, and alarmingly fast, just as Branwen had said. If only she knew what was coming. Something to do with that man... Damn, where had she seen that face before? And why would he be shown in a vision? Because, by God it was real.

It can't be.

It is.

She looked like the creature in Branwen's paintings. Uncannily, in fact, like the one on her mantelpiece – Immie!

She must speak to Branwen.

Rapt in thought, she hurried along the lane between the high hedges, listening out for a car or van hurtling round one of the many blind bends. Crows cawed and circled overhead and the sky darkened further. Rain was spotting more frequently now, great blotches dropping onto the tarmac; and from behind a raw wind blew off mountains still topped with snow. She put her head down, walking so fast her chest began to wheeze and her nose streamed. Why the panic? It seemed to come from a force outside of herself. And yet it was undeniable. She was almost running.

At long last the lane straightened and The Drovers Inn came into view. Hopefully Branwen would be in. She had to tell her what had just happened. Must describe the man now revealed to her. It was so bloody frustrating trying to recall where she'd seen him. Who the hell could it be? There'd only been that old guy in the pub on the first night and it sure wasn't him. So where? Who?

Surprisingly, it seemed the pub was open. The front door stood ajar and a light was on. The shop, however, was shut. A little sign had been hung on the door, saying, 'Back in half an hour.'

"Fuck!"

She looked around the square, hoping that the half hour was already up and Branwen would be hurrying back. But the village was desolate. Not a single car. And no one was walking along the lane in any of the three directions either. Perhaps the backyard? Branwen might be in the kitchen?

Here too though, the lights were off, the house devoid of life.

Cold and wet, she hugged her arms to her chest. Okay then, well there was nothing else for it but the pub while she waited.

Delyth stood behind the bar clutching a mug of something hot, taking perpetual noisy sips exactly like last time. The woman looked wrecked - old beyond her years – with wispy thin hair, a waxy complexion and rolls of excess fat. Definitely a thyroid problem. Her doctor should have picked up on it ages ago. Mervyn Fox-Whately, wasn't it? Yes, a wonder he hadn't asked her to pop in for treatment.

Delyth was deep in conversation with one of those men who liked to hog the territory – although of slight build he took a lot of space, leaning over the bar with his arms folded in a manner precluding interruption. There was also a conspiratorial air about him - the tilt of his head implying he and he alone be listened to. As Isobel was deciding whether to approach, Delyth fleetingly raised her eyes, and the uneasy, cornered look in them was enough. This conversation was an uncomfortable one.

Taking her cue she stepped back, not keen to have the man notice her. He had a beard. It could be Rhys Payne. Or perhaps one of his sons?

Turning swiftly away however, it was to once again find herself looking at the old photographs on the pub wall. These were the line-ups of village folk in Victorian dress - the ones with vacant expressions and a whole host of dark shapes hovering around their auras. Swallowing down the shock, she forced herself to examine them more carefully this time, and with far less fear.

Those people were ill, some of them epileptics or with Downs Syndrome – you've only to look at the photos on the pub wall...

Of course...these were patients from the asylum. She flitted from one face to another. Very few faces appeared more than once, the set of twelve in 1892 quite different from the set in 1893 and so on. Except for one of them, no two - a lady seated at the front in a long, taffeta dress, and a man of slender build wearing a top hat. She leaned in. His expression was hard to discern, the features blurred...then she drew back with a sharp intake of breath. Looked again. *Holy crap, that was him!*

"Interesting, aren't they?"

The male voice was hot against her neck and she whirled around.

"You must be our new neighbour? I'm Doctor Fox-Whately. How do you do?"

The floor was coming up to meet her. She clutched at the mantelpiece.

His voice seemed to come from far, far away. "Are you all right? You look as if you're about to faint."

Her vision! It was both the man in the photograph

and this one in front of her. She managed to form some words, "Sorry, I felt dizzy for a moment. I'm fine, honestly."

"Well, if you're sure. Perhaps if you sat down for a moment? I could ask Delyth to bring you some tea?"

"No, thank you, honestly. I was just looking for Branwen—"

His eyes bored into hers. Small and glass-like they had an unnerving deflective quality.

"I don't think you'll find her in the photographs."

Heat was crawling into her face, suffusing her cheeks, burning the lobes of her ears.

Still he stared.

She struggled, as if hypnotised, for something to say. "I…I was just…Sorry, it just struck me how alike you look."

"Alike?"

"Yes, to the gentleman in the pictures. It's really quite a striking resemblance. Is he your grandfather or great grandfather by any chance? The…what were they called back then, alienists or mind doctors?"

Mervyn's face blanched very slightly. A shadow passed behind his eyes and his mouth seemed to twist inwards. The man, she realised with growing disquiet, seethed with a quiet rage, albeit restrained and controlled, but perhaps all the more dangerous for that.

"What a good eye you have."

"Ah!" She affected a bright tone, a guileless demeanour. "I'm very good with faces. I had a resemblance to my great grandmother, apparently. It seemed to miss two generations. Quite uncanny."

He remained standing exactly where he was, glaring

now as if the very sight of her appalled him.

What was the matter with him? How could he possibly have taken offence? She smiled. "I suppose being a doctor must run in your family. Anyway, I must try and find Branwen, she might be back by–"

"Your friend's in the church yard."

"Really?"

"Yes, I just passed her. Oh, and you must come and see me – register at the practice. Lorna will book you in."

"Thank you, yes I'll do that."

Her heart was banging so hard she felt sure he could hear it, her footsteps loud on the flagstones as she hurried from the inn. His eyes were on her back until the very last minute. Goodness, did it matter that she knew who his grandfather was? The man was a dead ringer. What was far more disturbing was something he didn't know - that was he was the man in her vision, and the one the spirits tried to show her last night.

She had to find Branwen.

Outside, the rain had set to grim. God, how desolate this place in winter. There wasn't a single person in sight, no cars, no distant rumble of traffic, no muffled voices from within the cottages. Her lone steps clicked along the cobbles and down the path towards the church.

It only occurred to her as she neared the lytchgate, to wonder what Branwen could possibly be doing in the graveyard. In the rain. But as she cranked it open it was to find two women in the churchyard, not one. Perhaps she'd been half expecting Branwen to be knee deep in a grave digging up a coffin. Instead, she was standing by the porch with her hands on her hips talking to Mercy May, raven hair streaming behind her, facial expression set to grim.

Mercy was clutching a hymn book, her words carrying in fragments on the wind. "...absolutely cannot...against our Lord Jesus Christ...everything...completely forbid..."

"Who told you? Who told you?" Branwen was yelling.

"Never mind that, this is sacrilege."

At the sound of Isobel's approach both women turned.

"Sorry to interrupt. Sorry. I was told Branwen was here and I–"

Mercy glared. "Oh, I see. You couldn't wait for me to come over and bless the house, so you thought you'd try witchcraft instead, is that it?"

"Sorry?"

Mercy shook her head. "I simply cannot allow this to happen in my parish. I absolutely forbid it. It's the devil's work and I won't have either of you in my church if you persist in using the dark arts, do you understand? And you, Miss, will not dig up my graveyard. Not now and not ever. Do I make myself clear?"

"Oh sod off," said Branwen. "It was a handful of earth, that's all. You don't own it."

"We'll see," said Mercy. "We'll see what the rest of the village has to say about this."

"Is that a threat, because if it is it isn't very Christian," said Branwen. "Anyone would think I'd committed murder not dug up a spoonful of soil. Anyway, what's more important is who's spreading gossip? I have a right to know who's slandering my name."

"No, you don't. Suffice to say that Christianity presides in this village and there are loyal parishioners who keep an eye on people like you."

"What do you mean by people like me?"

"I'm talking about black witchcraft, Branwen Morgan. And well you know it."

She pushed past Isobel with a face set to granite, unlocked the church door and slammed it shut behind her.

"Good grief!"

"I know," said Branwen. "The thing is, I only got a smidgen of dirt from Olivia's grave, and it took less than a minute. Someone must have tipped her off."

"And someone was outside the house last night."

"Exactly."

"The doctor knew where you were too. I just bumped into him. Oh, and Branwen, I have to tell you something urgent."

Linking arms, they walked back down the path to the lytchgate while Isobel brought her up to speed. "What I don't get, though, is if Mervyn's grandfather was guilty of something or other and he thinks we might find out, why does it matter so much to him, because he was sure as hell freaked out, especially when I said they looked alike?"

Branwen was quiet, and for a while they walked in silence. Suddenly she stopped and said, "You saw the fae! Do know how lucky you are? I mean, you've only been here five minutes and you actually fucking well saw—"

"I thought you did – all the time? She looked like the

painting you gave me so I thought you must have–"

"No, no. I've worked on it for years, though. Offered them libations, alcohol mostly - but also bracelets and herbs…all sorts…you'll see them in the trees. Sometimes I'm rewarded with blinding insights. Or if I've offended them I'll wake up with my hair in hundreds of tiny knots I can't get out, or everything will be switched around the room. But what I paint, well, it's more like…how to explain…I hold the brush and that's what happens. They live in the umbra, the darkest part of shadows. God, Isobel…I've never actually seen one walking in the forest, although I know some folk said they have."

"Who?"

"To be honest, it's hearsay. Riana told my grandmother who told my mother. Some folk in the village would come home screaming from the forest if they'd strayed in too deeply or gone over the wall, usually courting couples and the like – said they'd seen tiny, wizened creatures with paper white faces. Everything changed apparently, once the Fox-Whatelys sealed off the woods. There used to be a track that ran all the way to the house and beyond, but now as you probably saw, it comes to a dead end. They blocked off their land around the time of the miners' uprising – no doubt to stop them coming near the house. Anyway, the track was completely dug up, traps were set and a stone wall built. And that was after all the deforestation for the mine itself. Some say the family angered the fae."

"Actually, it wasn't a nice experience at all. I felt ill. Everything blacked out and I had a horrific flashback to one of the bleakest, most terrifying times of my life, followed by a blinding close up of this man's face. I thought I'd be sick and my head was banging so hard I swear an artery was about to burst. It was horrible."

"That's them all right. They do evil shit to you but you'll get the truth. Thing is, they're wild. There's nothing gentle about it. But remember what I told you - there's always a price to pay."

"But I didn't ask for anything."

"No. But they have given and you must pay. As must I."

"I don't understand."

"They want us to do something for them and we have to do it. If you run away now one thing's for sure – you'll spend the rest of your life being shown what fear and madness really are. And they will take Immie."

"Christ! What, though? This is so hard. I mean, do you really think we'll solve this by raising Olivia's spirit? Meantime people in this village are watching us and I've been attacked twice already. I want out, Branwen. I really do. I want to go tonight."

"Listen to me, Lady! If we flee the village to escape Rhys Payne and the like we'll be plagued with the wrath of the fae for the rest of our lives. They get into your head, plant nightmares you won't recover from and send you insane. Don't think it won't happen. And I can promise you this - there won't be a psychiatrist on earth who'll either believe you or cure you. So I think I'll take my chances with Rhys and do the necromancy. You do what you like, but leave me the keys. And besides – you fucking promised."

Jeez, this girl's fire. It set the blood racing. "Right. Well, what if it doesn't work?"

"It will. And while I'm doing it you can talk to those poor spirits who've been desperate for your attention."

"The same folk whose bodies you say were never collected and therefore must still be on the estate grounds, maybe even underneath The Gatehouse?"

"Uh-huh."

"So they will be the spirits opening drawers and crawling around…quite insane…"

"And?"

"Insane, Branwen. So how will they communicate with me?"

"Maybe they aren't insane in the afterlife."

"All right then, let's assume this will work. Let's say all goes swimmingly. What about whoever's spreading gossip about us in the village? Might they try to stop us? I mean if Mercy May is–"

"That silly cow's being used good and proper but she'll put out the word, and you're right – there are those who'll not turn a hair at a bit of grievous. Rhys Payne's lads have done time for it."

"Okay, look I'm going to do this because I said I would. But I can't lie – I'm scared half to death, and not so much from the spirits anymore as the locals. I wouldn't put it past Rhys Payne or his family to come to the house. What if they turn up while we're tranced out doing the ritual?

"I'll do banishing rites before I come over. They should know better than to set me against the church, the lousy bastards. I'll make it so they can't get their arses off the sofa to take a pee let alone drive over to start a fight."

"Banishing rites…?"

"Look, I know you feel we're working totally in the dark, Isobel, and that you don't believe a lot of what I say but I am asking you now to trust me, okay? Things will be revealed and often it's never quite the way you expect or even what you think you're going to expect… if that makes sense…? But there will be a light shone on this, I know it. I can almost see it. Please don't go until I've tried."

"All right. Let's give it our best shot, it can't do any harm."

***

Chapter Thirty

Isobel

The remainder of the afternoon eased into evening, shadows merging with the dusk until light no longer reached the four corners of the room. From within the forest a vixen's raw cry ripped through the air, and once again wet fog sank into the valley.

Branwen was due to arrive after eleven once she'd taken Immie to her father; but the hours waiting were fraught. She sat by the electric fire, stood up, walked around, switched on all the main lights closing curtains as she went…sat down again…And still it was only seven o'clock.

Perhaps she'd write to Nina again.

Finding it hard to concentrate on even the simplest of tasks, she reeled off one ridiculous sounding missive after another before deleting them all and starting over. Everything would seem absurd to the reader. Who would not think her out of her wits with stories of fairies, visions, creepy photographs on the pub wall and a new friend who disinterred graveyard dirt? What had loneliness done to this woman who had once been sectioned in a psychiatric unit?

Instead, she kept to plain facts – the local doctor's resemblance to his grandfather, the mystery surrounding the patients' graves and the terrible lynching of Branwen's great-grandmother. About to relate last night's disturbance outside the window however, she hesitated. What was the point of worrying Nina by having her think she was in danger? She had offloaded far too much already. In the end she added the incident as an aside, making light of it. It was high time she sorted out her own problems, and preferably without the aid of alcohol.

Especially tonight.

Branwen had explicitly said not to eat anything and definitely not to drink alcohol. They must both be fully prepared. "Meditate. Ask for protection and stay grounded. I'll bring some oils and herbs with me."

"Do I need to get anything ready?"

"Yes, can you close all the curtains and pull up the carpet in the room we're working in? Let's have the floorboards exposed for a circle."

"Right."

Truth be told, she thought, this whole thing felt like crossing a line. Accepting you could see spirits was one thing. But actively meddling, as in conjuring, was quite another. Could it be worse than what had already happened, though? Could raising Olivia Fox-Whately from the dead actually be more frightening than events so far encountered in her life? Surely, once you'd peered over into the abyss there was nothing else left to fear. Was there?

The atmosphere grew more fractious by the hour. The house held an air of expectation as if it was waiting, the shadowy alcoves, niches and corners darker than usual, and the ghosts so quiet it seemed they held their breath. On the mantelpiece the clock ticked hypnotically and the electric fire cranked with a heat that burned her face but left the rest of the room cold. Nothing warmed this house. Beneath the soles of her feet the floors were particularly icy, as if suspended only inches above the hardened winter earth. And was it her imagination or did the painting of Immie seem to come alive a little? She would look and then look again, to find the eyes glittered a little more, the expression increasingly inquisitive.

Leaning back in the chair she took slow, deep breaths, forcing a meditative state that would not come. Her mind wandered, time passing without notice as she dipped in and out of the depths of her unconscious mind. All moments had led to this, came the message. What was happening now and the experience in the park all those years ago, defined her entire existence.

After a while she bent her head and prayed.

"Dear Lord, whatever rites Branwen is planning tonight, it is with good intent. Please protect us both from evil and forgive us both for what we are about to do. Thank you, Lord, and Amen."

A sudden and powerful burst of clarity flashed into her mind. There had been no official registers found for the asylum, fire accepted as the cause, so that had made it easy for people to disappear...but she had been shown a suitcase. A shabby leather case that smelled strongly of mould. A dark place. *There were papers...evidence of something...this was the question to be asked!*

A loud rapping on the front door catapulted her out of contemplation.

She looked at the clock.

Ten. Too early for Branwen.

On guard, she sat stone still, gripping the arms of the chair. This could be Lorna. Or Mercy. She would not be subjected to more verbal abuse. Had done nothing wrong. In fact, one had been paid rent and the other asked for help. So they could piss off talking to her like that. Anyway, she was entitled to privacy and for all they knew she could be in the bath.

Whoever it was knocked harder.

Oh, sod off!

A slight lull.

Then it started again. On and on and on. Insistent and prolonged.

"I know you're in there!" Lorna Fox-Whately barked. "And I won't have it, do you hear? You're a trouble maker and I won't have this going on in my property. I shall fetch the police."

Isobel's law-abiding heart slammed against her ribs. Until her inner rebel kicked in. Like they were going to come all the way out here - an hour-long drive in the dark and fog on winding narrow lanes because a middle-aged woman might be holding a séance? *Don't make me laugh!*

"I shall have you evicted. We are Christian people and this is absolutely against our agreement."

She gripped the chair until the knuckle bones shone through. *An agreement to what? Not to commune with the devil? Was that on the tenancy contract…?*

Lorna pounded on the door with what sounded like all her weight, which was considerable, the final thump so violent it made the house shudder. "Open this door at once!"

Fuck off.

That woman was like the worst kind of demon, but still it made her heart lurch sickeningly. Lorna could and would do her harm if she could. A thought occurred – what if they had a key and changed the locks when she went out? And they would keep her money. Stupidly she'd paid up front. And on the back of that one another thought crossed her mind…Was the front door bolted from the inside? What about the back? It wasn't safe here - and not as it turned out because of the ghosts of mad, unhappy people, but because of the neighbours. Lorna could easily call in the likes of Rhys Payne and his boys.

I'll do banishing rites….I'll make it so they can't get their arses off the sofa…

Pray to God that Branwen's rituals worked. If only she'd done them on Lorna too.

But all now was quite suddenly quiet. Like a thunder storm that had done its worst and was grumbling away to distant hills, leaving behind it the sharp, clear pelt of rain.

Tip-toeing into the hall, Isobel quickly checked the front door before scooting into the kitchen. The bolts were drawn across both. And all the windows to the ground floor had locks on them. She lay a hand across her chest. The woman could not get in, master key or no master key.

Even so, who still prowled around out there? And where was he - the quietly menacing family doctor? Well, it certainly seemed to spook them out if anyone either ventured onto their property or asked questions about their family. Their fear was palpable. Some displayed fear with physical aggression, some with barriers of authority, and others with thinly veiled threats. But fear was fear.

They shouldn't have rented this out if it made them so darned jittery, should they? Perhaps it was as Branwen suspected, and Mervyn was being pressured to align with a medical practice in town, and if he didn't agree it could leave both him and Lorna without an income. However, if he did agree then that would leave other doctors potentially opening his books, so to speak. So they needed the rent in order to carry on both running and guarding Lavinia House. What could it be that was so bad? Surely the past was the past?

The minutes ticked by painfully slowly. Isobel moved around the house from room to room, keeping in the shadows, peering through gaps in the curtains for signs of prowlers, ears straining for footsteps. The fog had closed in so completely that on occasion, the sight of her own face in the glass appeared as a spectre, making her catch her breath.

Had Lorna gone to get reinforcements? Would a mob arrive as they had for Branwen's poor great-grandmother all those years ago? Imagine, God imagine the sight of all those torch-bearing men outside demanding your blood! She shuddered. How terrible to look outside and see the hatred on their faces, see the rope...

Eleven-thirty. Branwen would be here soon.

Jumpy with nerves and still muttering to herself about Lorna, she decided to prepare for the ritual now and roll back the lounge carpet. Cheaply laid with no underfelt or grips tacked around the edges, it peeled back easily, releasing an immediate waft of damp and decay. She then set about moving the table against the wall and hunting for matches. God only knew what would happen next. Would Branwen arrive safely? Would this work? Would it reveal anything? Oh God, so many unknowns…her stomach was squirming.

***

At quarter to twelve a text flashed. Branwen. 'BACK DOOR'

She let her in, hastily locking and bolting it again.

"Nice and foggy out there, is it? Mind you, I was sure there was someone behind me. If not from this world then from the next. I don't mind telling you I'm nervous, lovely."

"Have you done something to keep them away? I've had Lorna here banging on the door."

"Don't answer. Don't let her in and don't speak with her."

"I haven't."

"Good. We don't need any weakening of energy. Yes, anyway," Branwen continued, as she eased off her wellies and threw an anorak over the kitchen table, "the Payne and Ash boys will be housebound for a while, a bit groggy with a nasty bit of blindness thrown in."

"Blimey, how do you do that?"

"I'll tell you one day, lovely, but right now we've got our work cut out. Oh, well done rolling back the carpet. Stinks a bit, is it?"

"Damp, I expect."

Branwen stood transfixed. "No, it's more than just damp earth and wood rot. That's the smell of death that is, like a graveyard."

"You said it had been a morgue."

"Yes, hmm…Anyhow, it's all good because that's what we need for this ritual. A place of death."

"Gulp. Okay, right, tell me what you need me to do."

Branwen was unpacking a rucksack full of candles, phials of oils, and little tins. "We haven't got long. I need to have this in place by midnight. Once I've drawn the circle you must not, absolutely not, whatever happens, move outside of it. Isobel, promise me! You must stay within the circle at all times because this is a binding ritual and it can be dangerous."

"Yes, I promise."

Branwen set to work, talking Isobel through it as she cast the circle and quickly salted the circumference. Three candles were then positioned in a triangle - one red, one white, and one black - with a blurred sepia photograph of Olivia in the middle. Taken when the woman was quite elderly, her eyes were hooded and unreadable, the angular planes of her face gaunt and somewhat masculine. Other than that her appearance was unremarkable. Although, as Isobel stared at the image, it did jar on some level, dislodging a sense of déja-vu.

While she was trying to recollect the ghost she'd seen in the parlour, assuming that was where the recognition came from, Branwen started smudging the room with rosemary before beginning the ritual. The sweet smell of the herb was intoxicating, and although it was meant to both cleanse the area and draw the spirits towards the circle, it also induced relaxation, and Isobel had to check herself from drifting into a dream.

Finally Branwen lit incense of wormwood and black henbane, inhaling the smoke and asking Isobel to do the same.

It hit her more powerfully than any joint she'd ever smoked in her life. "Whoa!"

"You all right, lovely?"

"Yes, wow, powerful stuff."

"Now don't forget what I said - on no account must you move out of this circle."

"I absolutely promise." A shiver crept up her spine. "I think someone's here, I've gone cold."

"Okay, sit tight now. I need you to note images, emotions and messages. Anything and everything no matter how small or insignificant you personally think it might be. If we're right and these spirits were blocked by Olivia then remember I've got all her attention whether she likes it or not. So don't get drawn into the darkness. Don't listen to lies or tricks. People like Rhys and Lorna exist on the other side too. So if you see an image of your late grandmother it's not her, okay? Let me handle the dark side."

"Okay." Doing her best to unravel the knots in her stomach, Isobel crossed her legs and closed her eyes, holding her palms upwards.

"Here – let me just put some of this on your fore-head. Hold still, it's myrrh, to help you connect. And a bit of this one on the nape of your neck. Same for me. Okay, now are you ready? You know what to do? Ignore me and my ritual. Just tune into the spirits that come forward."

"Yes."

Branwen placed the smudge stick back on the floor, its fragrant smoke curling into rings, then lit a stick of mullein and walked widdershins three times around the inside of the circle.

"Hecate, Great One, Mistress, Goddess of the Underworld, You of Many Forms...Come, Hecate of The Three Ways, You who with your fire-breathing phantoms oversee the dreaded paths and harsh enchantments. Come Hecate, I ask for your guidance and assistance."

Filling a chalice with lavender and dandelion mead, she then offered this to the Goddess before taking her place next to Isobel.

"Colpriziana, Offina Aha Nestra, Fuaro Menut! Olivia Fox-Whately, the dead whom I seek, thou art the dead I seek. Spirit of deceased, arise and answer my calling! Berald, Beroald, Balbin, Gab, Gabor, Aagba ! ARISE! I charge and call thee!"

With the yew wand she made an 'X' sign in the grave dirt she'd collected. "Olivia Fox-Whately, I call thee. Allay Fortission, Fortissio Allynsen Roa! Allay Fortission, Fortissio Allynsen Roa!"

Over and over the words were repeated, her voice deeper and more powerful with every command.

Through the haze of smoke and incense, Isobel was reminded of the drugged feeling she'd had many times as a disturbed teen. The ceiling was whirling, walls undulating, and a swill of nausea was rising in her throat. The vague notion came that someone was offering her a blood soaked rag, but it flickered only for the briefest of moments like a dream already fading. She shook her head. Had she fallen asleep? This was weird - the floor was rising and falling like a boat on the swell.

It must be the incense.

A girl appeared before her.

But I have my eyes closed…

Take note of everything you see…no matter how small or insignificant…

She was young, wearing a white nightdress, and very busy with her hands as if knitting furiously. Her words made little sense, like jabberwocky, but her eyes were imploring as desperately she tried to make herself understood.

Who are you? What is your name?

It sounded like Die!

You are dead, yes.

The spirit stamped her foot. Again it sounded like Die. The girl clutched at her tummy and, exactly as had happened with the girl on the stairs, blood began to seep through the girl's dress, dripping down her legs until it flowed in a torrent and pooled on the floor. And the sound of a baby crying filled the room – from every corner until it was screaming through her head.

You had a child. We are talking about a baby - yours?

The screaming quieted.

Again the girl's eyes and hands frantically gesticulated.

You were a patient in the asylum? You gave birth while you were in there? Did they take the baby from you or did you die in childbirth?

Frustratingly the image vanished, immediately replaced by another – a creature with a malevolent cackle, who skittered around the outside of the circle on all fours, gathering things from the floor. Before one by one her limbs snapped off like chicken wishbones and the vision dissipated.

The room was black now. The air crackling with static.

Suddenly an apparition appeared at such close range Isobel jumped back.

The old woman's appearance was highly disturbing, her eyes white and blinded. Despite that, there was the queerest feeling that the woman could see – not her face but rather into her thoughts, her mind. A moment of transmission, and then her whole body began to respond with waves of heartbreak, grief tearing through her in shards that ripped into emotions, leaving them exposed, raw and howling. And then the visions came in their hundreds - lightning quick flashes - bars at windows, lines of emaciated down-trodden creatures in filthy nightdresses, stick limbs being thrashed with nettles, tubes rammed down throats, freezing water dowsing shivering bodies, lungs full of ice…

Her body thrashed around on the floor, the screams stuck in her throat, tears streaming down her face.

Trying desperately to concentrate her mind, she threw questions in. *Who are you? What happened here? Where do we look? How do we help?*

On and on the scenes played as if a memory were being projected directly onto her own. She had to wrest control. *Please how do we help you? We are here only to help.*

One word. One word floated in on the chaos, as finally the energy level abated and the old woman faded.

Flora.

And it was this name, still echoing around the bones of her skull, that she was repeating when Branwen's voice broke through. "Tell me where the bodies are! Tell me where the registers are! You will tell me!"

"Flora! Ask her about Flora, Branwen. And an old suitcase...battered leather...against a wall, somewhere dark and cold..."

Instantly, a piercing metallic screech loud enough to burst eardrums had them both clamping hands to their ears. And a scraping noise behind them indicated the table was moving across the floorboards. Shocked, Isobel turned around in time to see it picked up by invisible hands and hurled across the room. Then she was slammed onto her back and to her horror found her dress being hitched up. Callous hands she couldn't see were touching her, violating her, a foul breath in her face. She couldn't get her breath, could not inhale. Her lungs had turned to iron. Worst of all the man in black had appeared, and was now standing in the corner of the room, the tip of his cigarette flaring in the dark.

The urge to break free of the circle was overwhelming.

Over the demonic screeching, Branwen's voice shouted, "Stay with it, Isobel. We are stronger."

At this all the candles snuffed out, and from out of the engulfing blackness a pulsating, palpable presence loomed towards the edge of the circle. Later, she could only recall the hatred, as whatever or whoever it was, leapt towards them repeatedly, flying at their faces with savage claws that left both of them bleeding from scratches. It picked up everything that was loose and threw it – candlesticks, a stapler, books – aiming directly for their heads. Prowling around the circle it re-iterated threats of eternal damnation and hellfire, of plagues and bad dreams, of running sores and madness. An echoing welter of bestial howls emanated from the creature's mouth, instilling oppression and terror, compelling them to weaken and run. On and on and on the presence circled – reaching in to pull at hair, rip claws down spines, spit and hiss.

You common little witch, how dare you!

"Tell us where the graves are! Tell us where the papers are!" Branwen shouted.

Her neck snapped like a wishbone and everyone cheered. All the people you think are your friends and neighbours, even family, they all cheered!

"Tell me where the graves are, you evil bitch! Tell me where the papers are! Tell me what your father did!"

Then quite without warning Isobel caught it. While Branwen battled with the force of hatred in the room, names and images came to her. Although they were faint – little more than vague impressions - she grasped enough to understand. But her strength was draining away rapidly. It had been hours. Her body slumped and her head pounded.

Flora!

The girl on the stairs was Flora. The image was just a flash, but a highly vivid one. Bound and gagged, a girl in a hideous flowery dress lay spread-eagled on a filthy mattress in a padded room. And on top of her lay a rough looking man with greasy hair and a reddened face. Flinching, she began to shut it down. This was a rape. A horrible rape…

Look, look again…more carefully…

Using every last vestige of concentration she made herself examine the finer details of the scene. Yes, there was a lit cigarette at the tiny window in the door. Someone watching. Someone witnessing the assault. A mentally unwell girl was being raped in a place where she was supposed to be cared for. And this person was watching. Someone who must have authority to be there…

That image. And the face shown to her earlier….Was that it? Had the doctor sanctioned this? But why?

"Tell me you're getting something because I want to send this bitch back to hell," said Branwen.

"Something to do with Flora – a girl called Flora! A suitcase, very old, shabby and box like. And there is someone hiding….a cupboard under the stairs."

Scrambling for a tin of powder, Branwen tore it open and hurled a handful of dust into the dark. Immediately the most disgusting stench of ripe excreta made both of them dry retch. With her eyes streaming, Brawnen began to chant once more. "Go, go departed shades by Omgroma, Epic, Sayoc, Satony, Degony, Eparigon, Galiganon, Zogogen, Ferstigan. I license thee to depart onto thy proper place, and be there peace evermore."

Slowly the light of the room lifted and the candles flickered back into flame.

"What was that?"

"Don't ask. Got rid of her, though, didn't it?"

"I'm not surprised. Oh God, that was horrible. I can hardly believe it happened. I feel terrible, wrecked."

"What did you get?"

"Olivia was terrified, absolutely out of her wits. That's what makes people as angry as that, isn't it? Usually fear or insecurity, someone making them feel inferior or jealous? And I think it has to do with a girl called Flora. Lots of girls were raped here. I don't know why except it seems to have been sanctioned by the doctor. Nor do I know where the bodies went or why they never left the asylum. But I do know the key is a girl called Flora. All the spirits told me that name. I also got a cupboard, or enclosed place where someone was hiding, and the suitcase again....papers of some sort, or letters perhaps."

Despite the fact that a whole night of intense psychic attack had passed, Branwen's green eyes were all aglitter. "Someone burned the asylum down looking for something they couldn't find. I think that's why they're so bloody nervous about the whole estate. One day someone is going to stumble on either a mass grave or a pile of papers that show how hundreds of people just vanished. I think Edgar kept the fees paid to him while pretending the patients were still alive. And I also think he had girls raped then sacrificed the babies."

"I really don't know about sacrifices. But I saw a heavy, ugly man. An uncouth sort that must have frightened those poor young girls to death, and he had really bad breath. I think he was the rapist"

"What did he look like? Tell me while it's fresh in your mind."

"Ruddy face, bulbous nose, bad teeth – like pegs sticking out–"

"Sounds like Hywl Ash. Rhys Payne's bessie mate. And both of them had grandparents who worked at

Lavinia House."

"But the thing I don't get, in fact my head hurts trying to work it out, is why. Why all the rapes and deaths?"

"I told you. Sacrifice."

"For what?"

Branwen stared her down. "The fae, Isobel. The Fox-Whatelys destroyed hundreds of acres of wild forest for the mine, then dug up ancient pathways and built a ruddy great wall across it."

"But how, I mean I don't understand how–"

They were quiet for a minute. Suddenly, Branwen said, "Can you smell burning?"

***

Chapter Thirty-One

Flora
All Hallows Eve 1893

Oh, but she fair stops my heart.

Stepping out of the cover of darkness, her face catches in the fiery glow - features chiselled as if from porcelain, long black hair coiling around her shoulders like a wild gypsy girl. More arresting than any physical beauty, however, is the powerful gaze from those glittering eyes. Startlingly direct, she takes in my pathetic appearance, prowling in a slow cat-like circle as she nears.

She is a heathen. A savage on her way to some ritual. I cannot run. I cannot...

Expecting the woman to lunge, to force me along to where people will laugh and torment me, I flinch and cower. I am breathless, too weak to fight. And yet her voice was soft as she watched from the edge of the woods, and she watched my flight. Perhaps she knows compassion? Oh dear God, please let her have compassion.

Drawing level with my face now, she peers in close. A more handsome woman I have yet to see. Those eyes are pale jade, the skin luminescent, the curves of her body strapped into a bodice of jet satin and lace.

"I...I need to make haste, I–"

She nods, her accent strong with the local dialect. "I saw you." It is quite as if she can read my mind for suddenly she throws back her head and laughs. "Escape!" Then without warning she grabs my hand and urges me to follow. "Come. Quickly."

"No, no, I must find a road."

"Ach..." She looks me over, shaking her head at my terrible attire. "But your dress."

Of course, her English is not fluent. "Mi Flora George."

She laughs again, a delighted giggle. "Mi Riana...." Indicating the nearby fire now burning so ferociously sparks are flying into the trees, she begins to chatter avidly in her native tongue. A few words I recognise, "coelcerth...plentyn...eglwys..."

Nodding to show I understand, that I realise they are all busy with Halloween celebrations, I finally take her hand and follow. Pray to God she has a good heart. Pray to God she is going to help and not thrust me before some drunken mob of savages, for her humour seems high and excitable.

The route we take is in total darkness, and Riana leads us through waist high bracken, snapping boughs and crispy leaves as swiftly as a fox. Away now from the heat of the fire, the air is cool and smoky, the ground underfoot becoming boggy. Although she flies, I stumble and trip, bump into tree trunks, all the while gasping painfully from the sharp night air hitting my lungs.

Abruptly she stops. Turns towards me pressing a finger to her lips. Ahead a small house squats darkly at the opposite end of the field. I am not at all sure of my bearings.

"The Gatehouse," she whispers. "To the asylum."

"No, no…What if–?"

"No, shush. They are out." She nods towards the fire behind us.

"At the coelcerth?"

My eyes must be filled with horror because softly she touches my face. "Clothes, money. You must have. Can you run?"

I feel sick, but nod. Yes, I will run because there is no choice.

"Come then. Run fast."

The field is miles and miles and miles, or so it feels, the ground shattering my joints with every thump on the turf. Every breath is a knife wound. I cannot go on… cannot….

Riana clasps me to her as I fall, strong arms around my waist, pulling me along until finally we reach an archway and the tiny stone house.

Thrusting me into the cover of dense shrubbery, she shakes me hard by the arms. "Wait here. Be quiet. Shush."

A few moments later a sash window scrapes open and she flies back. "Hurry now!"

Once inside she thunders up the stairs, clearly ransacking a bedroom while I sit on the bottom step, then thunders down with a pile of clothing. "Dress. Boots. Hat. Food now. Wait."

The clock on the mantelpiece in the parlour is tick-tocking far too rapidly. We must leave at once. "No!"

Too late, she is in the kitchen opening cupboards. She is right - there will be a long journey ahead, maybe for days and I am weak, a crumpled collection of bones with barely the strength left to put on the heavy woollen dress and lace-up boots. But I confess to being more frightened than I have ever been. If they should come back suddenly and find me here, there is nothing...

"I have to fetch my da's horse," she says, placing bread and cheese in my lap.

"No, no! Don't leave me here. What if they come back?"

And so tenderly then, she sits next to me as once my sister did when we were girls. It is quite as if I have known her all my life. Pointing to the cupboard under the stairs, she says, "Wait in there. The roads here are not safe. We have to take Drovers Pass - The Valley of Spirits, and need the horse. Now dress, eat, prepare. They will be back at midnight."

Yes, yes, of course. No one will be out on All Hallows Eve after midnight. Recalling the tale of the black sow it is strangely comforting to know there will be no other human beings present in the Valley of Spirits tonight. And I would rather take my chances with the black sow than Gwilym Ash and his henchmen.

But after she has gone the clock ticks ever more rapidly, and so much louder. It is the only sound in the house. Even here in the cramped stair cupboard, struggling to dress in oversized clothing, I can hear every second counting. Cling-cling...for the quarter hour. Cling-cling-cling-cling...for the half hour. Oh, God she has been gone too long. Say she ran to the village?

274

Galloped back on horse-back…would not she be here by now?

The bread and cheese lodges as a rock in my stomach.

The leather pouch of coinage contains enough for a journey and more - maybe a stay at an inn. I wonder who the woman is whose clothes I must wear, whose money I must pilfer - the wife of a gatekeeper? Do they know? Do they realise people arrive but never leave? Are they party to this? Certainly they are well paid.

Cling-cling!

Another quarter of an hour has passed. It is nearly midnight. The revellers will soon run home in terrified glee, perhaps returning in ten minutes or less.

I have waited until I can wait no more.

Something has happened to Riana.

Fear stabs at my heart. I dare wait no longer.

The cupboard door creaks alarmingly on opening. A gap is all. Enough to peep into the silent, shadowy hallway. What if the two of them are staggering up the driveway at this very moment? Will the sash window open for me as it did for Riana? Pray I have the strength. I must go. I have to.

The kitchen is pearly now with moonlight, as I stand here in the middle of the flagstone floor in these strange clothes, paralysed with indecision. Straining my ears for the slightest sound of another's breath on the night air, the moment weighs heavily. What should I do? And which way? Over to the village following Riana? But what if, about to take her father's horse, she was stopped and forced to explain why? And now men are on their way back here having extracted a confession? Something has happened to her I know it, and I cannot bear it. But I dare not follow. I dare not…

I think the route to take is the one Riana suggested - through Drovers Pass, or the Valley of Spirits as she referred to it - then over the moors by foot?

Food aplenty lies on the table for the doctor's servants - slabs of rabbit pie, scones, bara brith, apples – and a little will not be missed. Filling the pockets of this woman's skirts I care not for the theft. If they catch me they will lock me up for ever more and the punishment will be worse than death. So I will take my chances with the Black Mountains and stories of the Underworld. The doctor will not yet know I have gone. Oh, he will send for men with horses but they will be drunk and useless for a few hours yet.

So then, this is my one chance.

And I will take it.

***

Chapter Thirty-Two

Isobel
Present Day

"Christ Almighty - the bloody house is on fire!"

Like a match to gasoline the whoosh of flames was instantaneous. And in the seconds it took to realise what had happened, the whole place had become an inferno.

"It's everywhere – we're in the middle of it. They must have torched it all the way round."

Heat cracked the window panes.

Isobel screamed. "That's petrol. We have to get out."

"No shit!" Branwen opened the hall door to a fireball and slammed it shut again. "We're fucking trapped."

"There has to be something underneath – it's our only chance – to get under the floorboards."

"You said there wasn't a cellar? Are you sure? What about the cupboard under the stairs?"

Smoke was rapidly filling the room, and the ominous sound of splintering wood meant only seconds to make a decision.

"Let's do it," said Isobel, grabbing the tablecloth and throwing it over their heads. "There's a breeze coming from in there. Could be a basement or cavity underneath–"

"Hurry! Run!"

Holding their breath they pulled back the door, shot across the hall to the cupboard, wrenched it open, crammed inside and slammed it shut behind them.

"You okay?"

"Think so – you?"

With thick acrid smoke stinging their eyes they frantically began banging the floor and walls for signs of weakness.

"There has to be a cellar," Branwen said. "Just has to be…"

Isobel began ripping back the carpet. "Come on, let's get this up. Hurry." Heat scorched their throats and burned their lungs as they tugged at the plasterboard underneath. "Oh my God, the house is collapsing."

"It's coming up easily. Look it's all new…And yes! There is one. I knew it!"

As the first square snapped apart an icy dampness wafted into the smoke. They flew at the rest. "Come on, come on…."

"There's just enough room now. Quick - you first, Issy. I'll hold onto you as long as I can. Hurry, hurry!"

Fumbling with her feet for a ladder or a flight of steps, Isobel quickly realised there wasn't one. And in the confusion and haste, her hand slipped from out of Branwen's clutch like a loose glove, dropping her into the darkness below.

This was her nightmare – all these years - falling backwards into a bottomless pit, echoing with howls of the inhuman and icy blasts from empty tunnels.

Half expecting to find the man in black standing

there waiting for her with his back to the wall, the end of his cigarette flaring in the dark, she found herself instead lying flat on her back on a wet cobbled floor. Pain seared through her spine and her throat burned.

Beside her Branwen groaned.

Her voice was as raspy as a forty-a-day smoker's. "Are you all right?"

"No, I think I've broken my ankle. It's agony."

"Hang on a minute, there's some fallen chipboard here." Forcing herself into a sitting position, she tore a strip off the bottom of her skirt and fashioned a makeshift splint.

"It's bloody killing me."

"That should hold it straight and stop the bleeding. I know it hurts like hell but we've got to find a way out. Hold on, there's a pile of wood here." Scrambling in the dark on her hands and knees, still coughing and wincing with pain, she grabbed hold of a long stick. "Here, use this to lean on because you're going to have to walk."

"Can you get the matches and candles out of my pocket? I can feel a strong draft – there must be another room down here."

"Thank God you've got these. It's as black as a coal mine."

Branwen grimaced, managing a slight laugh. "Always. Fuck me, though. I knew there had to be a cellar."

Isobel struck a match and gasped. "I think you're right about another room as well - have you seen this?"

An elaborate archway heralded a flight of steps leading deeper underground.

"Looks like part of the old monastery."

Bit by bit they took it all in.

"I'll bet there's a tunnel to the house, as well," said Branwen.

"They all had them in the old days, didn't they? So people could hide or escape…"

Struggling to her feet, Isobel helped her friend up.

"Ouch, ouch!"

"It's about half a mile. Do you think you can make it or do you want to stay here? If we can get out at the other end we could call the police. I hope to God one of us has got a phone."

"Don't leave me here, no I'm coming. And mine's on the kitchen table, I know because I threw it on there when I came in the back door."

Isobel patted her pockets. "Shit, I haven't got mine either. Well anyway, we'll just have to take a chance and hope we can get out."

"Agreed. Can I hold onto you? I can't put any weight on this at all."

Together they hobbled down the narrow flights of steps, made smooth with moss and trickling water. A couple of squeals indicated rats, their pink tails scooting out of the candlelight.

"This bit must be twenty feet under."

"Hold the candle up, Issy. I want to see better."

The flame flickered and danced, sending shadows over stone walls and a cobbled floor.

"Can you see an exit?"

"I think so."

An archway at the far end loomed out of the dark, and they made their way towards it, coughing and shivering.

"Branwen, I feel terrible in here."

"Think how I feel. The pain keeps blacking me out."

She squeezed her arm. "Hold on. We're alive and we'll get you out of here. I didn't mean physically, though."

The sense of sadness was overwhelming and soon they realised why. At the far end of the chamber there was an incinerator, an old fashioned sort used in old hospitals, and neither woman could bring herself to speak when they saw what lay scattered around it; the only sound that of dripping water to break the silence.

After a while, Isobel said, "I think this is my abyss."

"Who the fuck do they think they are, these people?" said Branwen. "To just get rid of human beings like this - to dispose of them like broken toys? Who the fucking hell do they think they are, the self-righteous bastards?"

"I know."

The ivory smoothness of tiny human skulls, femurs and vertebrae shone in the buttery light. Along with a slight but distinct warmth emanating from the incinerator.

"He's still doing it!" said Branwen. "That's why there are so many still births, so many abortions…Bloody hell fire and brimstone, he's still fucking at it!"

"And why they won't move out of the house…but why, why…for God's sake why…?" Isobel's voice faded out as an overpowering series of images shot into her mind. One after the other. Limbs being snapped off crippled cadavers and thrown onto the fire, decaying bodies heaped onto the floor…

The stench of burning, rotting human flesh was nauseating and she clutched at thin air, the hard, shiny cobbles rearing towards her.

Now on her knees and retching violently, the relentless onslaught of images kept on coming. *Stop…stop…stop…*A rough, uncouth looking man with peg teeth was kicking ragdoll, broken bodies into the furnace, an expression of malevolent glee on his face as he stripped the female corpses and cracked their bones like dry tinder.

"Why?" Isobel wailed. "All this…all this…it's horrible, the dread, the pain – disgusting, terrible…"

"What are you getting?"

"Murder. Bodies left to rot and burn. Some weren't even dead yet. Smallpox sores, terrified eyes, faces eaten away, skeletal people still alive, wandering around in the dark trying to find a way out–"

"Come on, let's go, Issy. The police will find the answers now. We've done enough to get it opened up."

"I've got to be sick. I'm sorry–"

"Tell it to stop. You've seen enough. Try and stand. Come on, you need to get out of here now more than I do."

"It's freezing. I can't stop it, can't stand–"

"Yes you can. Power of the mind. Switch it off. Come on, stand up, lovely. Stand up!"

Trembling from head to foot, she pushed herself to her feet. "I can't stop shivering."

"It's a fucking hell pit, a death vault. I really hope that archway's leading to a tunnel. I don't want to come back through here."

Isobel swayed and grabbed her arm.

"You okay now?"

"Yes, stonking headache and really sick, but…God, that was the worst, absolutely–"

"Sorry, Issy, just a minute but what's that pile of stuff?"

She squinted into the lurching shadows. "Looks like bags, books, luggage? The deceased's possessions?"

Limping badly, Branwen gave Isobel the candle. "Hold it up. Let's just have a look."

Warily they peeled away blankets and rotted clothing. "Euw, no, this has been here a hundred years. They're old asylum uniforms and blankets. Like someone was having such a good time burning bodies he forgot about the rest."

"I can't say it would be a nice job raking through this. Come on, let's go."

"Hang on, what's that at the bottom?"

Isobel bent down and held the candle closer. Her eyes widened. "Bran, it's a little leather suitcase."

"You're kidding me."

"I bet one of the servants cleared out a room and it's been here all along."

"And they never knew!"

***

Chapter Thirty-Three

They hurried now towards the exit, Isobel clutching the case and the candle.

"It does look as though it's a tunnel, doesn't it?"

"Sounds like one too."

They peered blindly into the blackness, a waft of chill air whooshing past their ears. Here the dripping was louder, so too the scurry and squeak of rats.

"What if we can't get out at the other end?"

"I know. I'm worried about that too."

"I'm frozen to the bone."

"Logically it can't be too far now. We've got to try."

"Let me hold onto you, Issy. I'm on one foot here and it's really slippery."

The further into the tunnel, the blacker, colder and wetter. Their breath misted on the air and the candle kept snuffing out. "You all right?"

"Trying not to cry, to be honest," said Branwen. "Has it occurred to you that this might take us past the house altogether...on and on to–?"

"The lake? To where the ruins are?"

"Or to the graveyard underneath the island? Oh God, we never thought of that"

"No, no, it's okay – look, Bran, I can see a door."

"Steady, don't rush or you'll slip and we'll both go

down."

"Hold on, I need to relight the candle."

The flame ignited again and a weighty iron door appeared in front. "Hell – look at it. It's like that one in the pub - at the back."

"You mean the one to the cock pit?"

"Cock pit? You mean cock fighting? Do they still do that – I thought it was illegal?"

"Course they bloody do. Who's going to stop them? Oh, fuck, Issy, there's no way we're going to get through that, it's like a prison."

They climbed the steps and slumped onto the top one.

"I could cry now as well," Isobel said. "And you must be almost passing out with the pain."

"I've got some stuff in my pocket - I'm gonna smoke, it'll help."

"What are we going to do? Go back again? Assume that once the fire's died back they'll think we're dead and–"

"Yeah right, and how do you propose we get up there? We dropped a good seven or eight feet, remember?"

"I really don't want to go back through that chamber either."

Branwen lit her smoke, inhaled and coughed until she retched. "Damn, that's good. I know you don't lovely, but we might have to. Anyway, if we're going to die stuck down here we may as well take a look in the suitcase - see if it's what we were after."

"We won't die. We're strong and we'll find a way out. But we do need a rest. Okay, here goes."

The case sprang open on its hinges to reveal hundreds of beautifully scripted letters, all with wax seals still intact, along with various lockets and old photographs.

"Incredible calligraphy."

"Oh my word…oh my, oh my…And look, Branwen – they're addressed to Flora George of Lavinia House."

"And a lady called Amelia Lee in Derbyshire - sender, Flora George. All of these are between the two women."

"Lee?"

"Yeah, that's a bit of a coincidence, isn't it?"

"Hmm….Mind you there are lots of people with that surname where I come from. So Flora's letters were never actually posted then? And the ones sent to her never passed on. Do you really think Edgar was keeping the fees and not letting on the patients had either recovered or died?"

"Oh, definitely. I always thought that."

"And all the while Flora thought she'd been abandoned!"

"Bastards, they really were. Come on, let's open the letters - we have to. She wants us to, I feel it."

"Okay. But then we should hand these over to the police."

"If we get the chance."

They both stared back into the tunnel.

"You don't think anyone will come down here after us, surely? The house will be too dangerous for a long time yet. There's no way they can know we survived. In fact, they're probably dancing on our graves as we speak, drinking to it at The Druid."

"True."

Isobel sliced open the first envelope.

Dear Amelia,

How could you leave me in such a place? An asylum! Where is my child? Is he safe? I am beside myself with distress. The conditions here are dreadful, with scant sanitation, and I must share a dormitory with wild creatures that scream in the night and soil their beds. Last night a woman hit me hard in the face with a shoe...What did I do to deserve this? I beg you write to me. The doctor is not a doctor at all, but an alienist of enormous self-importance...

Dear Flora,

We have not heard a word from you but are assured by Dr Fox Whately that your response to treatment is most encouraging. I implored him to allow a visit but he was adamant it would set your progress back, and I must wait for an invitation from you in your own fair hand...

Dear Amelia,

I implore you to help me. I have a friend, Diane, who suffers greatly from some disease of the mind, but she alone holds my hand during the darkest hours, and she alone has confided what happens within these walls. She speaks of the devil, and at first I thought her quite insane, but now I see him too – the glowing tip of his cigarette at the peep hole to our dormitory. She is with child, Amelia, for the second time. How did she get with child in this place? It is he, the attendant, Gwilym, who does the doctor's bidding and with such rabid glee...

Dear Flora,

It is with such sadness I have to tell you of Samuel's passing. He died of consumption brought on, I am sure of it, by the fatigue of working all hours. We did not want to worry you but the exorbitant fees we pay for your private quarters and personal care have depleted the estate to such a degree. He never did have resources, which was why of course he sold off much of the woodland when you married. I know that bothered you enormously. You always said there were fairies in the forest, do you remember? When we were girls…

Dear Amelia,

Diane has gone. I know they have taken her. I dread to think it is to those higher rooms, the ones from where I hear such mournful wailing and terrible screams in the night. Again and again I recall the story she told of having a baby pulled from out of her body, of lying on a blood soaked mattress. But what of that child, and what of this one? Where have they taken them? Oh, Amelia, please write me. I beg you not to abandon me. I have a feeling I have done something I cannot recall. I see your face. I see Samuel's, but I cannot know what I have done?

Isobel put down the bundle of letters and pushed them back into the case. "I'm going to read them all. Every last word and get to the bottom of this. I cannot bear it. I feel as if I am her. I feel all the fear, the not knowing, the frustration."

"I feel hate. Real, serious hate - more than ever before and that's a lot. For that pig. The whole lot. All of them, but especially him, the doctor. These others might do the dirty work but it's on his orders every single time."

"And   Amelia's   surname   was   Lee.   I mean…hmmm…"

"What? I thought you said there were lots of people called, Lee?"

"Yes, but it's set me thinking – because when I was a girl we found this bottle tucked into the foundations of the house, a time capsule if you like, and there was a newspaper article inside about a missing woman…and it's just her face…I could be wrong, of course…"

"You think Amelia and her sister were related to you?"

"It's certainly a possibility."

Isobel picked up one of the lockets and clasped it to her chest, eyes closed.

"Is that hers? Flora's? Shall we see what she looked like? See if she is the same girl we've both seen on the stairs?"

With a fluttering heart Isobel clicked open the delicate, silver clasp, suddenly afraid to see her living and breathing ghost. On each side of the locket, however, a grainy sepia photograph had been set.

"Oh!"

"That can't be Flora and her husband, surely? They look really old and bald and wrinkly."

"And tiny."

The elderly couple were finely dressed. But their faces did not resemble the norm – the bones being small and delicate, noses aquiline with beaked tips, chins almost non-existent. And although perfectly formed, the heads were far too large for such narrow shoulders and totally without hair – no eyelashes or eyebrows. Miniature hands were clasped neatly on their laps, their large, protruding eyes staring into the camera flash.

Isobel read out the inscriptions underneath, "'Leonora Fox-Whately, age eleven,' And 'James Fox-Whately, age twelve.'"

"No!"

"Oh my goodness. These are HGPS children." She turned to stare at Branwen. "They must have been Edgar Fox-Whately's."

"What's HGPS?"

"Premature ageing–"

"Oh yes, I've read about that before. That's what Ophelia Fox-Whately had – her baby was born with that, apparently. It was all round the village just before she vanished. There must have been a court order or something to stop the press–"

"Did she? Are you sure?"

"Yes, absolutely. Is it hereditary then? Seeing as they all seem to be Fox-Whately's?"

"No, that's the thing. It isn't. Part of the reason for that is they rarely live long enough to produce another child but it could explain…"

"Oh yes…"

Both of them continued staring at each other in horror.

"…why they were sacrificing these girls' babies!" Isobel said. "They resemble, or certainly from a distance they might…what did you call…crimbils!"

"They don't just resemble them. They *are* crimbils. And that's why Edgar was sacrificing new-borns to the fae – to get his own children back."

"No, that's preposterous - tragic. These were children with a syndrome, not changelings or crimbils or curses from the fae. And to think what those poor innocent women went through for nothing other than superstition! What they did to those new-born infants. Oh my good God! At least Ophelia's child will be better understood and taken care of. "

Branwen was glaring at her.

"Branwen, don't you see? If anyone saw these children maybe taking a walk in the forest on the estate–"

"People did see them."

"Yes, but they weren't actually seeing crimbils. They must have seen these two – Leonora and James. It's superstitious folklore that made them think otherwise, especially when they knew what the family had done to the forest. Word would have got out that it was the wrath of the fae or other such bullshit."

"So what did you see then, yesterday, Isobel? Tell me that, if the fae don't exist!"

"An apparition. I'd been looking at your painting and I'd had nightmares, not slept, been drinking mead laced with magic mushrooms…I was having visions and that was what my mind chose to see."

"I don't bloody believe this. You were physically knocked backwards. You were shown a past that frightened you to the core. You've been given insight into who is at the heart of all this, shown what to do, felt the power. And how come Ophelia has a child with this when it's not hereditary then, if not for the wrath of the fae?"

Isobel shook her head.

Branwen's eyes were pools of misery. "You must feel

the magick of this place? How can you just dismiss everything like that?"

"I'm sorry. I'm just saying I think there have been terrible misunderstandings and some truly evil crimes here, when there was a rational explanation all along. As for the insights and the visions, you're right - I can't explain them and they did show me what I couldn't otherwise have known. Please don't be upset with me - I do feel the magick here, and I do respect how you live and what you believe. I do."

They sat quietly, shivering.

"I think we should go back. Somehow you're going to have to climb back up the way we came in."

"The worst of the blaze will be over, do you think? Will anyone in the village have called the fire brigade?"

"Yes, once it's burned to the ground and Rhys Payne and his boys have pissed off."

"I hope they catch them."

"Well they're thick as pig shit. They'll have left clues even Inspector Clouseau would—"

"I mean Mervyn and Lorna."

"So do I, Issy."

"I can't believe we've got to go all the way back."

"Me neither."

Half way down the tunnel Isobel stopped. "I'm truly sorry for upsetting you, Branwen. If it means anything at all, I should tell you that in the few short days I've been here I've gone from paralysing fear to welcoming my gift. If it wasn't for you I would have spent my whole life running from it."

"Thank you for that. It means a lot, actually. Will you stay here or go back to England now, do you think?"

"Are you kidding? As long as the rat boys are caught I'm staying. It feels like home to me. I don't ever want to go back."

"Good, I'm glad."

They linked arms. "We'll have to hurry through that death vault, though. I can't bear the thought of it even."

The smell of smoke as they exited the tunnel, however, was strong.

"I think it's out. Look, the place is swimming in water."

"Fire brigade! Thank God!"

"Lucky we rescued the suitcase as well – look all those clothes and books are floating."

On nearing the wreckage they speeded up, climbing back up the steps into what was a torrent.

"We're down here!"

"Help! We're down here. You trying to drown us or what?"

A man with a sooty face wearing a helmet peered through the hole. "Bloody hell! That's fantastic, that is. You all right, are you?"

"One with a broken ankle, the other with cuts and bruises, but we're okay."

"Be down for you in a moment ladies, hold on there." He turned to shout to someone for a stretcher. "Okay, lowering the ladder now….hang on a minute…what you saying, lovely?" He turned away in response to a woman's voice then turned back. "Lady here called Nina. She was the one who called us or we'd never have known, see?"

"No one from the village rang?" Branwen shouted

up.

"No, just this lady. Said…oh, she says are you all right, Isobel, is it?"

Branwen's eyes were full of tears. "They left me to die."

"I suspect there are a lot of people here terrified of Doctor Fox-Whately and his wife," Isobel said softly. "Not to mention Rhys Payne."

"No, well yes… but what they really fear are the fae, don't you see? That's why they let him do it. In case it's their child next. You've got to understand that, Issy. It's very, very real."

"Well, we're going to have to put a few folk straight then, aren't we? The fae, spirits of the woods, exist I grant you that, but they do not take people's children and replace them with their own, okay?" She grabbed hold of the ladder. "Bran, we're going to enjoy some hours debating this, but right now I don't know about you but I want to be taken to a hospital and knocked out for a week."

"Me too. But I'm going to hold you to that, Lady. We are going to thrash this out. And it'll be your turn to bring the mead."

"You're on."

***

Epilogue

Flora George
1st May, 1894
Bournemouth

I love it here. Loved it from the first moment I arrived at the station with only two farthings to my name. I think it was the seagulls, the salty breeze blowing off the sea and the tinkling bob of fishing boats. I almost kissed the ground and wept with joy, even when trawling the promenade guest houses for work as a humble chamber maid. Even then. It was life, you see, such an enormous sense of uplifting freedom. Oh, to be able to come and go as I pleased, to buy fresh fish and vinegary chips wrapped in newspaper, to walk on the sands barefoot, and lie in bed watching the moon dip over the hazy horizon. I will not return to Derbyshire. No, I can never go home now, knowing what they did to me.

Yet all the while this child has grown inside, and the time for change is as inevitable as the tide.

The infant lies now, over by the window in a cot, delivered safely by the midwife. But despite the brightness of the morning, it seems a gloom hovers over the cradle and the new-born screwing up its fists and kicking its feet is a most malicious one.

This baby is not mine, you see? Quite what it is about it I cannot say, other than the creature is not human. Perhaps the blackness of its eyes? Or the large head and sharp nose? The skin too, appears wrinkled as a reptile, the little feet claw like.

Turning my head to face the wall I find I am unable to respond to its tinny mewling, the thought of putting that rodent mouth to my breast utterly repugnant. And somewhere under the layers of memory, there is a sense of repetition. Of being back once more in the chamber.

They are here again, you see. In the pattern of the wallpaper. Faces reside in the woodwork and the very fabric of the curtains. And how horrifically enthralling it is to see, as hours and days pass by - how they begin to take form, how their eyes glint and their whispers grow louder. And the more the baby cries and works itself into a ball of rage the more the wood sprites in the whorls and knots of the bedposts begin to amass. Until a great crowd of chattering urgency fills the room.

Someone below thumps their ceiling. Another bangs on the walls. And the landlady raps repeatedly on the door.

"Are you all right in there, Mrs Lee? Is the baby sick?"

"We are both quite well, thank you."

"Only it's been a few days and she ain't stopped bawling."

Picking up the infant to dissipate their concern, the creature stares back with such evil as I have never seen. "She is hungry, that is all."

"That's all right then, Mrs Lee. Only I can call the

doctor if you—"

"No, there is no need. Thank you."

"I'll bid you good night, then?"

The baby, quiet now, observes me in a most unnatural way, its eyes as old as time in a face quite gnarled to walnut. And when thrown back into the cot it cackles as an ancient crone. No, no, no….this is not human. And now….now look…it has twisted into a stick figure, with a lopsided mouth and eyes set far apart, and a forehead so broad as to be of a most terrifying appearance.

What evil is this that besieges me so, when I have begun a new life with a new name? Am I never to be free? This…this ogre…cannot be. It cannot…

The thing thrashes and tries to bite, talons ripping into my arms. I will get it out of this room. Out! Out now!

A scream from somewhere… And the sash window sticks. But eventually gives, as wrenching it open with the evil creature's head upon the sill, I have to slam it down hard over and over and over…until finally its neck cracks like a nut….the little pink head dropping down-down-down…several storeys…before smashing like a water melon on the promenade below.

A woman stops in front of it. Her hands fly to her mouth. Blood spatters her long ivory coloured dress. Men are running towards her, holding onto top hats. There are others now too…all rushing to the spot.

"Mrs Lee! What in the devil's name? I'm letting myself in…"

Yes, I remember now.

Turning to face the door as it bursts open, suddenly it all makes perfect sense. "I remember now. It was a changeling, you see? A wood sprite! We chopped down the forest so they took my child and replaced it with an evil troll. I told them – my husband, the doctor, my sister - but no one would believe me."

She stares aghast - at the blood smeared over my arms, chest and hands, at the torn skin and gristle on the window sill. But mostly at the headless body of an infant lying at my feet, and the frothy crimson pool rippling across the floorboards.

***

Glossary of Terms

HGPS

Hutchinson-Gilford Progeria Syndrome (Progeria or HGPS) is a rare, fatal genetic condition characterized by an appearance of accelerated aging in children. Its name is derived from Greek and means 'prematurely old.' While there are different forms of Progeria, the classic type is Hutchinson-Gilford Progeria Syndrome, which was named after the doctors who first described it in England; in 1886 by Dr. Jonathan Hutchinson and in 1897 by Dr. Hastings Gilford.

HGPS is caused by a mutation in the gene called LMNA (pronounced, lamin – a). The LMNA gene produces the Lamin A protein, which is the structural scaffolding that holds the nucleus of a cell together. Researchers now believe that the defective Lamin A protein makes the nucleus unstable. That cellular instability appears to lead to the process of premature aging in Progeria.

Although they are born looking healthy, children with Progeria begin to display many characteristics of accelerated aging within the first two years of life. Progeria signs include growth failure, loss of body fat and hair, aged-looking skin, stiffness of joints, hip dislocation, generalized atherosclerosis, cardiovascular (heart) disease and stroke. The children have a remarkably similar appearance, despite differing ethnic backgrounds. Children with Progeria die of atherosclerosis (heart disease) at an average age of fourteen years.

Postpartum Psychosis

Postpartum psychosis, or puerperal psychosis, is a rare but serious and potentially life-threatening mental health issue. It takes the form of severe depression or mania or both.

Most women get postpartum psychosis in the first three months after birth. Usually, it happens within the first two weeks.

Postpartum Psychosis includes one or more of the following:
• Strange beliefs that could not be true (delusions).
• Hearing, seeing, feeling or smelling things that are not there (hallucinations).
• High mood with loss of touch with reality (mania).
• Severe confusion.

These are also common symptoms:
• Being more talkative, sociable, on the phone an excessive amount.

- Having a very busy mind or racing thoughts.
- Feeling very energetic and like 'super-mum' or agitated and restless.
- Having trouble sleeping, or not feeling the need to sleep.
- Behaving in a way that is out of character or out of control.
- Feeling paranoid or suspicious of people's motives.
- Feeling that things are connected in special ways or that stories on the TV or radio have special personal meaning.
- Feeling that the baby is connected to God or the Devil in some way.

<u>The Fae</u>

For many Pagans, Beltane is traditionally a time when the veil between our world and that of the Fae is thin. In most European folktales, the Fae kept to themselves unless they wanted something from their human neighbours. It wasn't uncommon for a tale to relate the story of a human being who got too daring with the Fae and ultimately paid their price for his or her curiosity. It is important to note that the Fae are typically considered mischievous and tricky, and should not be interacted with unless one knows exactly what one is up against. Don't make offerings or promises that you can't follow through on, and don't enter into any bargains with the Fae unless you know exactly what you're getting and what is expected of you in return. With the Fae there are no gifts - every transaction is an exchange, and it's never one-sided.

A considerable amount of lore about fairies revolves around changelings or fairy children left in the place of stolen human babies. In particular, folklore describes how to prevent the fairies from stealing babies and substituting changelings. The theme of the swapped child is common in medieval literature and reflects concern over infants thought to be afflicted with unexplained diseases, disorders, or developmental disabilities.

***

If you have enjoyed reading Hidden Company, please would you kindly leave a review on amazon? It would be most appreciated by the author

***

More Books by S. E. England

Father of Lies

A Darkly Disturbing Occult Horror Trilogy: Book 1

'Boy did this pack a punch and scare me witless..'

'Scary as hell...What I thought would be mainstream horror was anything but...'

'Not for the faint-hearted. Be warned - this is very, very dark subject matter.'

'A truly wonderful and scary start to a horror trilogy. One of the best and most well written books I've read in a long time.'

'A dark and compelling read. I devoured it in one afternoon. Even as the horrors unfolded I couldn't race through the pages quickly enough for more...'

'Delivers the spooky in spades!'

'Will go so far as to say Sarah is now my favourite author - sorry Mr King!'

***

Ruby is the most violently disturbed patient ever admitted to Drummersgate Asylum, high on the bleak moors of northern England. With no improvement after two years, Dr. Jack McGowan finally decides to take a risk and hypnotises her. With terrifying consequences.

A horrific dark force is now unleashed on the entire

medical team, as each in turn attempts to unlock Ruby's shocking and sinister past. Who is this girl? And how did she manage to survive such unimaginable evil? Set in a desolate ex-mining village, where secrets are tightly kept and intruders hounded out, their questions soon lead to a haunted mill, the heart of darkness...and The Father of Lies.

http://www.amazon.co.uk/dp/B015NCZYKU
http://www.amazon.com/dp/B015NCZYKU

***

Tanners Dell – Book 2

Now only one of the original team remains – Ward Sister, Becky. However, despite her fiancé, Callum, being unconscious and many of her colleagues either dead or critically ill, she is determined to rescue Ruby's twelve year old daughter from a similar fate to her mother.

But no one asking questions in the desolate ex-mining village Ruby hails from ever comes to a good end. And as the diabolical history of the area is gradually revealed, it seems the evil invoked is both real and contagious.

Don't turn the lights out yet!

***

Magda – Book 3

The dark and twisted community of Woodsend harbours a terrible secret – one tracing back to the age of the Elizabethan witch hunts, when many innocent women were persecuted and hanged.

But there is a far deeper vein of horror running through this village; an evil that once invoked has no intention of relinquishing its grip on the modern world. Rather it watches and waits with focused intelligence, leaving Ward Sister, Becky, and CID Officer, Toby, constantly checking over their shoulders and jumping at shadows.

Just who invited in this malevolent presence? And is the demonic woman who possessed Magda back in the sixteenth century, the same one now gazing at Becky whenever she looks in the mirror?

Are you ready to meet Magda in this final instalment of the trilogy? Are you sure?

***

The Owlmen

If They See You They Will Come For You

Ellie Blake is recovering from a nervous breakdown. Deciding to move back to her northern roots, she and her psychiatrist husband buy Tanners Dell at auction - an old water mill in the moorland village of Bridesmoor.

However, there is disquiet in the village. Tanners Dell has a terrible secret, one so well guarded no one speaks its name. But in her search for meaning and very much alone, Ellie is drawn to traditional witchcraft and determined to pursue it. All her life she has been cowed. All her life she has apologised for her very existence. And witchcraft has opened a door she could never have imagined. Imbued with power and overawed with its magick, for the first time she feels she has come home, truly knows who she is.

Tanners Dell though, with its centuries old demonic history...well, it's a dangerous place for a novice...

http://www.amazon.co.uk/dp/B079W9FKV7
http://www.amazon.com/dp/B079W9FKV7

***

The Soprano

A Haunting Supernatural Thriller

It is 1951 and a remote mining village on the North Staffordshire Moors is hit by one of the worst snowstorms in living memory. Cut off for over three weeks, the old and the sick will die; the strongest bunker down; and those with evil intent will bring to its conclusion a family vendetta spanning three generations.

Inspired by a true event, 'The Soprano' tells the story of Grace Holland - a strikingly beautiful, much admired local celebrity who brings glamour and inspiration to the grimy moorland community. But why is Grace still here? Why doesn't she leave this staunchly Methodist, rain-sodden place and the isolated farmhouse she shares with her mother?

Riddled with witchcraft and tales of superstition, the story is mostly narrated by the Whistler family who own the local funeral parlour, in particular six year old Louise - now an elderly lady - who recalls one of the most shocking crimes imaginable.

http://www.amazon.co.uk/dp/B0737GQ9Q
http://www.amazon.com/dp/B0737GQ9Q7

***

Monkspike

A Medieval Occult Horror

1149 was a violent year in the Forest of Dean.

Today, nearly 900 years later, the forest village of Monkspike sits brooding. There is a sickness here passed down through ancient lines, one noted and deeply felt by Sylvia Massey, the new psychologist. What is wrong with nurse, Belinda Sully's, son? Why did her husband take his own life? Why are the old people in Temple Lake Nursing Home so terrified? And what are the lawless inhabitants of nearby Wolfs Cross hiding?

It is a dark village indeed, but one which has kept its secrets well. That is until local girl, Kezia Elwyn, returns home as a practising Satanist, and resurrects a hellish wrath no longer containable. Burdo, the white monk, will infest your dreams....This is pure occult horror and definitely not for the faint of heart...

http://www.amazon.co.uk/dp/B07VJHPD63
http://www.amazon.com/dp/B07VJHPD63

***

Printed in Great Britain
by Amazon

47399313R00179